SEEN BY THE HUNTER

Seen By The Hunter

CHERIE SIM

Cherie Sim

Cover Design by SelfPubBookCovers.com/LaLimaDesign

Edited by Christine Haines

Paperback ISBN-13: 978 0 6457076 1 8
E book ISBN-13: 978 0 6457076 0 1

First Printing, 2023

This book is dedicated to Craig, Kyle, Bradley and Angelina.
I couldn't do it without you.

Thanks also to my mum for all of her help and advice.

My thanks and apologies to my sister Julie who told me all about how nursing works, which I have immediately forgotten or ignored.

Contents

Contents ~ ix

Chapter 1

Dusk - City outskirts

My hands ache on the steering wheel as the highway widens and farmland morphs into creeping suburbia. I can't quite believe I'm finally here, in this city hiding behind a long, windswept mountain range. Out of sight and mind of the rest of the country.

The icy pool of dread swelling in the pit of my stomach oozes down into my legs. Either that or I'm going numb from sitting in one position for the last twelve hours. I remind myself moving here is a great choice for me, I have a place at a top university and a job at the hospital next door.

Still, it's hard to ignore all the warnings. It seems like everyone thinks Adelaide is all bad. It doesn't help that it's the serial-killer capital of Australia, but most of those famous cases are from way back. They haven't caught any for years now.

The housing developments here look the same as they do everywhere else. Homes are set back from the wide highway behind tall, noise-reduction walls and long bands of scrubby trees. I pass a few large shopping centres. It's all pretty standard stuff.

Yet the tension inside me grows until my fingers tingle from gripping the steering wheel way too tight. I blame the hushed whispers my family use to talk about this city, the place I was born.

Darkness descends just as the clouds that have been threatening for the last couple of hours finally strike. Even with the wiper blades set to maximum I can barely see the road.

I must be getting close to the city itself. The buildings lining the road are older and bigger here. Two and three storey structures with multiple chimneys and thin, pointy windows are hiding behind old-fashioned brush fences. For some reason they remind me of the nightmare that woke me before sunrise. I get a lot of nightmares and this one was particularly bad. It forced me from my bed two hours earlier than planned. My parents weren't happy, but they were going to cry no matter what time I left.

I turn a corner and I can see the wide concrete-arch bridge that leads into the central business district. The city looks great from here. It's shiny-bright in the rain and the mixture of old stone and new glass and metal buildings, as well as a few larger-than-life statues, gives the place a grand feel I could grow to love. I turn left at the first major intersection and drive past museums, galleries and the university I am enrolled in, before I see the old hospital ahead. The nurses' quarters I'll be staying in are somewhere behind that.

I take the next left and find a park under a tree with a trunk so thick it'd stop a runaway semi. It's sure to drop sticky sap, or a limb, on my car, but that would just be an artistic addition to all the bug guts already there.

It's still pouring and I haven't brought an umbrella. My singlet and denim skirt combo are no match for this cold, coastal weather, but at least they won't take long to dry. I get out of my car, go around to the hatch and drag out a red, clothes-stuffed backpack. I'm already shivering when an enormous drop of water slams onto the nape of my neck and slides down my spine like some outward manifestation of the dread I feel inside. Okay. The rest of my stuff can wait here until the rain stops and I know where I am going.

I jog from shelter to shelter until I am at the door of a dark and deserted-looking, three-storey building. I think this must be the nurses' quarters. It looks old, but still much nicer than a building scheduled for demolition should look. There are no broken windows and no graffiti anywhere. The walls are built from actual stone and they even have those pretty little decorations around the windows and eaves.

The windows are like dead shark eyes staring out at me, but that darkness does check out with what I know about the place. The building manager told me on the phone that nearly everyone has already moved out. They're knocking the whole thing down in eight weeks.

I press a button next to the keypad. Instead of a tinny voice from the intercom speaker, I hear the thud of fast-moving footsteps inside and the door is flung open. My first impression is the guy giving me an exhausted smile is probably hungover. Then I see he is wearing scrubs with no shoes, every one of his pockets are overflowing with nursing bits and bobs, and his short, dark hair is sticking out at weird angles, as if he has just pulled something off over his head. Like the lanyard still hanging from his pocket.

Just finished work then.

He sticks an entire triangle of toast in his mouth and offers his now empty hand for me to shake.

"Hi, I'm Lily," I say, shaking his sweaty hand.

He chews hard, swallows and then smiles at me again.

"Sorry," he answers. "I'm Sam. I spoke to you on the phone. Come on in."

He ushers me through a cavernous, tiled foyer and up a scuffed, wooden staircase to the first floor. At the first door on the right of a seemingly endless hallway, he hands me a key.

"This is your room," he says. "The door at the far end of the hall is the bathroom for this floor. You'll have it to yourself. I'm on the ground floor in the old matron's rooms. Ellie's on the top. It's just you, me and Ellie here now."

He goes quiet so I glance over at him. I figure he's wondering why I'm bothering to move in when everyone else is headed in the opposite direction. He warned me on the phone that the facilities are pretty dismal, built in a time when employees didn't have as many rights as they do now. But the room is short term and furnished, so it suits me perfectly. Also, I'm drawn to old things, probably because I don't have much of a past of my own. None of this was Sam's business though, as nice as he seemed, so I don't feel obliged to explain.

"Thanks," I say, opening the door to my room.

It's tiny.

It looks like someone took a cheap hotel from the nineteen fifties and shrunk it. Maybe this is why the building is being torn down. It'd be too hard to open up these tiny rooms and make them useful for anything else.

The room has glossy-painted walls, a single bed, a tiny fridge and a small wardrobe with a long bench attached to it. I think that last bit is made of real wood. The bench has drawers under half of its length, doing double duty as a kitchenette and study desk.

I throw my handbag on the bench and my backpack on the naked bed.

"So, not from South Australia then?" Sam asks.

"My family have a farm about three hours south of Sydney," I answer, dodging the question out of habit.

Feeling guilty I change the subject.

"So what's the hospital like?"

"Which one?"

"The old one I guess," I say. "I've got a job as a nurse's assistant there."

"It's old." Sam shrugs. "New one's better."

"I'll bet," I answer. "I transfer over there in a few weeks when all the patients have been moved."

I stop talking abruptly. I've been annoying everyone for weeks, babbling about my big move and new career. Don't want to scare off a potential new friend by over-sharing.

"Well, let me know if you need anything," Sam says as he turns away. "Oh, and the code for the main door is one, two, three, four."

Sounds safe.

I thank him, shut the door and have a quick look around before making a half-hearted attempt to put my clothes away. I'm too cold to concentrate. I'm still damp from the walk here and I have to clench my jaw to stop my teeth from chattering. All of my towels and bedding are still in the car, so rain or no rain, I'm going to have to go back out for the rest of my stuff.

I grab the keys and open the door to the hallway. The lights must be on a timer, or Sam switched them off, because the hallway's now almost pitch black. The stairwell on my left has a weak green glow coming from a flickering exit light. To my right is a scene out of a horror movie. All down the long hallway doors gape open and the unused rooms are in perfect darkness. There are a million places for something to hide.

I have no idea how I missed that when I came in. I wait for the hallway to lengthen into the distance or for some unnameable creature to come slinking out of a doorway. Nothing happens.

Of course the bathroom would have to be right at the far end of that. I'll have to get used to not drinking after dinner, so I can make it until morning without going down there. Maybe Sam and Ellie wouldn't mind if I leave the lights on in the bathroom.

Figuring out where the light switches are will help too.

I can't see anything helpful or immediately harmful, so I head downstairs. The foyer and ground-floor hall lights are off as well. Acutely aware of the yawning blackness behind me, I open the heavy front door to see it's stopped raining. With warm orange lights lining the road it feels far more welcoming out there than inside.

Unloading my little car only takes two trips, and when I lock it up, I look around the street wondering if it'll be safe here. Mine is easily the oldest car here tonight. A person would have to be desperate to steal my twenty-year-old hatchback instead of the shiny-new Audi or Lexus parked either side of me. Those nice cars might not stay there all night though. Their owners could be a couple of blocks over in the city at clubs and restaurants. They could even be visiting someone at the hospital, though it's getting a bit late for that. The street parking sign says I'll have to move the car before work tomorrow, but this park will do for now.

My stomach growls. I look dubiously back at the car and the half-eaten packet of Twisties I know lies on the passenger floor, because it fell out of my reach while I was driving.

Nah. The packet was wide open. They'll be stale.

I need to go out and get some food or starve until morning. Hunger wins, it always does. I can already feel the shakiness and headache I get when I need to eat. I know I can't leave it much longer or I'll get a migraine, or worse.

Anyway, it'll be nice to get a feel for my surroundings before I start my new job in the morning.

I carry the last load of my things up to my room and dump them in a corner to clean away later. I check a map on my phone, looking for supermarkets and restaurants in the area. Usually I would just walk where the mood takes me, knowing I could find my way home with my phone, but Adelaide has a reputation for dodgy utilities like power and water. It'd be just my luck the Internet would go down and I would wander around lost until one of the local serial killers found me.

Of course Mum and Dad, my adoptive parents, Margaret and Gary to their friends, would prefer I starved in my room rather than go walking around at night. Actually, considering their opinion of this particular city, they would probably brick up the doorway to keep me in here tonight. We haven't been back once since the day my adoption was completed.

Mum failed badly at hiding her dismay at my choice to move here, but she didn't try to stop me. Dad even told my older sister Corinne to lay off the subject. They really shouldn't have bothered trying to spare my feelings though. I'm used to it. Corinne's favourite game is teasing me about my biological father. And following her lead, my sister's school friends were pretty painful too.

Corinne isn't as cruel as she sounds, it's mostly normal, sisterly teasing. She just has way better ammunition than most.

True to form, last week she insisted we watch a documentary about some of Adelaide's more notorious crimes. Finding out the city has an entire television series dedicated to its murders is a bit of a worry, but I didn't let Corinne know that. I'm just grateful my bio father's name wasn't mentioned. I guess one murder isn't unusual enough to get much attention here, no matter how strange the news reports about his trial got.

Chapter 2

Early evening - My room

I throw on a pair of jeans and a jacket, put my room key onto my key ring, and head outside. There are so many other people out here tonight that, at the very least, I would have plenty of witnesses to my murder.

At the railway station I cross the road into the city to find a restaurant that does takeaway. I'd like a proper meal, but everywhere looks busy and I'd feel weird sitting alone. I settle for two serves of chicken tenders and some hot chips with chicken salt and vinegar from a small cafe. I wander aimlessly, eating as I walk, keeping to the brightest, busiest roads for safety's sake.

When I run out of food, I stop in at a cramped convenience store and buy an apple cider and a packet of chips for dessert, as well as some supplies to get me through the next day or so.

Exploring isn't as much fun now I'm carrying my groceries and this city looks like all the rest I have seen, so I head east looking for a major road to take me back to my room. I ignore all the dark alleyways and soon reach the eastern edge of the city centre. On the other side of the road, lush parkland stretches away in both directions. Winding pathways beckon me into the peaceful surroundings that seem the complete opposite of the bustling city behind me. But as I can't see anyone else over there wandering around, going in alone might be too big a temptation to the local bad guys.

Instead I head north for a few blocks and, in a small miracle for my navigatory talents, I see a cluster of old, mismatched hospital buildings across the road to my left. I'm home, almost. The closest hospital wing is already wrapped in scaffolding, so it looks like the demolition crew aren't waiting for the whole place to be empty before they start tearing it apart.

I cross the road, still basking in the satisfaction of correctly reading a map, when I stub my toe on the curb and stumble headlong into a group of pedestrians gathering for the next change of lights. A businessman dodges to my left as I get my feet under me and say about thirty sorries. I scuttle through the crowd, finally reaching a space where I can catch my breath and stuff any remaining dignity back into my chest.

When I have studied my feet long enough for my face to stop glowing redder than the stoplight over my head, I look up and am instantly distracted by the fairytale in front of me. I'm standing in a grand entranceway that is set back in a little bay off the main road.

There are ornate iron pillars with large glass lanterns at the top that look like they were stolen straight from Cinderella's carriage, if Cinderella was a giant.

Between the pillars are decorative cast-iron gates wide enough for cars. There are also smaller, pedestrian-sized gates on the outer sides of the pillars. The whole thing is intricately decorated with flowers, leaves and beautiful scroll-work. I fall instantly in love.

Signage informs me this is the Botanic Gardens.

Excellent.

It's a public space, I'll be able to go inside. It closes pretty early, but I'll find some time. It looks like the gardens butt right up to the hospital I'll be working at. Maybe I can come here in my breaks.

I am not particularly planty. None of the ferns Mum and Dad give me every year survive more than a month or two, but I'm not against greenery in general as long as I don't have to weed it.

I pull my phone out of my pocket and search up a map of the area. It's a pretty big place. There are quite a few buildings in there and even a little stream.

I get back into the flow of pedestrians on the footpath and follow the outer perimeter of the gardens away from the hospital. My path takes me away from my room, and the shopping bag is getting heavier by the minute. I won't walk the whole perimeter, just this front bit.

An old stone wall soon replaces the iron one, but as it's only chest high I'd still be able to see into the gardens if it weren't too dark, and if there weren't too many trees.

I'm walking far slower than any of the people around me. I must be the only tourist in the crowd. I stay as close to the wall as possible so I don't annoy all these busy people with places to be. The rushing pedestrians are so focused on their destinations that not one of them reacts when the sound of heart-rending anguish sets my nerves jangling.

It's a woman's voice. She's somewhere inside those dark gardens and she's in trouble.

Another scream is disgorged from the darkness and my skin prickles in response, but still no one around me seems to care. Not even a head twitches in the poor woman's direction. I hope I don't get so hardened by city living that I could ever ignore someone in trouble.

I can't see anything inside the gardens except trees and shadows, but I'm about two seconds from vaulting this stone wall and finding the cause of that terror. Only the total lack of reaction from the people around me has me second guessing my instincts. Finally there's a gap between the trees and I can see the silhouette of a large three-storey building about a hundred metres into the park. The building's long flat roofline is broken by four sharply pitched gables that are not quite towers, but still manage to evoke castles, ghosts and bats. A few windows glow with a flickering yellow light, but most are dark. The screaming is definitely coming from that direction.

The stone wall is getting taller the closer I get to the castle-like roofline and soon I can't see inside the gardens at all.

The screaming stops. Not slowly, as if the woman found help. But suddenly, mid breath, like someone forced her to stop.

At last I see another tall, cast-iron gate in the wall. It's smaller than the last one, but still impressive with large glass lanterns atop brick and stone pillars. I stop walking and peer through the thick, black bars, reaching out one hand to steady myself on the brick pillar. As soon as my fingertips touch the rough brickwork, the sound of the wind whispering through the trees swells and morphs into human voices. People inside that building are crying in sorrow and some are keening in despair. More than one is furious. But all of them are desperate.

The trees seem to have shrunk and the Gothic-style building brightens as if the moon has appeared from behind a cloud.

Dread descends over me. The same dread I would feel if I were looking at a snake or over the edge of a cliff. Some primal instinct is warning me there's danger here.

The cry I heard in the beginning, that poor tortured woman, starts again. Her voice is clearer this time. I can hear the scratchy hoarseness of her throat, like she's been screaming for a while. And she's closer than the rest of the voices.

Her next scream makes the muscles on the back of my neck clench, and I flinch away from the pillar. The building darkens. I can still see it, but it looks less real now. The voices fade back to a whisper.

Through all this, no one around me reacts beyond a quick glance if I'm in their way. Is this normal here? Am I the one overreacting?

Maybe there's a simple explanation. Like an outdoor cinema with really great speakers and a really big screen.

My phone will tell me what I'm looking at.

I check a couple of different maps, but there's nothing that remotely matches what I can see.

Eventually, a middle-aged woman with wild hair and wilder clothes takes pity on me and stops to see if I need help.

"I am not lost exactly, but I think I have the wrong map," I say.

"What are you looking for?"

"I'm wondering what that building there is." I point to the distinctive roof line in the distance.

She turns and looks in the same direction as me.

"Which one?" She searches the dark.

I lean in a bit closer and point into the gardens when I'm jostled from behind. I put my hand on the woman's shoulder to catch myself from completely slamming into her. I see her searching eyes open wide and the silhouette of a Gothic roofline is reflected across them for a split second before she gasps and jumps away from me.

"I am so sorry," I say. "Someone pushed me."

But the wild haired woman is already hurrying away from me. She must think I'm some kind of weirdo.

I turn away from the ghostly building and start walking back the other way, towards my room. As the scream-whispers fade I start feeling worse and worse about the whole thing. It's more than the embarrassment of scaring that woman.

I just can't let it go. The thought that perhaps the building isn't real and I'm seeing things keeps niggling at me.

It certainly isn't the first time I've seen things that aren't there.

Sometimes for a few minutes after I wake up, my dream doesn't quite stop. I can be awake and looking around, but the dream plays on.

The doctors told my mother it probably isn't related to PTSD or anything like that. At the time I assumed 'anything like that' meant mental illness.

Now, I wonder.

I yawn, which cheers me up like chocolate and a great book on a stormy winter's night. I'm just really tired. It has been a terribly long and stressful day. I'm going to go back to my room and get some sleep.

Chapter 3

Dawn - My room

He's right behind me and I'm not fast enough. I feel the sharp tip of the knife against the small of my back as my bloodied hand slips from the door handle. I knew he would catch me. He always does.

The blade grates upwards across my spine and ribs before piercing my flesh. My muscles cramp around the blade and I wake in pain. It's another damn nightmare. I roll onto my side, curling up into a fetal position to stretch out my back.

I look around to reassure myself I'm safe in my new room in the old nurses' quarters. Wooden furniture, glossy white walls and my suitcase are all visible now. Unfortunately, so is the anonymous-faced killer. He is standing over me, watching, waiting for me to die.

He doesn't fade away, it's more like the dream gets harder to see. I don't know what the difference is myself, but it feels important. Either way, within a minute he is gone.

I've been trying to wake up for hours. Even while in these vivid dreams, I know I'm asleep. Sometimes I can even force myself awake.

Mum made me go and see a therapist back in primary school. She said the man in my nightmares represents my biological father, and because I don't remember him, my mind just puts anyone's face on the attacker. Sometimes it's a guy I know, like a friend from school, or my dad. Sometimes it's not, like today.

I am used to the nightmares, but that doesn't make them any easier to deal with. It only takes a minute or two before he fades away, but it feels much longer when you're being punched or stabbed.

When it's bad I can have five or six nightmares in a row and I spend the entire night fleeing houses, climbing over fences, and trying to find a hiding place safe enough. And if I manage to wake up, when I finally get the courage to go back to sleep, a new dream will start up straight away.

It often feels like I've lived through a week in one night, and I'm more tired in the morning than the night before.

The therapist said it's because I haven't processed what happened. She reckons I should be learning all I can about what happened back then. Dealing with the truth.

I'm calling bullshit on that. Why would I put myself through it? I don't want to think about how that stranger to me, killed my bio mother. Yes, I read a headline or two when I was younger. I know he tried to blame the whole thing on her, and that his version got more and more outrageous over time. But I have never read the court transcript Mum got for me. I've kept it, even bringing it here to Adelaide with me in case the day comes when I want to know more. That's not today though.

I still have an hour to go before I need to get up and start my morning routine, but I haven't got the energy to face the murderer again, so I get up and get ready.

The Hallway-Of-Doom and cold bathroom at the end of it have lost their spooky feeling now the sun's shining through the long line of open doors. Oh, this is why they were left open, to save on electricity during the day.

The sickly-green, tiled bathroom seems designed to discourage people from spending any time here. If so, the architect would be happy to know it's still working perfectly, even after a hundred years.

One side of the large room is lined with a row of showers with those filmy, white curtains that stick to your legs while you are trying to get clean. The other side of the room is wall-to-wall, heavy-wooden doors that are so short they barely come up to my chin and I can see the toilet under them as well. Awkward. I'm glad I have this bathroom to myself.

I rush through showering and getting dressed into my brand-new scrubs because it's like the Arctic in here. I tie my long, brown hair up into a ponytail and check I have some hair clips in my pocket in case the hospital is strict and I need put my hair in a bun.

On my way back to my room I see movement out of the corner of my eye as I walk back past the long line of open doorways. As usual no one is there when I turn my head, but it's a good reminder that I'm physically and mentally exhausted after driving across the country yesterday. No matter how much the adrenaline of first-day nerves has me tingling.

I need to find some caffeine and food ASAP.

I let myself out of the building into the crisp morning air. The leaves of the plane trees sparkle with a golden shine that tells me the sun hasn't been up for long.

Since I got up before my alarm, I use some of the extra time to move my car to a free all-day park a few blocks away. It's a bit of a hike to get back to the hospital, but I find a cafe on the way with plenty of spread-out, empty seating. I know the stereotype says that overweight people don't like to eat in public for fear of being judged. But trust me, some of us skinny people aren't too keen on it either. Everyone always checks what I eat, and how much of it I eat, to see if I am purposely starving myself. I'm not.

I'm a bit fussier now since I lost my sense of smell years ago. Cinnamon tastes like dirt now, which is a shame, because I really miss hot cinnamon-sugared donuts. I sigh, savouring the memory of scalding my fingers and tongue on a cold winter's day at the rural show. With ever-present optimism I order cinnamon toast and a coffee. Unfortunately, my sense of smell hasn't improved. It tastes like sweet dirt on toast. I should have gone for the full English breakfast like the couple sitting next to me did. Even the full-fat, flat white I drink on my walk to work doesn't completely satisfy me.

As soon as I get to the main entrance of the old hospital, I decide I hate it. Not the whole hospital, just the foyer. It's a wall of glass wedged strangely between the sides of two, red-brick buildings. The glass has a dark green tinge that makes me think it's old, so it might be original, but the way it sits between the buildings makes it look like an afterthought.

I cross the foyer checking for signage as I go. I should be concentrating on where I'm going, but I'm distracted by the history of this old place, so I'm quickly lost in the confusing mess of green or white hallways that all look the same. It doesn't help that the hospital is comprised of many different buildings that might have been built where they could fit on the block, rather than to any efficient plan.

I eventually find the human resources office and join a small group of new employees. We stand around nervously introducing ourselves while we wait, it turns out all the other people in this group are temporary workers too. We're here to boost numbers while the normal hospital staff are divided between this old hospital and the new site down the road.

After a short wait a brisk, humourless woman storms into the room and introduces herself as Jan. She begins by telling us we won't be getting the full orientation package because we're all on short term contracts and we will be supervised carefully.

My name is called, and I raise my hand. I have to concentrate on controlling the blood flow to my warming cheeks when everyone turns to stare curiously at me.

Jan tells me I will have to do a proper orientation in six weeks, when I start at the new hospital. For now, the abbreviated version is only a few hours long, leaving us free to work on the wards in the afternoon.

We are ushered into a conference room where Jan sits us down and puts a stream of short training videos on a Smart Board. They are all the usual stuff: OH&S; ethics; and a short history of the hospital and its staff. Everyone looks relieved when the lights are switched back on and we are led out for a tour of the hospital.

We are barely two wards from our starting point before I am completely lost. We are being barraged with fairly useless information that sounds so rehearsed that the inflection on the words has shifted weirdly. Jan's speech is emphasising words like in, or the, distracting me from what she is actually trying to say.

Everything looks the same as all the other old hospitals I've been in. Same green and blue of the older wards and white and beige of the newer ones, same unremarkable patient rooms.

I try to keep it all straight by noticing small details that set the wards apart; like the higher ceilings and smaller doorways that are particular to the oldest buildings. A few of the wards here and there are already empty, patients having been moved to the new hospital already. One whole wing is closed.

The elevators are small, so our group needs to split into two to go up to the top floor. I hang back with the smaller second group, which proves to be a mistake.

Jan sidles up next to me and starts chatting like we are best friends. I am the only newbie whose name she knows. This might be the closest thing the woman experiences to an actual friendship.

I nod politely while she tries to impress me with her experiences with famous people who have stayed in the hospital in the twenty years she's worked here. I ooh and ah appropriately, not that I think she notices.

I've completely tuned her out when I realise I've missed something important. She's looking at me expectantly. I rewind the conversation in my head and find I've been invited on an after-dark tour of the hospital.

"Oh sorry, when did you say it was?" I ask.

"Nine o'clock tonight and tomorrow night are the last tours I am giving."

I am actually interested in the history of this old building, but the thought of spending an evening with this woman leaves me exhausted.

"Oh, that's such a shame. I'm in the process of moving right now and I've already arranged to catch up with relatives tomorrow night." I stop talking before I give the lie away.

"Are you sure?" Jan tries again. "There's some really cool stuff the public aren't allowed to see down in the basements, a lot of leftovers from the nineteen hundreds. This was a teaching hospital as you must know, and there's even an old theatre down there they used to demonstrate autopsies in. It's one of the last of its kind left in the world."

I nod politely. I can't tell if this woman really likes history or whether it's the macabre she's into. I look closer at her face trying to imagine her as an aging, closet Goth.

Luckily we join the group again and Jan immediately reverts to ignoring me as she drops back into her much-rehearsed routine.

I give up trying to remember where everything is and resign myself to being perpetually lost for the next few weeks.

When we finally return to HR we are all told our assigned wards. I am excited to find out I will be in the surgical ward, since that is a specialty I'm interested in.

I try to remember how to get back to Surgical from here, but the only thing that comes to mind are the double doors at the entrance.

We are finally dismissed for lunch and told to report straight to our wards in a half hour.

I am trying to decide whether to stick with the group or leave to find food when my stomach growls loudly. Finding the kiosk it is. I ask directions and slip away before I get roped into getting things for others.

I'm walking briskly around a corner while scanning for directions on the wall beside me when strong hands grip my upper arms and I'm stopped in my tracks.

Unfortunately, my feet don't know about the change in program, and I lose my balance. I would have fallen on my butt if the hands hadn't immediately switched from holding me back, to holding me up.

I look up into a handsome face which would be an inch from mine if he weren't so tall. Late twenties, medium brown hair and the darkest, richest, chocolate-brown eyes. His jawline alone could bring tears to my eyes.

I sigh.

Not my type.

How could you ever relax and be yourself around someone so perfect. He would never even know I existed if I didn't nearly body slam him.

The beautiful man lets go of my arms like he has been burned and steps back a pace. His full lips morph from a grim line into a polite smile. I assume he was angry at my complete uselessness but has now remembered politeness is necessary at work, at least in public.

"Sorry for that," he says in a deep voice that flows over me like a warm bath. He should be a voice actor.

I'm not sure why he's apologising. Maybe he is afraid I will claim assault or something.

"No, I'm sorry. I wasn't paying attention. It's totally my fault," I mumble, looking down as my face reddens.

I notice his hospital lanyard. His name is Nathaniel Cain and he's a doctor, a surgeon in fact.

Typical. Why couldn't I have crashed into a nurse's assistant, or anyone else who doesn't have the power to fire me.

I have to get out of here. He's still standing in my way, so I skirt around him, heading anywhere but here.

Out of the corner of my eye I see his hand rising. I don't know whether it's due to my nightmare this morning or just because I'm out of my comfort zone here, but for one split second I think he's going to hit me.

I flinch away from his hand while he's looking right at me. Too late I realise he was getting a phone out of his top pocket. I am such an idiot.

The surgeon's jaw drops slightly as he stares at me. I think he is horrified to be judged so badly by me, until I see the corners of his mouth lift slightly.

Apparently, I am entertaining.

"Ignore me, way too many horror movies lately," I say and smile. I hope I look amused. The way I feel right now I probably look like one of those television chefs grinning stupidly at a bowl of whatever inedible muck they are mixing.

Dr Cain gives me a polite smile, probably already forgetting I exist, and walks away in that way beautiful people do. Not a hair out of place and, you know without having to check, even their socks match.

I check my watch. I am due on the ward in twenty minutes, and I now doubt I'm clever enough to find the kiosk at all. I grab two full-sized chocolate bars from the nearest vending machine. I eat while I walk, a skill I've perfected since eating is one of my favourite pastimes. With only one wrong turn I make my way to the ward. Hopefully being early will make a good impression.

Chapter 4

Noon - Surgical ward

I walk straight up to the reception desk and introduce myself to the woman working there. She's older than me with a shock of bright red hair and a cheerful, slightly-harried demeanour. Her name is Jennifer, Jenny to me, and she is sorting paperwork into file boxes in between answering the phones and manning the desk. She greets me warmly and sends me off to find a woman named Kaye.

As well as being my boss for the next few weeks, Kaye turns out to be the Team Leader who will be in charge of me at the new hospital.

I can't work out if it's good luck to meet her now, before it really counts, or incredibly bad luck that I will be fumbling around as a complete newbie in front of her today.

Kaye is a friendly, middle-aged woman, who is so intensely efficient she's scary. I'm probably being unfair. It's my first day and I am feeling intimidated by anyone who knows what they're doing.

Since I'm a nurse's assistant, I am basically an extra set of hands for anyone who needs me. I follow Kaye around for a while as she does her job perfectly while also acting as my tour guide.

When Kaye is satisfied I know my way around and can be trusted with simple tasks, she takes pity on me and lets me help out. I spend a few minutes helping a young business-man organise himself so he can work from his bed. As soon as I've put everything he needs within reach, he's on his phone making a business call. I leave him shouting angrily at some unlucky employee and go looking for Kaye.

I grin at Jenny as I walk up to the reception desk. She smiles back before squinting at my face and looking me up and down.

I sigh. I think I know what I'm in for. The second I met her I could tell she's a mother hen, and I'm worried she has singled me out as a particularly urgent case. She's already mentioned how skinny I am to Kaye.

"You look terrible," she says.

"I feel fine."

Which is true. I'm tired, but everyone's tired, right?

"Sweet, you are blue." She reaches over the counter for my hand and examines my definitely-blue fingernails.

"I go blue real easy, it's fine." I take my hand back gently and rub them together a bit to try and improve the circula-tion. "Any idea where Kaye is?"

"Actually, she needs you to sit with a patient. Apparently, they're getting a bit restless."

I give Jenny a nod and head down in the direction she pointed.

I don't know if it's because I'm actively looking for some-one, or if I desperately need caffeine, but I can see shapes moving in the corner of my eyes. It's not the usual dark shadow I sometimes see either. This is more like a blue smudge. The movement vanishes whenever I turn to look at it straight on though, so I'll ignore it for now.

Finding Kaye in a patient's room, I wait quietly in the hallway until she's finished. When she sees me waiting for her, she gives me a big smile. It feels nice to be wanted.

"Ana in room 10 is worrying me," Kaye explains as she walks me down the hallway. "She's quite frail, even for an older lady. She is still bleeding internally and needs to go back to theatre as soon as they can clear a space. The problem is she has very little English, so communication is a bit iffy. You just need to sit with her, make sure she doesn't try to leave again. Okay? Call me if you need me."

Kaye hurries off to be efficient somewhere else. I mask and glove up before heading into the room. There's no one in there but the patient, and a quick glance around reveals no cards or flowers either.

"Hi Ana," I say quietly to the shrunken figure on the bed.

The old woman's head turns sharply towards me and her eyes search my face. She seems shocked. I hope I didn't wake her up.

"I'm Lily and I'm here to keep you company for a while," I continue.

"Lilijana." The woman whispers. I recognise the name, I've had someone ask if my name is short for it before. I think it's European.

"No, just Lily," I reply.

We try to communicate for a while but Kaye is right, the woman's English is not good. Finally we resort to hand signals. She beckons me closer.

When I lean down, she sweeps one bony finger under the elastic of my face mask, tearing it off my face. I freeze in shock for a moment before taking a step back, out of arm's reach. She clearly meant to do it because her face is triumphant.

Heading back to the door to get a new mask gives me a chance to think through my options. Getting Kaye seems like a bad move. This lady is obviously going to be a problem, but I don't want to look like I can't manage a simple task either.

Still, it looks like the woman's getting more agitated. She's saying something I don't understand, so I am grateful when she points to her phone. That's something I can do.

I hand it to her and she fumbles around for a while, before managing to dial the number correctly and putting it to her ear. After a short wait she talks in a language I don't recognise.

I've got no idea what she's saying, but I feel better for her now I know she has people who care for her.

I guess I could be wrong. She could be talking to her landlord, or even her bank manager, but I don't think so. The tone of the conversation was friendly at the beginning, before becoming excited and even a little demanding now.

Ana looks straight at me while she talks, and I start to fidget with my uniform. What if she's telling them I'm useless? I busy myself around her, hoping to look like I know what I'm doing. Maybe she's telling them the hilarious story of how she souvenired another nurse's face mask. It's nice to see her heart rate come up a bit while she's talking. A bit of passion is just what she needs to pull through another operation.

Finally, I hear her dismiss the person on the other end and she hangs up. She calls my name, she actually says Lilijana which is close enough, and holds out the phone for me. I take it carefully, staying an arm's length away and then sit down on the seat beside her.

"That was a nice long conversation," I say, knowing she probably won't understand, but I can try. "It must be nice to talk to people you know after being stuck in here for weeks."

Ana doesn't respond. Maybe a shorter sentence.

"Was that your family?" I ask.

She smiles and nods.

"Grandmother," she murmurs.

She must mean she's a grandmother.

"That's nice," I answer.

Ana seems content now. She watches me out of the corner of her eye, but makes no attempt at conversation. She's just about to drift off to sleep as Kaye comes in to tell us Ana's surgery is scheduled for the next hour.

I pat Ana's arm and her filmy eyes blink open, focusing on my face. A wide smile wrinkles her thin, powdery skin, like I'm her friend rather than someone paid to take care of her. My eyes start to prickle, and I smile at her for a second before I have to look at the ceiling to make the threatening tears stay put.

Kaye sends me out of the room to find a new box of latex-free gloves. Finding the box barely takes a minute and it's only a few seconds more to put fresh gloves and a mask on, so it's a surprise to find Ana's room bursting with people when I get back. A quick glance over the uniforms and I identify the extra people crowded around Ana's bed as an orderly and two doctors.

A balding anaesthetist with a deeply lined forehead is leaning over Ana. I don't have time to figure out why, but there is something about his posture as he whispers to her that makes the hairs rise on the back of my neck.

But I am soon distracted by the doctor with his back to me. He's talking to Kaye and my cheeks burn as I recognise the deep, rich tones. I groan softly under my breath.

Ana hears my misery and looks up to see me standing in the doorway. The resigned apathy on her face changes instantly to unmistakable fear and she starts struggling to raise her upper body off the bed. Kaye, who is in the process of taking Ana's blood pressure, grimaces slightly but stops what she is doing to let Ana shift her position. I take a step forward to help, but Ana's bloodshot eyes are still fixed on mine as she speaks clearly, in a rising tone of desperation.

"Go."

I freeze in the doorway. Is she talking to me?

The doctor on my side of the bed turns around to see what triggered Ana's reaction. I was right. Even with his mask on I recognise Dr Cain, the surgeon I walked smack into.

He recognises me too. I see him frown and his eyes narrow as he stares at me for just a second too long before he turns back to his patient.

The balding doctor on the other side of the bed doesn't even look up. He ignores me, leans closer to Ana and continues whispering to her.

I assume he is trying to settle her down, but she just becomes more and more agitated. She puts her arm up, elbow in the anaesthetist's face, as she repeats the same word over and over.

"Go, go, go."

I stand frozen for a second more before I obey her wishes and flee the scene of whatever the hell my crime was. I keep going until I am far enough away that Ana can't see or hear me anymore.

Someone has followed me out of the room, I hear their footsteps. I turn around and find Dr Cain towering over me with a thunderous frown on his beautiful face.

Kaye is one step behind him and she calls the doctor's name. He stops a little too close to me for comfort and they discuss the plans for Ana's operation. I don't know why no one is asking me what I've done to Ana, but I'm absurdly grateful to not be the centre of attention. I end up carefully examining the white, rectangular box of medium-sized, latex-free gloves I'm still holding. My sweaty hands are leaving grey hand prints on it now.

I try backing up a short distance, but that just attracts Dr Cain's attention. I risk a peek up at him just as Kaye follows his gaze in my direction, so I see the exact moment she remembers I exist. I'm obviously not the only one affected by the doctor's good looks.

Kaye dismisses me to help one of the enrolled nurses at the other end of the ward, so I hand her the now-damp box of gloves and make my escape, fast.

As I walk down the hallway, I feel a crawling sensation on my skin. Trying to act casual, I glance back down the hall as I turn the corner towards the reception area. Dr Nathaniel Cain is standing with his arms folded tightly across his chest, glowering in my direction. I snap my head back in the direction my body's facing.

Looks like I've made an enemy there.

Chapter 5

Late afternoon - Surgical ward

I help a patient with their dinner for about a half an hour before Kaye comes to find me. Ana's finally consented to the operation, so I need to tidy and secure her belongings while she's away. I head over there straight away, wondering about the earlier incident. I thought we were starting to get along. She even smiled at me when she woke up. Maybe she thought I was someone else.

I give Ana's room a quick clean and put her phone and purse into the little lockable cabinet.

They said theft is down lately, with the hospital emptying out, this part of the building is pretty quiet now. Still, you can't be too careful.

I search Kaye out again and assist her with her next patient, a middle-aged man who's recovering from bowel surgery. Kaye's focused on her job with grim pleasure as she pulls the long drainage tube from the patient's abdomen. The poor guy collapses in on himself with a grunt.

Kaye notices his discomfort, but her hands are full. She has to deal with getting rid of the contaminated waste. Distracting the patient from his pain is my job. I tactfully ignore the tears gathering in his eyes and pat his arm, tell him he's brave and make jokes with him. I get him smiling again in under a minute.

After we clean up, Kaye tells me I can go as she hurries away. I thank her, but I don't know if she hears me. She's always so busy.

I'm walking up to the staffroom to get my things from my locker when I see a tall guy with unruly, dark hair walk quickly out of Ana's room. He's only a few years older than me, but his hard expression sets me on edge.

He's not staff. He's wearing work boots and hi-vis gear under a large navy-blue jacket. Maybe he's one of the construction workers?

Hi-Vis Man freezes when he sees me staring at him. Up this close his face is surprisingly expressive; I can almost see his thoughts. His eyebrows lift and mouth opens a smidge. I don't think he expected to get caught. He still looks angry, but now he's angry and surprised.

He looks down at my ID and back up at my face, weighing his choices before settling on one.

He leaves, walking swiftly past me towards the exit.

I am super glad I locked all of Ana's things away earlier. I wonder if I should alert someone. I check the room first. The little cabinet next to the bed is still secure and everything else is exactly where I left it. Looks like there's nothing to report.

I gather my things from my locker, wondering if I can sneak in a nap before dinner. I shouldn't, because then I might not wake back up until two in the morning and then

I'll eat junk. The eating junk could happen either way to be fair. All I have at my room is a frozen Beef Stroganoff.

I head out through the main entrance even though I know the nurses' quarters are somewhere behind the hospital, because I don't want to get lost. Once I hit the road I remember the beautiful gates I saw the night before are only metres to my left.

I'm exhausted, but that's pretty standard for me.

Deciding I'll survive a half-hour detour, I turn left towards the Botanic Gardens rather than right towards my room. I have to know if there is some horrific Gothic edifice eating people alive in there.

I strongly suspect I was having some sort of waking dream, I refuse to call it a hallucination, but I'd like to know for sure.

The beautiful wrought iron gates are just as impressive in the daytime. I push through one of the small pedestrian entrances and follow the main path deep into the park. These gardens have been here for a long time because the garden beds are full of mature trees and plants. Many of the trees have trunks too big to wrap my arms around and even the plants I'm used to seeing in small pots are taller than I am.

The lawns are a lush, deep green and there are heaps of man-made structures in here as well, all sorts of fountains, statues and gazebos, and some old stone and brick buildings. I am walking past an old wooden rotunda when I get a prickly feeling right between my shoulders.

Someone is watching me.

I glance back over my shoulder. There's no one close by. Even further away, no one seems particularly interested in me.

I veer off the path and make my way across the deep, spongy lawns. I don't really have a plan, I'm just following my heart. An avenue of trees leads me away from the path and up a small rise. These lines of hundred-foot-tall pine trees must have shaded a driveway once. Now they just lead to another large lawned area.

I still can't shake the feeling someone's following me. Sometimes I even hear the crispy leaves crunching under furtive footsteps.

The cool breeze is growing stronger now and the pine trees are whispering their warnings to me.

I cross a bitumen path and walk up to a small plaque set into the grass. It says the Adelaide Lunatic Asylum once stood here. Obviously quite a while ago, with a name that politically incorrect. There's no sign of it now, it was knocked down before I was even born. As I haven't seen any other creepy Gothic mansions here, this seems like the best candidate for the building I saw during my evening wander.

I look around trying to locate the boundaries of the garden and the road I was walking along last night. There are too many trees and this place is big. I can't tell if I'm in the right area.

Nothing even remotely close to a vampire's summer palace is in sight. There are some smaller buildings ahead of me, but they are very different looking.

No, there's nothing here to explain what I saw. I must have known this was the site of an old asylum, some sort of subconscious memory of something I read once. I do watch a lot of documentaries.

From what I've seen mental health facilities back then were pretty horrific places. It's hard to believe there was one right here as it feels so peaceful standing in the sunlight, surrounded by this carefully-perfected landscape. Even the shadows under the trees are not truly dark and it's almost closing time.

I imagine being locked in here as the sun goes down. The golden glow retreating as the darkness slithers in. The shade under the trees darkening to hide a world of evil, or just one man. The wind whispering through the pine trees rises to a shriek to drown out my screams.

I have to get out of here.

I'm barely back on the path before I hear footsteps behind me again. I veer to the left to let the person pass, but the sound remains a steady distance behind me.

I brace myself to check. I think I'm allowing my imagination to run away with me again. No one is going to be there.

Wrong again.

My feet stutter to a stop. The scruffy Hi-Vis Man I saw coming out of Ana's room is about ten paces behind me. The work gear is gone now, replaced by casual wear, but I recognise him by his unruly hair and grey-blue eyes.

A fleeting impression of guilt crosses his face, before it is replaced by a stony, neutral expression as he looks straight at me. His stare feels like a challenge as he closes the gap between us.

I'm torn between running and fighting until, at the last moment, he breaks eye contact and strides past me as if I'm not there.

I stand and watch him walk away while my heart acts like the drummer at a rock concert.

I have got to get my shit together.

I don't know why I let myself get so worked up. Why would anyone bother following me? And why would Dr Cain notice me long enough to hate me?

And of course, there's the thing last night.

I know I'm tired and stressed, but this is getting ridiculous.

What's worse is I can't let anyone know what's going on with me, because I already know what people will say.

I'm just like my father.

Chapter 6

Dawn - My room

I feel the attacker's hands claw into my shoulders as I wake up. I'm face down in my own bed. I can see my cream-coloured pillowcase and the glossy, white wall beside the bed. But still, an appalling weight presses me deep into the mattress, burying the lower half of my face in the pillow.

I can't breathe.

I know this is only a dream, but the lack of oxygen feels real. I can't help trying to fight him off. Twisting to escape his grasp I choke out a sob in between gasping for air.

Soon the pressure on my shoulders lessens and I know he's gone. I lay still for a moment to reorient myself to the real world. This is the third morning in a row I've been chased awake. For variety, this time the attacker was the grim-faced man I thought was following me yesterday.

But right now I've got bigger problems. I haven't had the courage to brave the long walk past all of those pitch-black, hell-mouths in the hallway to get to the bathroom and I've needed to go for several hours.

I check the window and I'm relieved to see milky light spilling in around the tattered edges of the blind. I get up and gather the things I will need to get ready for work and brave the now harmless hallway.

After I shower and dress, I check the time and head out to find food. I am shaky with hunger after only having a tiny frozen meal and a few chocolate bars for dinner last night.

Living in the city centre has its advantages. I find an open cafe only a block from my room and order a full English breakfast with extra bacon. The beauty of this meal is that even with no sense of smell all of the flavours are still perfect, particularly the meaty deliciousness of the bacon. I am still not quite satisfied when I finish, so I order a coffee to sip as I walk to work. I am going to have to hit the shops soon. With my appetite, I'll go broke eating at cafes.

It's less than a five-minute walk to the glass entrance foyer of the hospital, even while carefully sipping the coffee-lava. I'm looking around for a rubbish bin when I hear my name spoken in a deep, melted-chocolate voice.

My heart skips a beat or two. I could blame the two coffees I just drank, but I know the sudden arrhythmia is because I recognise that voice.

I slow my pace and look at a small group of impeccably-dressed men standing just outside the hospital entrance. Dr Cain excuses himself from the group and takes a step towards me.

"Oh," I manage, and my foot catches on the perfectly-smooth path. I stumble forward a step.

"Hello Lily." The doctor stands perfectly still with his hand stretched towards me, like a man trying to coax a bird to fly onto his hand.

He knows my name.

I put my hand out, expecting to shake his, but he catches mine and clasps it between his hands.

"Uh," I breathe.

I feel my face burning. I hate being the centre of attention at any time, but now my conversational skills seem to consist purely of vowel sounds.

I cast around for something intelligent to say. A task which requires I stop looking at him. I look down at the surgeon's chest, which is no help. He's not wearing a jacket today, just a slim-fitting, dark-blue, business shirt and tie. I cannot avoid noticing how wide his shoulders are compared to his waist. I am staring at our hands between us when he speaks.

"I wanted to talk to you."

I figure that much is obvious and I can't think of any clever replies, so I resort to monosyllables again.

"Oh?"

"I'll walk you inside, are you still in Surgical today?" He ushers me forward into the hospital.

To improve my chances of intelligent conversation I look around for anything to distract me from my anxiety. I see a green-tinged reflection in the foyer glass of the group of men the doctor was talking to. I think one of them is the balding doctor in Ana's room yesterday. I didn't see him before because he had his back to me. Without his mask on I can now see his narrow face and long teeth match his thinning hair and I adjust my impression of his age up a decade into his mid-to-late sixties. If I am about to be told off for upsetting Ana yesterday, I'm glad it's Dr Cain doing it rather than that guy. I feel like Baldy would just have me fired.

"You just moved to Adelaide," Dr. Cain states.

I nod.

"Yeah, I've been here two days now."

Yay, a full sentence. It helps that I'm not looking at him. We walk swiftly through the hospital, at least I won't get lost today.

"Where from?" he asks.

"New South Wales."

"That must be hard, moving away from your parents? How do they feel about it?"

"Relieved probably," I say with a smile.

He's silent for a minute, so I have to assume he doesn't have a sense of humour. I try again.

"They're happy for me. I've wanted to be a Registered Nurse forever."

He glances down at my Assistant In Nursing uniform, so I feel I need to explain.

"I did a cert' three in high school. I'm starting my Bachelor degree in the mid-year intake."

"So what made you choose Adelaide? Couldn't you find anything closer to home?"

My defensiveness rises. I've been asked why I would move here by too many people. I try to keep the annoyance from creeping into my answer.

"I had other offers but getting the nursing assistant position here was too good to pass up."

We arrive at the hallway that leads across to the surgical ward. I expect him to walk in with me, but he stops, frowning down at me. Did I say something wrong? I rummage around in my thoughts looking for a red flag. Nothing. He's probably trying to think of a nice way to fire me. I'm not going to help him with that, so I shrug internally and turn towards the ward.

"Wait," he says, stepping across to block my path.

I am suddenly feeling the difference in our size in a totally different way.

Less hot, and more threatening.

The top of my head doesn't even reach his throat. The department we have just walked through has already been transferred to the new hospital, so it's silent and empty. There's no one else at all in this hallway, and the doors to Surgical are kept shut this early.

I glance towards the doors, judging the distance, and then look back to his face trying to read his mood.

He is watching me intently. The corner of his lip lifts ever so slightly. It could be the start of a smirk, but it doesn't feel that friendly.

"I could definitely catch you before you got to that door," he says.

I laugh automatically. He is joking, right?

I see a predatory glint in his eye, before he flashes a smile and steps away from me.

"I'll be on the ward later," he says, walking off and leaving me with a racing heart and no idea what to think.

Chapter 7

Morning - Surgical ward

I am paired with Sophie for the morning. She's been a registered nurse for about five years, so she's new enough to feel sorry for me and experienced enough to be a great mentor. She's pretty cheeky, making her patients laugh with off-colour jokes. They love her.

Our morning is showering and feeding the patients. Sophie shows me how to input data into the patient charts and a few other things that I will get to do while on placements once my university course starts.

We work well together and the morning races by, so I'm disappointed when Sophie runs out of tasks and sends me off to find someone else to help.

Sadly, Jenny isn't at the reception desk. The girl there today is even younger than me and she hates her job, I can tell. It's like she's trying to be fired. At first I thought it was just me, but then I heard her smart-mouth a patient's adult son when no one else was around.

I'm standing at the desk waiting to be acknowledged when Kaye walks up and sends me off to keep Ana company for a while. Apparently, Ana's operation the day before was successful, but she's still combative and disorientated.

As I walk down to her room, I can't help feeling a bit anxious. I still don't know why she took such offense to me yesterday. I can only hope she's in a better mood now.

She's asleep.

And she has a visitor.

I check my patient first. Ana's breathing is laboured, and her skin has a pale grey tinge, but she looks healthier than she did yesterday. Doesn't look like there's much she needs from me just now, so I turn my attention to the visitor standing on the other side of the bed.

She's holding a long coat and a tiny handbag, so she's either just arrived, or is about to leave. Her clothes look like she came here straight from a nightclub, though the bouncer would have to be mad to let her in. She looks younger than I am and I'm barely legal.

The girl is tiny, not much more muscle mass than me. She looks healthy though, her long sandy-blonde hair is a perfect complement to her light, natural tan. Her face lights up with a wide smile, like she's been expecting me.

"Hey there," I say, giving her a genuine smile in response. "I'm Lily."

The girl gets one of those expressions particular to teenagers who are being told what to do by adults. I even see the beginning of an eye-roll before she catches herself and her expression becomes carefully neutral. It feels weird being on the adult side of that interaction at the ripe old age of nineteen. Will I be called a boomer next?

"I'm Amber. You're Ana's nurse," she says, smiling again.

"I'm one of the nurses looking after her," I reply.

I don't want her thinking I'm the one making decisions.

"How do you know her?" I ask.

"She's my grandmother."

This is great, the girl might be able to interpret for us.

"So have you spoken to anyone yet?"

"I just got here," she says, shaking her head.

"I'll go and get someone who can tell you how your grandmother is doing."

Amber looks like she has something to say, but as I probably won't be able to answer any of her questions, I continue in a rush.

"Make yourself comfortable." I gesture to the green vinyl-covered chair next to the bed. "You know, that chair pulls out into a bed if you want to get some sleep while you are waiting for your Nan to wake up."

The girl looks at the chair dubiously. I don't blame her, it's probably not a great idea to sit in a dress that short.

"I'm fine."

"Okay, I won't be long," I say, heading out of the room.

The brat at the reception desk watches me walk up while still typing on the keyboard. I'm impressed by her skills, pity she's such a bitch. I wait until she pauses and I say "Hi," and give her a smile. I've decided to use my most polite behaviour around her to see how she reacts.

"Yes?"

"I'm watching Ana in room 10 and her granddaughter has just arrived. I was wondering-"

"Pretty sure she hasn't," the brat interrupts, shaking her head. "I've had that file out twice today, trying to find an emergency contact. No husband, no kids. She has no relatives at all."

"File must be wrong then, I guess." I raise an eyebrow at her, daring her to fight me on it. "Anyway, I have to get back. Could you please let Kaye know? Someone needs to update the granddaughter on Ana's condition. Oh, also I'm not sure if I need to keep watching her now or not."

I give the pouting brat a big smile and wave as I turn my back on her and head back to Ana's room.

Ana is awake and talking to her granddaughter in that language I don't recognise when I walk in. I don't think it's Italian or German based on my primary school lessons, so I can't guess at what their heritage is. They both give me a big smile when they see me.

I'm glad to see Ana looking so lively, but I still can't get my head around her mood swings. One minute we're friends, the next she can't stand to be around me.

I busy myself changing the water in the jug and doing other unnecessary tasks to give them an illusion of privacy. After a few minutes Amber breaks off her conversation and turns her attention to me.

"My grandmother says you look like someone she used to know. She was wondering if you remember her at all." Her voice is hesitant, a bit apologetic.

"Sorry, she must be thinking of someone else," I reply. "I've lived in New South Wales pretty much my whole life. I only just got into town."

Amber looks disappointed and has a quick conversation with Ana before addressing me again.

"But you're from here, right?"

I nod, wondering how she could tell.

I'm still trying to decide how much to reveal about myself to a patient's family, when I hear voices in the hall. Amber springs out of the chair and gives me a desperate glance before dashing into the tiny bathroom and locking the door behind her.

Ana's panicked face watches Amber hide and then turns to me.

"Go," she whispers.

But I'm still frozen in place trying to understand what's happening when Kaye enters the room with the intimidating Dr Cain a pace behind her.

My heart flip-flops in my chest, and I wonder if Amber has room in that bathroom for me.

"Hi Ana, Lily," Kaye says. "I hear your granddaughter has finally come to pay you a visit Ana."

Ana shakes her head, her lips pressed grimly together. She stares at me for a long second before lying back on her pillow and closing her eyes in dismissal. Kaye and Dr Cain both look to me for an explanation.

I'm usually pretty good at thinking on my feet, but a rational explanation for Amber and Ana's behaviour escapes me. Still, the instinct to cover for a young girl in obvious distress overcomes my rational self and I make excuses.

"Sorry, uh, there was a young girl here earlier, so I uh, just assumed..." I stammer.

Kaye looks only mildly disappointed in me, but the fleeting anger I see on the surgeon's face startles me. Luckily, Kaye dismisses me to go help someone else. Damn. I don't think I am making a very good impression on her.

Dr Cain watches me leave and by the look on his face, I'm pretty sure he doesn't believe a word I said.

Chapter 8

Noon - Surgical ward

Unfortunately Sophie was on top of all of her tasks, so I'm helping a different nurse change a wound dressing when Kaye comes in and tells me to go for my lunch break.

I apologise to Kaye again, but she doesn't seem too upset. Our patient, who had been lying back with a bored expression on her face, perks up a bit at the whiff of a scandal. I'm almost sorry to disappoint her by not wasting any time getting out of there.

I'm starving as usual, so I head straight for the kiosk. I'm three deep in the line at the counter when I see Amber walk in. She gives me a long look and then walks to one of the small tables outside and sits watching me. When my turn finally comes I get a pie, a bag of hot chips, and the obligatory chocolate bar for a cheeky snack later, and take them outside to Amber's table.

The wind is a bit too brisk to be comfortable here, particularly in my lightweight uniform, but Amber pushes a chair out with her foot, so I don't feel like I have much choice.

I sit gingerly on the icy metal chair and grudgingly offer to share my chips with her. She takes a couple, juggling them between her fingers to cool them down. I take a bite of my chicken pie and chew slowly.

Since it looks like she isn't going to broach the subject, I start things off.

"Are you on the run from the cops or something?" I ask with a smile, so she knows I'm joking.

She doesn't smile back. Instead, she nibbles at a chip, looking at anything but me.

"Wait, you aren't actually in trouble with the police are you?" I ask.

She shakes her head and reaches into her tiny handbag and pulls out an even tinier stainless-steel drink bottle and sets it carefully on the rickety table.

I try again.

"What's wrong? Is there something I can help with?"

As soon as the words leave my mouth I worry I'm getting myself into something I'll regret. My fear deepens when I see the way Amber sits forward and her expression brightens.

I try to dig myself out of the hole.

"You don't need to be frightened of the staff at the hospital. Nurse Kaye, who is looking after your grandmother, is my boss. She's really nice. She's the woman who came into the room with the surgeon just before."

Amber chews her lip for a moment before confessing.

"It's not her. It's him."

Amber being scared of Dr Cain doesn't really shock me. I find him pretty nerve-racking myself, probably for different reasons though. He's possibly too old for me, so he's definitely too old for her.

"Oh, how do you know him?" I ask.

She plays for time by picking up another chip and blowing on it before she explains.

"Our families don't get along."

Okay. That goes a long way towards explaining why Ana is so combative about being treated by him. It must be awful being so vulnerable around someone you don't trust.

It might also be why none of Ana's family are visiting.

Part of me wants to reassure Amber that Dr Cain is a great doctor, but I don't actually know anything about him. I settle for trying to convince her to come back in and talk to Kaye. Now I know what the problem is, I feel confident we can sort something out to make them both feel more comfortable.

I look at my watch; I have to be back on the ward in fifteen minutes.

"Why don't you come back in with me," I suggest. "I could get Kaye to speak to you by yourself."

Amber doesn't look convinced, but she doesn't say no either.

"If you don't want to see the doctor you can wait outside the ward until I make sure he's gone."

Amber shrugs noncommittally, so I eat quietly to give her a chance to think. I finish my pie and am dipping a hot chip in tomato sauce when I see the grim-faced, scruffy-haired guy from the hospital and Botanic Gardens yesterday. He is hurrying towards the kiosk when he scans the eating area and we lock eyes for a split second. I don't have time to look away before he freezes on the spot, does a quick 180 and walks swiftly back in the direction he came from.

I'm trying to decide if the stranger's weird behaviour is something to be worried about when Amber sees my frown and turns to follow my gaze. She must see nothing of interest in the guy, because she turns back to me, picks up the little drink bottle in front of her and holds it out in my direction.

"Would you like some? I made it. It's homemade cordial, my own recipe."

"No thanks," I say, giving her an apologetic smile.

It feels rude to say no, but nothing is going to make me drink something I can't even see, handed to me by someone I have known for ten minutes.

"Go on, it's really nice, I used fresh raspberries."

I shake my head firmly. I stuff the last couple of chips into my mouth and look at my watch to end the discussion.

"I have to go in." I stand and look at her. "Are you coming?"

She shakes her head and I'm disappointed, but I head inside.

And I don't even get lost.

I'm not on the ward for five minutes before I step out into the hallway and bump into Dr Cain, not literally this time though. Still, I am not quick enough to smother the little gasp that escapes my mouth, or the flinch. He stops walking and frowns down at me.

"Did I scare you Lily?"

I am so relieved that Amber hasn't come with me that I can find a weak smile for him.

"No, sorry Dr. Cain. Like I said earlier, I'm just jumpy."

"Do you have a moment?" he asks.

"Sure." He outranks me here by only about a thousand levels, what am I going to say? "I do have to help Sophie get one of her patients into a wheelchair though."

"Fair enough. Would you like to come out to dinner with me tomorrow night? We could continue our conversation then."

I have to work very hard to keep my face from betraying my shock.

"I don't even know you." My reply is a little abrupt.

I hate how flustered I am around him.

"That is the precise problem I am trying to solve, Lily," he answers patiently.

I nod.

"Okay," I answer, mostly because my cognitive processes have deserted me, and okay is one of the few words I can remember.

All my boyfriends have been in my own age group, you know, guys. Guys that are so entranced with themselves, their teams, or their cars, that I can just hang out and have a good time without being made the centre of attention. Which, in hindsight, probably explains why none of my relationships were ever super serious.

And now I think about it, I am not even a hundred percent sure this is a date. Maybe it's just a work colleague thing. Can a surgeon even ask an Assistant In Nursing out on a date? I feel overwhelmed.

"Shall I pick you up at seven?" he asks.

"Seven's good. I'm actually staying in the old nurses' quarters here," I answer. "The one they're pulling down."

I feel weird giving a stranger my address, but I can't think of any way of getting around it without insulting him. Then I realise I could have just met him in a cafe around the corner from the hospital. Never mind, I'm moving in a few weeks anyway.

"Tomorrow then," he says.

I nod. I should have ample time to get home, shower and try on and reject my whole wardrobe at least twice.

"Good." He smiles at me, turns away and walks back down the corridor.

Little butterflies are fluttering around in my stomach. Too late I remember Amber and Ana's family have major issues with the man. It can't be that bad, can it? The butterflies inside me start careening around, ricocheting off the walls of my stomach.

I remind myself he's a surgeon. He holds people's lives in his hands all the time. I'm being an idiot and I have to get back to work. I put tomorrow night firmly in a tiny box in my mind and hurry up the scuffed and tired old hallway to help Sophie with her patient.

Chapter 9

Before dawn - My room

I know I'm awake, because I can see the walls of my bedroom lit by a blood-red glow from the power board on the floor, but I can't move yet.

I have no option but to lie still and listen to his whispering. He's a featureless shadow even though he's so close I can feel his breath on my cheek. He tells me I'm worthless, a monster, and my death will make the world safer, happier. He tells me there is no one left to miss me.

Rough fingers brush my temple and stroke softly down the side of my face to my neck. The killer's hands circle my throat and his crushing grip chokes off my breath.

I lie paralysed with my head pounding and my lungs burning until finally my fingers twitch, then my arms. I can move. I thrash frantically, fighting for air until the agonizing weight on my throat vanishes and I am alone.

I gasp for air and try to rub away the residual pain in my neck. It takes a good ten minutes to recover my sanity. These nightmares are getting worse and worse.

It's only five o'clock in the morning, but I'm not going back to sleep after that. I get up and pop on my Bluetooth headphones. I could use something a little heavy, maybe even a little angry, after my fourth bad sleep in a row. I select Parkway Drive's new album. It's nearly impossible to be afraid while listening to metal.

But I'm still going to need to wait for daybreak before I can brave Satan's Hallway outside my door. I put the kettle on and make myself a coffee and some instant noodles for breakfast.

The instant coffee tastes like heaven after only five hours sleep but I'm only halfway through it when I realise exactly how big a mistake I've made. I badly need to pee.

I stick my head out of the door to check on the Hallway-Of-Horror's current status.

Each doorway is etched out in charcoal grey down the length of the inky-black hallway. There isn't even a hint of dawn.

But I'm desperate. I leave my door open and dash over to the stairs and hit the timer for the overhead lights, before jogging down to the bathroom at the other end of the hall.

My Bluetooth connection drops out as I enter the only stall with a working lock, and all my artificial courage in-stantly deserts me. Moving at a speed only adrenaline can provide, I am finished and back out of the stall in seconds.

I wash my hands over a chipped white basin while keep-ing my eyes carefully away from the row of mirrors. I'm not stupid, and I've seen plenty of horror movies.

I dash back through the door to race the light timer back to my room. Of course, luck is not on my side this morning or I'd still be safely tucked up in bed.

The overhead lights click off the instant I enter the hall. I skid to a stop in the bright pool of light leaking from the bathroom and look down into the almost perfect darkness stretching away from me. The golden glow of my open door in the distance only seems to make the long hallway even darker.

I hit the timer outside the bathroom. Nothing happens. The switch doesn't work.

I see a shadow move across one of the doorways about halfway down the hallway. I tell myself it's just my eyes trying to cope with the almost complete lack of stimulus, until the shadow crosses another doorway. It's headed my way.

My hands shake uncontrollably as I consider my choices. I dismiss the bathroom behind me immediately. With its see-through shower curtains and doors that any monster could just slither under, there's nowhere to hide.

My only option is to calm down and admit it's probably my overactive imagination terrorising me again. I take a deep, steadying breath and step out into the dark, towards the closest open door. I reach my hand inside and slide it up the door frame until I find the light switch and flick it down.

Instantly a warm yellow light spills out into the hall. The glow only reaches a few metres, but I move from door to door switching on every light on the right side of the hallway as I go.

I don't see anything that would explain the movement I saw. Still, I lose my nerve near the end and pelt past the remaining few darkened doorways and throw my door shut with a crash. I collapse onto my bed ashamed of my behaviour. Am I ever going to grow up?

My brain has only just started dredging up every shameful thing I have ever done when I hear swift footsteps coming up the stairs and a tentative knock at the door.

"Lily? Was that you? Is everything alright?"

I groan and sit up. I'm such an idiot, how am I going to explain this? I pull a pale-blue dressing gown over the old shorts and singlet I sleep in and open the door.

Sam's standing in front of me in loose grey pj pants with no top. He has tattoos. Lots of them.

I remember my headphones are still uselessly covering my ears and pull them forwards off my head, dragging my hair onto my face.

"I'm so sorry to wake you," I say shamefaced and try to scrape my hair out of my eyes. "The door slipped out of my hand."

Sam looks up the hallway at all the blazing lights wasting electricity. Luckily, he just scratches his chest distractedly and shakes his head.

"Nah, it's fine I have to get up now anyway, I'm working a double at the new hospital today," he says.

"Oh?" I'm curious as I still haven't seen the new site.

Also, if I change the topic maybe I won't have to admit I have the courage of a three-year-old.

"What's it like?"

"Don't know yet. There are some teething problems for sure. We're trying to get them sorted before the rest of you lot move in. That's why I've got the overtime."

"That's no good, I hope you get it worked out," I say. "Oh, and say sorry to Ellie too if you see her before I do. I still haven't met her yet."

His friendly expression shuts down and he starts looking as shady as a toddler who's been in the lolly jar.

"Oh, she's real busy. I doubt she's even here right now." His voice trails off as he turns to go.

At the top of the stairs he gives me a quick half wave and takes the steps down two at a time.

I wonder why he got weird when I mentioned Ellie, maybe they don't get along. I need to pop upstairs and introduce myself to her when I get the chance. Right now though, I can finally see pale grey light shining around the blinds in my room, so it's time for a shower. As usual the hallway's lost all its spookiness in the light, and I shower, dress, and get to work in less than an hour.

The ward's busy when I get in, and because it's a Friday it'll only get busier as the day continues. Patients and their families are always hoping to get out for the weekend. I decide to drop in on Ana if I get time. I want to let her know I talked to Amber.

Kaye assigns me to Sophie for the morning. We shower, dress, and feed our patients so they are ready to face the world. The busy morning races by and it's early afternoon before I'm sent for my lunch break. I am, as usual, absolutely ravenous, but I head down to Ana's room first. There must be something we can do to make her feel safer here.

I'm only one room away when Kaye walks briskly out of Ana's room, stopping when she sees me.

"Where are you off to?" Kaye asks me.

Her words seem like an accusation, but her tone is friendly.

"I was going to say hello to Ana. I haven't had a chance to see her today yet."

Kaye's lips become a thin line.

"Come with me first," she says.

Something is up. I trawl through my memories of the last few days, searching for any mistakes. We walk into the staffroom. Kaye plonks herself down in one of the chairs and points to another. I sit down with my jaw clenched and my heart fooling around with some interesting Ska beats.

"I wanted to talk to you in private because you're new to this. You might need a moment to yourself after I give you some bad news about one of the patients," Kaye says.

"Oh no, who?" I ask automatically, feeling a wave of relief that I'm not in trouble and then shame at my heartlessness.

"Ana died just after midnight last night," Kaye replies. "I know you spent some time with her."

No, please not her. I feel blindsided.

"Oh my god, really?" I blurt.

I can feel my face start to burn. I try hard to act professional in front of my boss, but I had thought Ana was doing better. And then there's Amber.

Kaye is looking at me sympathetically.

"She looked really good yesterday," I say.

"It was a surprise to me too," Kaye says. "But Dr Cain and another doctor were on the ward at the time, and they worked on her themselves."

"Dr Cain was here at midnight?"

"Yes, it was quite lucky. He'd stayed back for a meeting and came in to collect some paperwork. It's a shame he couldn't save her, but at least she won't have to be a coroner's case, they can drag out for weeks," Kaye says.

I sit quietly for a moment, then realise I have a confession to make before I'm in even deeper trouble.

"Her granddaughter really was here yesterday. Her name is Amber, but when she heard people coming, she left. I think she might be shy," I end lamely.

I don't want to tell Kaye the girl was in the bathroom and make all of us look like idiots.

I feel guilty betraying Amber's secret, but knowing your family member has died, and being able to claim their body, is surely more important than any issues they have with Dr Cain.

"Well, someone will need to come forward and claim her body soon. Burton Funerals have already picked her up and they'll cremate her as soon as the police clearance comes through," Kaye says. "Wait here."

She walks out of the room returning seconds later with a piece of paper and a pen.

"Write down the details and I'll add it to Ana's file and let the funeral home know as well. Maybe they can track the family down. In the meantime, keep an eye out for the granddaughter and let me know immediately if you see her again."

I write everything I know about Amber on the lined paper. Kaye gives me a firm look, an unspoken warning not to screw up again.

In which case, I have something else to tell her.

"Dr Cain knows them, Ana's family. Amber said their families know each other."

Kaye frowns.

"I don't think so. He has asked me several times if we've managed to find any relatives."

I nod miserably. I've done what I can. I must look as lost as I feel because Kaye sends me off to lunch and tells me to take an extra half hour if I need to. I hurry down to the kiosk in the hope Amber might try to meet up with me again.

She's not there.

I'm not hungry, but I order some hot chips and a roast beef and gravy roll to fuel my afternoon. I sit down and force myself to eat while I look around for Amber.

A woman at the next table gives me a sympathetic smile and I realise I must look like my date has stood me up.

I'm surprised when my plate is clean at the end of my break. It seems like nothing can really harm my appetite, not that I remember eating. I'm disappointed that Amber hasn't come here, but I'm also a bit relieved. I really don't want to be the one to tell that poor girl her grandmother is dead.

Chapter 10

Late afternoon - Hospital foyer

On my way out of work that afternoon I run into Jan from HR as I am crossing the foyer. At first I pretend I don't see her, but she's annoyingly persistent.

"Coming to the hospital tour tonight?" she asks in a friendly tone.

"No sorry, I have plans."

It's like I flipped a switch. All of Jan's forced friendliness is gone, replaced with utter contempt. She must really have her ego tied up in her superior knowledge of this place. And while I don't really care for the woman, I don't want to make any enemies at work. I look for a way to smooth things over.

"I might be able to make it tomorrow night if you are doing one then?"

"I hadn't planned on it," she answers. "But you aren't the only one who's asked, so I'll see if I can get approval. I'm working all day tomorrow, so drop in and let me know if you still want to come."

Even though I don't have a shift on Saturday I figure this is as good a place as any to bail from this conversation.

"Okay then." I give my best attempt at a genuine smile and hurry away.

The route back to my room takes me along a picturesque avenue of old plane trees already decked out in their autumn colours. There are enough leaves on the ground now to start collecting in piles in the gutters and corners of buildings.

Winter isn't far away. I need to start looking for a more permanent place to stay. The old dorms will turn absolutely frigid soon.

I eat a Snickers bar as I walk because I don't know how long it will be until I eat, or whether it will be edible. Not that I am a fussy eater, I'm too hungry for that.

I don't have long to get ready for my dinner date. If I had seen Dr Cain at all today I might've tried to call it off. Maybe. It's easy to feel brave when he's not actually here staring down at me.

Still, I really should've planned to meet him out somewhere. That also would've given me the excuse to go and check on my car. I haven't even seen it since Wednesday morning, it might not have any wheels left by now.

Actually, considering how sketchy the buildings over there looked, my little car might be someone's house by now. At least it doesn't leak and the heater works.

As I walk into the building I debate heading upstairs to introduce myself to Ellie. No, I really need to get moving if I'm going to have a shower before the sun goes down and this place makes its nightly transition into a Gothic horror set piece.

After my shower I use the rust spotted mirrors in the bathroom to add a smoky touch to my eye makeup. It's hard when I have to keep one eye looking out for any unusual movement in the mirrors. It's still sunny outside, but I feel like mirrors can be tricky, so it's best to be careful.

Choosing my outfit takes the longest time. I cycle through a few dresses, discarding them all because they send the wrong message: too eager; completely disinterested; lost teenager; vamp.

I finally settle on a modest, but figure-hugging, black dress. If I had curves this one would be a bit too much, but I am so thin that the snug fit is the only thing saving this dress from looking like I stole it from my nan. I would describe it as a classic look, but I know more about animal husbandry than fashion.

I add small silver earrings and a few silver rings that I can never wear to work, before completing my look with a small clutch that I wear with a chain shoulder strap. A careful balance between date and work dinner.

I look in the mirror and groan. Sure, I look great. But I must have been taken over by a demon to accept this date. I've never dressed up like this to go out with a guy. Jeans and a nice top are more my style, and all my usual dates expected.

What if Dr Cain shows up in jeans?

He's impeccably dressed at the hospital, but people are always more casual in their spare time, particularly when they are forced to wear a suit at work.

My stomach starts to churn. I should have asked where we were going, that might have helped with the clothing choice. I think I would rather be over dressed than under dressed though.

Because Sam isn't home to answer the main door, I put a light coat on over my dress and head outside to wait.

The sun has set and the street is dark except for small pools of amber light every fifty metres or so. The breeze has picked up a little and the dry leaves are skittering around like mice in a plague.

I am scanning the street for Dr Cain when I see a man standing motionless in the darkness under a plane tree on the other side of the road. There is something vaguely familiar about his silhouette as he stands waiting for some-one. I don't know anyone here yet, so it's easy to dismiss the stranger from my mind as a sleek black sedan pulls up to the curb in front of me. It's not a legal parking space, but the driver stops the engine and climbs out of the car.

A frisson of nervous excitement shivers through me as I recognise my date.

Dr Cain is wearing a dark, slim-fitting suit. I was stupid to think this man might dress down for dinner. For all I know he's come straight from work.

He walks around the car and stops a step or two away and holds his hands out to me. I wonder if he is standing back in a deliberate attempt to not intimidate me. Even outdoors he dominates the space impressively.

I step forward and hold my hand out to him. Again, rather than shaking my hand, he draws it closer to his body and holds it between his, as if warming me. It warms my face alright, my cheeks are on fire.

"Hello, Lily," he says, his eyes searching my face.

I try to will my cheeks to behave. I am desperately trying to create the illusion this is all normal for me, as if I'm always picked up for dinner by accomplished and attractive men.

"Hi Dr Cain." My traitorous voice is hoarse.

I look down and cough lightly.

He raises our hands to my chin, forcing me to look up into his too handsome, too close face. Even now I can't tell what he is thinking.

"Call me Nathan." His deep voice feels like a caress.

Yeah, I don't think this is a work dinner.

"Nathan," I repeat.

His shoulders relax slightly and he smiles the first proper smile I've seen on his face. I instantly want to be the cause of more.

He ushers me into the passenger seat of his car.

Now that I'm no longer looking directly at him, I'm disappointed with myself as I watch him walk around the front of the car. I can't just fall for a man because he has a beautiful smile, and other very attractive attributes. Particularly when, of the little I do know of him: his mood varies between indifferent to unfriendly; we work at the same hospital; and he knows at least one family who would hide in a bathroom to avoid him.

Nathan gets into the driver's seat, starts the car and indicates to pull away from the curb. A car stops to let us pull out almost immediately. An expensive car like this might even be worth the price if that's normal behaviour.

I watch Nathan driving while I try to think of a conversation starter.

"Nice car," I say.

I can't blame it on tiredness. My heart is racing, you would think I was about to jump out of a plane.

"Yes," he replies.

I guess I deserved that. I figure I have given it a try and he can take it from here if he wants to chat.

We are only a few blocks into the city when Nathan turns the car into a multi-storey car park with ridiculously expensive special rates and pulls into a reserved park on the ground floor.

I get out before Nathan can make it around to my side of the car. He frowns. He is obviously used to a more passive date than me or, if the look on his face is anything to go by, he's wondering why he forgot to lock me in. His face smooths out and he holds out his hands for mine again. I give him my right hand and he rubs it absently while we walk outside. When we approach a small restaurant Nathan tucks my hand around his arm so he can open the door.

"A friend of mine owns this place," he explains. "She's great."

The restaurant is high end. It has long white tablecloths and thick, cloth napkins. There are three types of silverware and a choice of wine glasses already set on each table.

The host greets Nathan by name and we are led to a small table towards the back, where it's quieter. As soon as I sit down, I check the menu. It has blood-red roses painted down one side to match a tiny vase of fresh rosebuds in the centre of our table.

The colour of the rosebuds is such a deep red I wonder if they have been dyed. I know not all roses have a fragrance, but I bet if I could smell, these would smell delicious. Would I taste anything if I ate one? Definitely not the place or time to try that.

I don't recognise many of the items on the menu and the prices are a little nerve-racking. I am definitely going to still be hungry after this meal. Nathan hasn't even glanced at his menu; he's sitting watching me.

"The duck is very good," he suggests.

I find it on the menu. It's cooked in sour cherries which sounds interesting.

I've never tried duck because I used to keep two as pets on the farm. While they were holy terrors in the yard, I just couldn't bring myself to eat them. No matter how often Dad suggested it.

"Thanks, I'll try that then." I put the menu down, feeling partly proud of my bravery at trying something new, and partly guilty about the ducks, but I can ignore that.

When the waitress comes over to our table Nathan orders for both of us, including starters and wine. I usually protest at that sort of arrogance, but the waitress is flirting shamelessly with him. He seems oblivious, but I choose to let her believe I am intimate enough with Nathan that he knows what I like. He waits until the waitress saunters off to get our drinks before speaking to me.

"So Lily, tell me about yourself."

The question is pretty vague, but his demeanour is not. He's watching me as intently as ever, as if the immediate future hangs on my next words.

"Um, what would you like to know? I grew up on my family's cattle farm a few hours down the coast from Sydney, so I can ride a motorbike or a horse better than I can ride a push-bike." My voice trails off as I realise I am talking about riding things on a first date.

Awkward.

I hope his sense of humour isn't as crude as some of my friends back home.

I check his expression, there's not even a hint of a smirk. I had wanted to surprise him, and it worked. Everyone from the city is surprised when I talk about farm life. I think people see my tiny size and think I'm dainty, breakable. They're wrong.

Sure, I've had a few broken bones and I'm not as strong as most people, but with a bit of extra energy applied there's always a way around that. That's probably why I eat my weight in protein every day. Also, being small has its advantages. Cows don't see me as a threat, so they are almost never aggressive with me.

Our salt and pepper quail entrees arrive with a glass of white wine. I have never eaten quail before and I probably won't eat it again if this is quail at its best.

I pick at my food while I answer Nathan's frequent questions about farm life and my childhood. He seems genuinely interested in me. He doesn't just tune out my answers while waiting to talk about himself like some people. I'm starting to think the bad vibes I got off him the first couple of times we met might have just been because I made myself look like a complete idiot.

Our starter plates are cleared as our main meals arrive, complete with a matched red wine. Nathan sips his wine, waiting for me to try my meal.

I am ready to hate the duck when I see it doesn't look anything like chicken. It is much redder and still bloody in the centre. It's served in a pool of dark sauce that I think I can see a few mushy cherries in. In fact my meal seems much bloodier than Nathan's. I don't know if that's normal, but as he doesn't mention it, I assume it's fine.

I cut off a small piece of the meat and use the knife to scoop extra sauce over it before bringing it to my mouth.

The first thing I taste is the sharp, sour flavour of the cherries but as I chew, the savoury notes of the meat coat my mouth with a tangy, almost metallic, aftertaste which leaves my mouth tingling. The combination is surprisingly good, fantastic even. I put a much larger piece in my mouth and suck on the juices, before chewing it thoroughly.

"What do you think?" Nathan asks.

"It's delicious," I answer.

He responds with a satisfied smile and finally shifts his attention from me to his meal.

"What are your parents like?" Nathan asks, cutting a piece of his duck.

"They're great." I answer so enthusiastically that Nathan's eyebrows twitch slightly upwards. "They both work the farm, even Mum."

"Do you take after her?"

"No," I admit. "I mean, I work hard too, but I don't look anything like her. She's way taller than me and she's got masses of red hair, even longer than mine. And she's covered in those beautiful big freckles that redheads get."

"So you must take after your father then?"

This is starting to get awkward now. I usually don't volunteer the information that I'm adopted if I can avoid it. Partly as it's no one's business, but mostly because it leads to questions about my bio parents.

But if I don't say something now it'll be weird if he does eventually find out. I can't believe it's come up so soon. I've known some people for years before I needed to tell them. I try to think of a way to minimise the issue.

"No, my dad is a giant bear of a man with a bushy beard and even bushier eyebrows." I laugh lightly, stalling for time.

"My sister and I are actually adopted," I add finally, hoping the inclusion of my sister will lead the discussion in her direction.

Instead of showing surprise, which is the normal reaction, Nathan just nods. My anxiety flares as I realise his reaction is like I'm just confirming something he already knows.

I look down at my food again. I have finished my duck already and I am using the vegetables to mop up even the tiniest smears of the sauce left on my plate.

Even though the meal isn't hot my tongue feels scorched. I can't taste the vegetables at all when there's no sauce on them. I would think my tongue has gone numb if the sauce wasn't still amazing.

I pick up my wine glass for the first time and take a large sip. I am not a big drinker, and I am not particularly fond of wine either, but my nerves are looking for any distraction.

The wine tastes bland and a little bitter. I don't want to lose the flavour of the food I just ate, but I swirl the wine around my mouth in an attempt to revive my taste buds.

Nathan still isn't speaking, and I can't help sipping more and more of the wine so I don't fill the silence with nervous chatter.

Why would Nathan know or care if I was adopted? I can see now that a lot of the questions he's been asking have been leading straight to this topic. He can't have seen my personnel record at work or he wouldn't have needed to ask. Unless he just wanted to see if I would admit it.

I wonder what else he knows.

Chapter 11

Dinner - Sahra's

I am sipping my wine with abandon when Nathan looks over my shoulder and smiles warmly at someone behind me. I turn to see an attractive woman in her mid thirties walking up to our table. She is wearing a more tailored version of the restaurant's uniform.

"Lily, I would like you to meet a friend of mine." Nathan introduces us. "This is Sahra, the owner of this place. Sahra, this is the girl I told you about. She's new in town."

Okay. Not sure how I feel about him talking about me to his friends. Flattered he knows who I am, scared about why?

Sahra nods in greeting and studies my face closely before giving me a guarded smile.

"The food was really delicious," I say.

Her face transforms into a wide self-satisfied grin.

"Of course," she answers. "You don't mind if I sit for a minute do you?"

Without waiting for an answer, she moves a chair from the nearest table over to ours and sits down. Nathan doesn't seem surprised. I have to assume they are quite close and this is normal behaviour for her. I wonder if they've hooked up.

"You seem familiar, have we met before?" Sahra asks me.

"I don't think so."

Sahra wrinkles her aquiline nose at me.

"Are you sure? I feel like I know you."

"I think I just have one of those faces," I suggest to her. "People often make the mistake of thinking they know me, particularly since I moved here."

"Indeed."

Sahra sits back and looks over to Nathan, her shoulders rise and fall by a few millimetres at most. I would have missed the shrug if I hadn't been staring at the woman's long silver earrings at the time. Or more specifically, the dark rubies hanging at the ends of them like heavy blood drops ready to fall.

"So, Lily is a lovely name. Your mother must have great taste." She smiles and waits.

"I've always liked it," I reply cautiously.

This is dangerous territory for me. I keep my background to myself. I want people to know me for who I am not for some stereotype built up by society. But I've already told Nathan I'm adopted and he's looking at me expectantly.

"Lily's adopted."

"Ah." Sahra seems as unsurprised as Nathan was. "Where have you been?"

I find her word choice unusual. Does she mean here in Adelaide or where am I from? I choose the latter.

"I lived on a farm in New South Wales until three days ago. I just moved here for uni and to work at the hospital."

"You are very brave." She shudders slightly. "How do you cope with the blood?"

"I'm not afraid of blood," I answer.

Sahra snorts a laugh and I stare at her. I'm having trouble believing someone so calm and confident made that noise. If I had to describe her in one word, I would choose serene. Before the laugh that is.

"Of course you aren't." She leans over and pats my hand. "So how old did you say you were when you moved away from Adelaide?"

"Under a year old," I say in resignation.

These two obviously know more about me than strangers should and it's probably in my best interests to find out why, and what they want.

Also my head is starting to swim. I look at my nearly empty wine glass. I really shouldn't drink.

"So you wouldn't remember anything about your life here at all then." Sahra seems to be waiting for a response, so I shake my head.

She pouts slightly but then brightens.

"Never mind, Nathan will take care of you while you figure things out."

Sahra gives Nathan a significant look and then stands and sets her chair back at the other table.

"See you later," she says, walking back towards the kitchen.

I turn back to Nathan with a question on my lips when I see a faint outline of Sahra still sitting in her place at our table. My head whips around to watch her walk away. Shivery lines are sloughing off her skin and hanging in the air behind her. I try to blink them away, but the lines continue to shiver in the air, transparent but still somehow solid as if I could reach out and grab them like a spider's web.

It's hard to focus on Sahra now. I can see her solid form passing through the door to the kitchen, but she has left a trail of ghostly Sahras behind her, like a long exposure on a photograph.

I try to find something stable to focus on, but Nathan's outline begins to blur as well.

I figure my deteriorating vision means I've had enough wine to be brave.

"Why did you ask me out tonight?"

"To get to know you." Nathan answers with a smile.

"How's that working for you?" There is a bit too much snark in my voice for my liking, but I'm feeling ambushed right now.

I thought Nathan might actually be interested in me, but instead he has some secret agenda.

"Really well actually. I know who you are, I know your family." He waits until I hold his gaze in astonishment before he continues. "And I know what you are."

Okay, now I am confused. Not about the first part. I told him my name myself, and I've got a bad feeling I know which of my families he means. But the bit where he 'knows what I am' is a problem. If the next comment out of his mouth is something about being hot, a tease, or anything to do with sexiness at all, this will officially be the most awkward date of my life. He doesn't look like the type for such a clunky attempt at a compliment but what do I know?

I raise my eyebrows at him and wait it out.

"I know Jak, your real father," Nathan tells me quietly.

I flinch so hard my right hand knocks my empty wine glass over. I try to set it upright, but my hands are shaking so badly I crack the glass against the edge of my plate.

Nathan takes the glass from me and sets it aside. When he reaches towards me again, I place my hands in my lap.

I am literally speechless. I have a million questions. And none.

I want to ask if he knew my mother as well. I'm curious about her. All the usual questions: what was she like; do I look like her; would she approve of me? But I can also feel a creeping desperation in that curiosity. A yearning that could grow until it consumes me.

I have to push those thoughts away. It's one of the reasons I never tried to learn more about what happened that night. And of course, that way lies knowledge about my bio father. The less I know about him, the happier I will be.

Now I am thinking about that night eighteen years ago, Nathan would've only been a kid when my mother died. I guess he met my bio father in jail, hopefully as a visitor. I try to picture Nathan as a criminal. No, he's a surgeon, surely you can't be an ex-con in that job.

I still haven't thought of anything to say and Nathan is obviously not in any hurry to explain.

I want to get up and stalk out, give myself time to think, but my vision is seriously messed up. I can't focus on Nathan's face at all. I look around the room and there are blurry lines everywhere. I can almost see a translucent shell of a person within some of the sketchy lines. Most of them look like Sahra, but not all.

"I'd like to go home now," I say in a firm voice.

To my relief Nathan doesn't argue and waves the waitress over to pay for our meals. I try to pay for my share, but Nathan assures me he gets a great discount so not to bother. He retrieves my coat and helps me slide into it before taking my hand and leading me outside. The hand holding feels weird, but I don't have much option if I don't want to fall face first onto the road. We walk the short distance to the car in silence.

I think he knows I don't feel well, but he doesn't comment on it at all. Maybe he just thinks he crossed a line mentioning my bio father. Which he has.

I don't know how I feel right now. Scared, definitely. About what Nathan knows about me and what he wants to do with that information. Maybe Corinne was right when she said moving back here was too big a risk.

In the car, he checks I am safely strapped in and then sits still in the driver's seat. I risk a quick glance at his face, but the blurry lines are still there. I look back at my hands in my lap.

"I only want to help," Nathan says quietly.

His voice does sound sincere, but I have no idea what he's on about.

"Why do I need your help?" I ask, trying to sound strong and independent, whatever that sounds like.

"You'll see."

And this time his deep, chocolaty voice is not calming at all.

Chapter 12

After dinner - On the road home

To avoid seeing any more shivering lines I keep my eyes closed on the drive back to the condemned building I call home. The one time I risk a peek, even the shimmering stars are leaving long, white streaks behind them in the dark sky. I feel like someone accidentally swapped my settings to time-lapse photography.

What's weirder, when I close my eyes to shut out the confusion, I don't even feel sick. I feel kind of strong and energetic, like I could run, like I should run. My muscles are twitching and I rub my hands up and down my thighs, trying to settle my nerves.

I've been drunk before and it took a fair bit more than the one glass of wine I've had tonight. And this isn't how it felt. The drunk dizziness was always swiftly followed by throwing up and that feels extremely unlikely right now. I could eat a horse, particularly if it was cooked in that sour-cherry sauce. My mouth starts watering.

Nathan's silence is becoming physically painful. That little voice in my head I usually pay close attention to is screaming at me to get away from this man. Which I intend to do when it's convenient, but in the meantime it's important to keep him sweet.

I try to make conversation.

"You should ask your friend for the recipe for that duck dish for me."

I check Nathan's reaction through squinted eyes. Several of his mouths become grim lines as he pulls the car up in front of the old nurses' quarters. I'm home. When he turns the car off and unstraps I realise he intends to take me to the door, or further.

"I can make it from here. Thank you for dinner," I say, struggling with the seat belt.

Nathan ignores my attempt to brush him off and comes around to help me out of the car with a tight grip on my elbow. While I am annoyed at the presumption, a teeny part of me is also grateful. It is surprisingly hard to keep my balance with all the hazy streaks hanging in the air.

The shivering lines are worse here. The air around the door to my building is so thick with lines it looks like cobwebs leading into some enormous spider's lair. Only my conviction that they can't be real and I must have developed some rare medical problem, keeps my feet moving towards that horrifying entrance. Pulling my arm from Nathan's grip, I put my hands out in front of me to protect my face.

"What's happening?" he asks, his voice carefully neutral.

"You don't see anything unusual here?" I ask.

"No."

I believe him, but there is something off in his tone. As if he expects me to ask strange questions. He does know my father, maybe he expects me to be mentally ill? I don't even know if my father's brand of insanity can be passed down. He can't have been very believable, or he'd be in a mental health facility right now and not prison.

We reach the big wooden door and I stand in front of the keypad to block Nathan's view while I type in the code. When the door clicks, I push it open and then plant myself right in the middle of the opening to make it obvious Nathan isn't coming in. Unfortunately this position puts me in the thickest part of the translucent, cobwebby lines running through the doorway. All the muscles in my back and neck creep and cramp up as I imagine a human-sized huntsman spider crawling up behind me in the dark.

I can't see Nathan's face at all now. He is just a fuzzy, black silhouette against the orange street lights outside. And he is standing so close to me I could rest my head on his chest by simply leaning forward. I can almost feel the smooth material of his jacket on my cheek and the pressure of his strong arms wrapping around me.

My brain is telling me this man is trouble, but the rest of my body is willing to give him a chance.

For about the millionth time I wish I could smell. I bet he smells as perfect as he looks. I inhale deeply. Something reminds me of leather and a wood fire.

Occasionally, when spray deodorant or something like that is really strong in the air, I can taste it in my mouth. Mostly a bitter chemical taste. That's not what this felt like.

I inhale again and there is definitely a flavour in the air around me, the impression of outdoors and a new saddle. Clearly, I am homesick, which isn't a surprise. Or worse, my nose has joined my eyes' hallucination party.

"Thank you for dinner," I say.

I am trying to broadcast to Nathan that he should leave, but I don't want to be rude. Right now, I can't decide if Nathan is a threat or the best thing that's ever happened to me. Either way, it's important not to annoy him.

And it now feels like every nerve end in my body is jangling. Though that could be because I just felt Nathan's breath on my forehead.

I tell myself firmly I need a good sleep. I'll see if things look any different on a clear sunny day, without the enormous huntsman spider crouched behind me.

"Anytime, Lily," he says, not making any move to leave.

I back into the darkness and shut the door softly in his face.

I hear his footsteps walking away as I fumble in the dark for the ancient light switch. I don't find anything on my first sweep and my imagination runs wild in the complete darkness. Relief floods through me when I finally locate the large toggle switch and click it down.

But instead of providing safety and comfort, this time the light confirms my fears. I freeze in place, staring at the cobweb of blurry lines that fills the space, running into every doorway and even up the stairwell. Thousands of moving translucent strands overlap to create a thick tangle of muted-colour and movement.

If I concentrate on one spot I can see ghostly shapes coalesce from the blurry mist. A pale impression of a young woman wearing an old-fashioned, white nurse's uniform complete with a folded cloth cap appears before me and then slides instantly back into the haze.

My mind rattles to a stop and I stand helplessly watching apparitions form and fade away. Most of the ghostly shapes appear to be women and none of them seem to be aware of me.

Maybe this is what they mean by ghosts just being memories of what has happened in a space. They can't think or act, they are just like a movie, remembered in the place they occurred.

I am just deciding this is all a harmless hallucination brought on by exhaustion and stress, when the shape of a young woman about my age appears at the bottom of the stairwell. She's thin and fragile looking, with shoulder length dark hair and she's wearing one of those awful nurse's dresses I remember from when I was a kid. She has no blurry fuzz around her. She looks as solid and real as I am. I can even see the woman has the same lush green eyes as me. Hers are sparkling as she laughs at something I can't see.

I step sideways out of her path as she gets closer. The apparition stops at the closed front door beside me and moves as if she is opening a phantom door. She smiles coyly at someone she can see on the step, before her hand reaches out and picks a small bouquet of blood-red roses out of the air. She is saying something I can't hear when her hand suddenly moves in my direction. Too late, I guess she is reaching for the light switch behind me. I bring my arms up in a futile attempt to fend her off, but her hand passes through me like I don't exist. Or like she doesn't.

She pulls away and even though I couldn't feel her touching me, there's an emptiness where she's been. I am confused by the sudden loss I feel and my arm moves instinctively to stop her from leaving. My hand catches on the edge of her shoulder for less than a heartbeat before it passes through her form like mist. As if triggered by my touch, the apparition immediately begins to fade away. But in the split second before she's completely gone, I see the woman's mouth pop open in shock and her eyes meet mine.

She sees me.

My mind stutters and starts with unhelpful suggestions: run; hide; scream. I'm not sure what good any of that'll do. I can see the shivery lines stretch right up the steep stairwell, there's nowhere to run to. Screaming will bring people here, possibly even Nathan if he's still out there, and that will require explanations that could land me in a straight jacket.

I take a deep breath and close my eyes. I must be hallucinating, but I don't know if I'd be able to feel a hallucination. Then again, I shouldn't be able to feel my dreams once I wake up either.

I should go to the hospital and see someone. There's at least some chance I've been Roofied. My vivid imagination takes off running with the idea. I imagine the scene where I am at the hospital I work at, telling a doctor that I think the ridiculously handsome surgeon, our co-worker, took me on a date and drugged me. My eyebrows rise as I can't help mimicking the look of disbelief on the imaginary face.

What would happen if they can't find any drugs in my system? Straight jacket time.

And worse, if they did find drugs, they might think I took them for recreational purposes. Then I get to lose my job.

No. I'd rather track down the six-foot-tall huntsman spider that's still lurking somewhere in these webby lines, and fight it armed with nothing more than a tub of peanut butter and a spoon. Obviously in this scenario I am hoping spiders are allergic to peanuts.

And I'm hungry again.

Keeping close to the wall because the blurry shapes are thinner there, I skirt the foyer and slowly make my way up the edge of the stairs. I need to step out from the wall once to avoid a slightly more solid apparition that's about half-way to looking real. I reach the first landing and see the outline of my room in the dark. I debate turning on the light timer but decide not to bother. That'll only make the shivery shapes more real.

What if the ghosts are in my room? What if they're in my bed?

I look down into the malignant darkness of the long hall-way and see shadows coalescing in the middle. I squint as the central mass appears to be growing taller, its silhouette more solid than the ghostly lines around it.

I leap for the light switch and the growing form is revealed as a man striding towards me with a determined grimace on his face. An electric shock of recognition runs through me. Memories of the guy leaving Ana's room and scaring me at the Botanic Gardens are followed by an image of a figure standing in the dark when I was waiting for Nathan. He's been following me. Stalking me.

My eyes flick between the man, with his clenched jaw and his expressive and unhappy face, and the door to my room. Too far. I start scrabbling for my phone, but my tiny clutch is too small and the phone sticks tight across its jaws.

The stalker sees me struggle and breaks into a run. I whirl around and hurtle up the stairs. Please let Ellie be home. I know Sam's still at work but maybe I'll get lucky and Ellie will be a six-foot-tall, former wrestler.

The man shouts something behind me, but I can't make sense of his rough voice in my panic.

I reach the top floor and try to slap the light timer without slowing my desperate flight, but my fingertips just slide ineffectually over the button. I hear footsteps closing on me, so I pelt headlong into the near-perfect darkness of the hallway.

All of the doors I can see in the sickly glow of the exit light have been left open, same as the floor below. I'm nearing the bathroom at the end when I realise none of the doors are shut, none of these rooms are in use. There's no one here to help me.

I slow a little, preparing a new plan. I'll get inside one of these rooms and lock the door behind me. Then I can call the police before he kicks the door in. It's not much, but it'll have to do.

Pity I'm not quick enough.

I feel a fist close on the back of my dress. The weight unbalances me and my feet tangle. I crash headfirst towards the door frame. I throw my arms forwards to catch myself but I'm out of time. My hands land on either side of the wooden barrier so I take the full force of my falling weight on my temple and the real world vanishes like a bad dream should.

Chapter 13

Later - No idea where

I am trapped in a small, stifling room. The inky blackness only relieved by three, weak strips of light infiltrating a barred window high above me. I am curled into the fetal position on the corner of the rough wooden platform that passes as my bed. I have no mattress and only one rough, grey blanket to soften the undressed wood.

They have taken my clothes.

Even so, sweat trickles down my bare stomach and my damp hair sticks to my neck. I stretch out one arm and let the starlight glisten on my skin, flexing my fingers in the pale bands of light. I imagine a breeze cooling my skin.

I can hear the deep breaths of sleep from the woman in the cell next to mine. I'm so tired my mind is starting to slip, my strength is ebbing away, but I still cannot sleep. I need to hear them coming.

Help is hundreds of metres away behind dense, stone walls and heavy wooden doors. And no one will come if I scream anyway. Screams are expected.

We are here in this horrific place because they think people need protection from us. No one has thought of our safety. Why should they? We are useless to them. I am useless to my husband. He is at home now, with my baby. My poor baby girl has no one to understand her and protect her from these things now. I wish I had lost my mind like some of the wretched women around me, then I wouldn't know what was coming for me.

In the distance I hear a door grind open and then the snick of metal as it is closed and locked. Heavy footsteps on gravel approach the small wooden building I am confined in. I feel guilty for even hoping for it, but maybe tonight I will be lucky. Maybe they won't choose me.

My heart is already racing as I quietly wrap the blanket around my naked body, clutch it tight at my breasts and hips and try to disappear into the wall behind me. The sound of a metal key being forced into a rusty lock cuts through the night and I flinch when a harsh voice greets me.

I was wrong. This is not one of the usual, opportunistic sadists who come each night to these distant, unprotected cells.

It is him.

The knowledge cleaves my mind in two. What rational thought is left begs me not to give up, to find a way to defend myself. But instinct takes over and I scream in vain for all the people who will not come for me.

I wake up with a start.

I feel the next scream still building inside me, but I'm afraid I wouldn't survive the noise. My head is pounding in time with my heartbeat. It hurts to even move my eyeballs, so I concentrate on breathing slow, deep breaths until I can think straight.

The pain doesn't get any better, but soon I can shove it aside and take in my surroundings. The last thing I remember was being chased.

I'm lying on my back in a bed I don't recognise. This isn't my room or even my building. The ceiling is covered in grey plaster that hangs down from the roof in rough spikes that look like rampant mould through my migraine blur.

The thick quilt covering me has a red, grey and black geometric pattern printed on it. That, and the lack of throw pillows, lamps, or decorations of any kind, tells me this is probably a man's bedroom.

I'm trapped in the evil lair of my stalker.

It's not much of a dungeon though. Where are the bare stone walls, boarded up windows or fluttering moths?

In fact, the door just beyond the foot of the bed is ajar and a large window to my left is open, allowing a cool breeze to flow through the room. This doesn't mesh well with my conclusion that I've been kidnapped by some psycho. Isn't he afraid I'll get away?

Oh, and it's daylight outside. If I was due at work today, I'd already be late and someone might start looking for me. But my luck isn't that good.

I lift the covers and look down at myself. Still fully dressed, thank God. My shoes are gone, but that isn't really that sinister.

I roll slowly to a sitting position with my legs hanging over the edge of the bed. I wait there for the throbbing in my head to settle back into an agony I might live through. After hearing nothing for a minute or two I creep quietly across the dark carpet to the door and peer out into the next room.

Two people are sitting on blue sofas in front of a silent TV. One person is slouched low with their back to me and their feet on a low coffee table. The other is little more than a blurry haze to my defective eyes.

Actually, considering what was going on last night, the second person might not even be real.

On the far side of the room I can see a door that, based on the three large deadlocks fixed onto the wood, must lead outside. I draw a deep breath in through my nose as I prepare to run for the door.

Bacon.

I can taste freshly cooked bacon in the air around me. No, I'm smelling it. I hesitate, momentarily distracted by intense hunger. I push the thoughts away, but my stomach can never be ignored. A growl like a rampaging bear erupts from my torso.

I hear a gasp and freeze in place as the blurry mass on the far sofa jumps up and moves in my direction. I stagger backwards looking for an escape until I realise the approaching shape is familiar.

"Thank God, Lily," Amber laughs and throws her arms around me.

When I don't return her embrace, she releases me and I stare stupidly at her.

"We were so worried," she says, turning to scowl at the man rising from the other sofa. "I thought he'd killed you."

My stalker comes around the sofa to stand next to Amber. He's even taller up close and I try unsuccessfully not to cringe. His expression softens as he looks at Amber.

At least, I think it does. His hard, angular face is still very blurry.

"Sorry." He isn't shouting at me this time, but his voice is still rough.

I assume he screams a lot.

"I didn't know who you were gonna call," he adds, as if that's an explanation for anything.

"Lily, this is my stupid brother Alex," Amber says, punching his upper arm.

I have trouble believing the two could be related. This grave-faced man is the opposite of the friendly, pocket-sized blond. Sure, their eyes might be the same pale shade of grey-blue, but Alex is tall and he certainly doesn't have the thin frame his sister and I share. He is wide and strong with long, athletic-looking muscles, like he is not unfamiliar with running. Actually, I already know that about him.

"What the hell were you doing with him, anyway?" Alex's rough voice rises in exasperation.

My mind is racing, and it takes me longer than it should to understand he means Nathan.

"It's called a date," I snap at him.

I don't like confrontation, but I'm not sure I owe politeness to the man who kidnapped me. Also the stabbing pain in my head is making me mean. My hands shake from the excess adrenaline coursing through my body.

"And what business is it of yours?" I demand. "What the hell is going on? Why did you kidnap me?"

The sunlight pouring in through the windows is hurting my head and I can't keep my eyes open. I blink rapidly and my blurry eyes clear for a moment before I see in double vision and then triple vision.

I close my eyes for less than a second, but that's long enough for my balance to shift. I stagger to the side until Alex steps forward and catches me neatly in his arms.

"Put her on the couch," Amber tells her brother as she runs into the bedroom I've come from.

Alex carries me to the nearest sofa and lowers me gently to the soft cushions before spoiling it all by giving me a scathing look. I get how Ana felt in the hospital when she was forced to trust Nathan to take care of her.

I don't like feeling helpless, and to make it worse, traitorous tears start dribbling down my cheeks.

Alex looks down at me and huffs.

"You and Nathanial Cain are my business because I have been looking for you for years," Alex says.

Wow, he's some kind of super stalker then.

"Looking for me in particular or just any woman you can sell into slavery?" I ask, embarrassment making me both brave and stupid.

"Don't you recognise me at all?" Amber interrupts as she comes back into the room and arranges a pillow and blanket around me.

Amber's all business, as if she is the nurse and I'm her patient.

"Of course I recognise you from the hospital." I wince as I remember why I was trying to find her. "Have you spoken to anyone from the hospital today?"

"If you mean do I know Ana is dead? Yes, I know. That's another reason we needed to talk to you."

"I am so sorry. I tried to find you." My emotions are getting all mixed up and I blink hard to clear my vision.

"Thanks for that."

I think I am more upset than she is right now, but then I am the kidnapped prisoner.

"That doesn't matter for now," Amber continues. "What I really need to know is if you remember me from before. We've known each other since long before the hospital."

I study her face carefully, but I already know she is not familiar to me at all.

"Sorry, I've only been in South Australia for a few days. I really think you must be thinking of someone else," I say.

"I told you, Amber." Alex finally leaves his position looming over me and settles on the far sofa.

He puts his feet back on the coffee table and slouches down to a comfortable position before continuing.

"You're gonna scare her off."

Amber scowls at her brother again.

"There's no time to pussyfoot around," she tells him. "Go get the food I made for her."

Alex frowns at her and gets up and ambles across the room to the kitchen area. My stomach growls again at the thought of food but, if they are intent on playing host, I have more pressing needs.

"Actually, if you have any painkillers I would be really grateful?" I ask as I scooch up into a sitting position against one arm of the sofa.

"Oh, sorry. Are you in pain? From where you hit your head?" Amber replies.

I assess myself before answering.

"Yes and no. My head does hurt." I glance over to the kitchen where Alex is spooning something into a white pasta bowl. "But I guess I started feeling pretty bad before that anyway."

Amber sits next to me on the sofa and studies my forehead where I connected with the door frame last night.

"Feeling bad how?"

"I don't know. Something is wrong with my head. I think I'm dizzy or something. Everything is blurry."

Amber gives her brother a long look as he walks over to us and hands me a large bowl containing a thick, meaty stew with a fork stuck in it. My newly active sense of smell identifies this as the source of the bacon I noticed earlier.

Alex returns Amber's look with a grim one of his own before turning his attention back to me.

"What do you mean by blurry? Is everything still blurry now? When did it start?"

It's hard to find the right words to explain what I can see. I don't mention the people I saw in the blur, that'd be crazy talk. I just describe the blurry edges and tangled lines hanging like misty webs. I know I mangle it, but the siblings just look at each other again.

"You know what's going on with me?"

"Maybe," she answers while Alex shakes his head at her. "First, you need to eat. It's an old family recipe for healing. I made it because you slept for so long, I got worried about you."

I look down at the bowl. The smell reminds me a little of the sour-cherry sauce I tried last night. As usual, common sense loses the battle against hunger, and I gather a small amount of the stew onto the fork and set it warily onto my tongue. Rich, meaty flavours flood my taste buds. I close my lips and drag the fork out of my mouth.

A tangy, mildly metallic flavour in the succulent juices set my nerve endings pinging like a sparkler. This food is literally the best thing I've ever tasted. I scoop up a larger forkful of the meat and pop it into my mouth.

I'm obviously starving, because even if I was told this contained arsenic right now, I would probably still consider finishing it.

"How did Nathaniel Cain find you, anyway?" Amber asks.

"I just bumped into him in the hospital," I say between bites. "To be honest he scares me a little."

"He should," says Amber.

Alex's scowl deepens.

"What did you do on your date?" He asks me.

"He took me to his friend Sahra's restaurant."

Alex and Amber look shocked.

"Is that bad?" I ask.

"Probably," answers Alex. "It explains why your vision has changed."

"Oh, why?" I ask.

When Alex hesitates, I frown at Amber.

"Why?" I ask again.

"We think they put something in your food," Amber replies.

"Like what? Poison or something?" I think back to what I ate. "I don't think so, the food was fantastic. Nearly as good as this."

I hold my almost empty bowl up for them to see.

Amber nods at Alex, the expression on her face unmistakable. She just won an argument.

"Look," I say to them. "I know you have some sort of feud going with Nathan's family, but I really don't think he would hurt anyone. What exactly do you have against him?"

Alex replies.

"Well, he killed Ana, for starters."

Chapter 14

About noon - Alex's place

Alex stands up to prowl around the room.

"Ana was sick," I protest. "She died of complications from her surgery."

"The surgery Nathan performed," Amber says sadly.

"No, that can't happen. He's not the only one in the theatre you know. There are other doctors and nurses in there with him."

Amber just sits looking at me with her eyebrows raised.

I decide not to mention that Nathan was actually with Ana when she died. I'm certain he would've tried to save her, but I don't want to give Amber any more ammunition.

I try again. "You hid from Nathan before your grandmother died, so you already didn't like him."

"That's cos Ana's isn't the only death he's responsible for," Alex growls at me from across the room.

"Anyway, it's more important to find out what their plans for you are," adds Amber. "What happened when you met them?"

And finally my patience is up. I know I'm the kidnappee, so I can't be making demands of the kidnappers, but I'm starting to think these two aren't going to hurt me. So I don't think I need to hang around buying into their delusions.

"Look, how about you give me back my purse and phone and I'll call myself a taxi and get out of your hair."

"No, no please, we're only trying to help," Amber pleads with me. "Just stay a little longer and then we will take you home ourselves. I promise, it's for your own good."

"If you want to talk to me, you could call and we could arrange to meet like normal people. When I don't have a raging migraine."

"Does it still hurt?" Amber asks.

My mouth is halfway through a yes when I realise it's a lie. My head's actually fine, like nothing ever happened. Even the lump on my head isn't as tender. My vision has also cleared and I didn't even notice it happening. I consider lying as an excuse to get out of here, but I'm not great at it at the best of times. Omitting a detail is about as much as I usually get away with.

"Actually no, I feel much better thank you." I answer with a clear conscience.

"That's-"

Alex interrupts Amber before she can finish. "That's the food Amber made for you."

I hope not. It would have needed opium poppies in it to clear up the migraine I had.

"I told you, we're trying to help you," Amber pleads. "And it'd really help us to know what you told Nathaniel and Sahra about us."

"I didn't tell them anything about you. Why would I?"

"What did you tell them?" Alex asks.

I think back to last night. It seems so long ago now.

"Almost nothing really, I like to keep my past private."

"You didn't need to tell them anything about your past," says Amber. "You're the only person who doesn't know who you are."

I'm lost as usual. I know who I am. I keep my true identity secret from the world not myself, not that she could know that. But I've been wrong a lot lately.

Amber sees my confusion.

"We are distantly related to your late mother," she says, giving me a reassuring smile. "We have the same heritage; that's how I knew how to make you better."

And I was feeling much better, until she said that. Now I'm getting a leaden feeling in my gut. I put the empty bowl onto the coffee table in front of me.

"How did you find out who my bio mother was?" I ask.

But my mind is already thinking back to Nathan's similar revelation. He knows who I am as well. They're linked of course.

"Ana recognised you," Alex says.

"She told Nathan," I say.

Amber gasps. "No, of course she didn't. She would never have told him."

"Nathan didn't know who you were for sure, until Sahra confirmed it," Alex says in a confident voice. "He must have suspected for some reason, so he wanted to see if she recognised you."

"I've never met her before," I say. "How would she recognise me?"

Amber reaches into a drawer in the coffee table and pulls out a worn photo album. It's the old-fashioned type, filled with black and white photos held in with little cardboard corners. She opens the album to a page marked with the album's faded red ribbon. A couple of loose, colour photos are sitting between the pages. Amber holds one up for me.

"This is your mother."

I look at the photo curiously. The woman in the photo is younger than me. She has the same colour hair as I do and the same heart shaped top lip as well.

As I look closer, I realise she looks a lot like the apparition I touched in the foyer of my building last night. In fact, they are scarily similar.

Amber then holds the little album out towards me and points to the page on the left. Two women are standing together. They are wearing period-costume dresses with aprons over them. The photo is small and faded so I have to squint to see it properly, but I recognise the women. The old woman on the right is Ana and the slightly taller woman on the left is me.

If I had memory issues, I would assume Ana and I had dressed up and had this picture taken. But I don't have any trouble with my memory, so someone must be very skilled with Photoshop.

"That woman is your great, great, grandmother," Amber says.

"Ana?" I ask. That would explain the special interest the family's shown in me.

"No, Lilijana, the woman Ana is standing next to." She points to the woman who looks exactly like me. "You remember how I said we come from the same heritage. We are Renascent, the reborn."

Amber waits a beat, but when I say nothing, she continues.

"One of our oldest and most important beliefs is that death isn't the end for everyone. Some people come back to us, like you."

Okay, this is all sounding a bit far-fetched.

"What do you mean?" I ask.

Amber speaks slowly like she would to a rabid animal. "It's pretty clear that's you in the photo."

"I don't know where you got it from, but it's obviously doctored. Even if it was a real photo from a hundred years ago, it just means the genes in our families are strong."

I stop talking abruptly. I am starting to feel a bit awkward, like I'm sliding into racist territory. I don't want to insult their cultural beliefs.

Amber shakes her head at me. "I get that it's hard to believe. We've grown up knowing our traditions. It'll be hard for you to accept you're different from everyone else."

At least she's aware how unbelievable she sounds. Suddenly a terrible thought occurs to me. An idea that would explain everything that is happening, much more nicely than anything Amber and Alex have said.

I close the obviously-fake photo album with a snap and put it on the coffee table next to my empty bowl.

"If you know who I am, you know that my father killed my mother." I am matter of fact about it. I don't remember my parents after all. "You know he was mentally ill."

Amber makes a non-committal noise and shrugs her shoulders. Alex comes over and stands next to her, I guess for emotional support. He doesn't tell me what he thinks of my having an insane father.

"Why are you two trying to make me think I've lost my mind?" I ask them.

Amber shakes her head again and starts to speak but Alex interrupts her in his rough, angry voice.

"I told you Amber. We're wasting our time. If she doesn't even believe this, there's no chance she's gonna believe the rest."

I look from Alex's face to Amber's. There's more to this outrageous story? I wait to hear what is less believable than I am my own great, great grandmother.

My vision has been almost perfect for nearly ten minutes now and I can see their faces clearly. So I am looking right at the two of them when their edges begin to blur and they vanish out of sight.

Chapter 15

Not sure - Alex's place

I stare stupidly at the empty cushion beside me. Is this a new phase of my eye problems? I reach out to see if Amber's still there, but my hand waves through empty air. They are actually gone.

There are other changes as well. My empty bowl and the battered photo album have disappeared from the coffee table and the light streaming in from the windows has a different quality. The room is now washed in an apricot blush, like it's sunrise or sunset outside. Also, the shadows in the room are longer and slanted towards the bedroom I slept in.

I hear the whisper of voices. Not like they are far away, more like they are trying to escape detection. I stand up silently and let the quilt fall to the floor. Tip toeing around the sofa, I peek into the bedroom.

Amber and Alex are standing beside the bed whispering to each other. They are looking down at a person-sized lump covered by the red, grey and black quilt. The same quilt I just left on the lounge room floor. I glance behind me and sure enough the quilt is still crumpled on the floor in front of the couch. Are there two?

I step into the room to ask what they're up to, but neither Alex nor Amber show any reaction to my presence.

"Hey," I say.

Neither of the siblings even blink. Soon their whispering stops and they creep out of the room, Amber leaving translucent, shivery lines hanging in her wake.

I walk down beside the bed so I can see the sleeping figure. My skin is already prickling with possibilities, but it's still a shock to see my own sleeping face lying helpless in front of me.

I reach out to see if I'm real, but as soon as my finger is close enough to my cheek to feel the warmth of my skin, the scene changes.

I'm still in the bedroom, but I'm not here now. The other me.

Even the quilt is gone.

I startle backwards and bump into the only other piece of furniture in the room. The large rickety wardrobe tilts backwards and hits the wall before rocking back towards me. I put my arms up and shove it back into position before it can knock me to the floor. Luckily, it's very light and settles back into place easily, but not before I hear the tinkling of cheap metal coat hangers falling. One of the doors pops open allowing a mound of clothing to ooze out at my feet.

I have to overcome my instincts to clean up the mess I've made. Alex would not be happy if I played around with his stuff. I head back out into the living room, but Alex and Amber aren't here either.

The front door is open. I briefly contemplate escaping, but I still don't have my shoes, or my purse. I sit back down on the sofa to wait until one of the siblings comes back.

As soon as I have finished wrapping the warm quilt back around myself Alex and Amber blink back into place like they had never left.

I flinch at their sudden appearance. Amber raises her eyebrows at me, but I don't know what to say just yet.

I sit thinking. Mulling over everything that has happened in the last twenty-four hours. Putting together what just happened, with the time-lapse images I saw last night, and the shivery lines some people leave behind when they move, leads me to one obvious answer.

"I think I just time travelled."

I don't know how I expected them to react to an obviously-outrageous statement, but Alex's face doesn't change at all and Amber gives me a wide smile.

"I told you we're different," she says.

I frown. Yes she did, but she wasn't talking about time travel was she? Still, maybe I need to keep an open mind and reconsider what she said earlier.

"Was it the first time?" Alex asks me.

"Yes, this is the first time." I reply, my voice possessed by a three year old having a tantrum. "You two vanished and I went back in time to sometime this morning when I was still asleep in the bedroom. You were in there checking on me."

"Oh great." Alex is annoyed. "She believes that right off, but reincarnation, which is central to a few religions, is crazy."

I feel guilty. I did blow off the reincarnation thing pretty quickly. But experiencing time travel, being able to see and

touch the evidence is very different from being told something by someone you hardly know.

"I'm sorry," I say to Alex. "I guess I had evidence of
travelling in time because it happened."

Alex huffs a breath and points to the photo album.

"That right there is evidence. And anyway, you could
always be crazy, couldn't you?"

He's not wrong. I could be crazy. Lots of weird things
have been happening around me lately. My dreams are
spilling into the real world more than ever. And there's the
eyesight thing.

Alex sees my concentration and rolls his eyes.

"For Christ's sake, you aren't crazy."

"No," says Amber. "What just happened is proof too.
Don't you see? Lilijana was psychic as well."

"Wait, psychic not time travel?" I feel deflated.

"Yeah, her ability could seem like time travel, but it was
actually a vision of the past. She couldn't really affect anything there."

I'm already shaking my head. I don't think that's my
situation.

"If Lilijana could time travel, why hasn't she just popped
in to explain this to you herself?" Alex interjects.

I am starting to feel like I must have imagined the whole
thing now anyway, or it's some elaborate trick of Alex's.
Amber doesn't seem that cruel.

"Cos it doesn't work that way," Alex continues. "You
can only see into the past. I think it's more like watching
a movie, you can't affect anything there. Or at least that's
how Ana said Lilijana described it. Also, your ability has
been weakening over the last dozen or so generations. There
are too many gaps in the line."

Something in his explanation bothers me, other than his tone I mean.

"No wait, I have proof I can affect stuff."

I get up and walk into the bedroom with Amber trailing after me. The wardrobe is neatly shut and when I open the door, I see all the clothes are hung up. I put out my hand and touch a suit jacket just to confirm it's real. The tiniest pressure from my hand is too much for the rickety furniture and everything comes crashing down, again.

"Don't worry about that," Amber says. "That's always falling down. Alex already cleaned it up once today."

"I knocked this down when I was in here before," I say uncertainly.

I don't know what to think now. It feels so real, not like a vision. I walk out into the living room and sit back down.

"So you have visions too?" I ask Alex.

He shakes his head.

"Being Renascent is mostly carried on the female chromosome," Alex explains. "Males born to Renascents are strong and great at making things go their way, but we don't have special abilities other than that. And we aren't reborn like you are. Evolution has just given us blokes a little bit extra so we can protect renascent women."

"You need protection?" I ask Amber.

"We do," Amber replies, with an emphasis on we. "We are quite easily killed. Disease and accidents are the norm. We have issues with nutrition." Amber looks pointedly from her thin arms to my even skinnier ones.

I'm used to people complaining I should eat more. So it doesn't take much to make me defensive.

"Hey, I eat like a horse."

"Yes," Amber replies. "But are you ever satisfied?"

I decide to ignore that for the moment.

"So can you see the past?" I ask Amber.

"No. Everyone's gift is different, and our line has even more gaps than yours, so I don't have any power left at all."

"Wait, like magic powers? Are we witches?"

Amber pouts and rolls her eyes at me. Alex chuckles. I think I have hit a nerve.

"No, we're not witches," Amber says. "But it's possible that idea came from someone's misunderstanding of what we are."

"Really?" I ask.

"Dunno. But I can tell you we aren't flying around on brooms, or casting magic spells in cauldrons and I absolutely love garlic."

"Wait, I thought the garlic thing was vampires?"

Alex cuts in, clearly trying to get the conversation back on track. "You get her point though. Things get distorted. That's why we try and stay anonymous. It prevents issues."

I'm still confused. Amber and Alex look from me to each other, clearly trying to decide what I most need to know.

"You inherit your old self through your mother's genes," Amber explains. "And we have a way of passing down the memories and abilities of recent female ancestors. So renascent women are essentially reincarnated with the memories of all their previous lives intact...usually."

I want to tell her I don't even remember my mother, let alone her memories. I stare at them dumbfounded for so long that Amber's skin starts getting blurry. I look around at anything else, hoping my eyes will settle down. I pick the photo album up off the coffee table. As I open it the colour photos fall out onto my lap. Glancing back up at Alex or Amber to see if they mind me looking at the album, I'm startled to see both of them have multiple layers again. It looks like spiders have been running all over them, trussing them up in sticky, shivering webs.

I squeeze my eyes shut, but I know it's not a long-term solution. When I've summoned enough courage to open them again, I find Alex has disappeared and Amber is now standing over the kitchen bench with blood running down her arm. A bloody knife is discarded in front of her as she starts screaming for Alex.

I blink, missing the transition back into the present. Alex is back in place with Amber and me in the lounge room and their edges are crisp again. Neither of the siblings seem to know anything just happened.

"What did you do in your vision when you saw us in the bedroom?" Alex asks me.

I struggle to remember what we were talking about.

"I don't know. I didn't try to do anything. It's completely out of my control."

"I think we might be able to help you with the control thing." Amber looks thoughtful. "Renascent women need to perform a ritual over the bodies of our ancestors to complete the transfer of their memories and abilities. Any direct renascent ancestor is good but the most recent direct relative and the earlier version of yourself are crucial to you gaining full control of your abilities."

I shake my head. The one thing I do know about my mother is that her body was never found. My father admitted to killing her, but he never confessed to where he put her afterwards.

"Which is why I was coming to speak to you," Alex says. "Our line has more gaps in it than yours does and Ana and

Amber's health has always been sketchy because of it, even though their ability is to heal people."

Amber takes over from Alex. I'm starting to feel like I'm facing a debating team.

"Ana was never able to trace the last time I lived. And she only had three generations of her own direct line passed down, so the power to heal was very diluted in her and non-existent in me.

"We need your help to find out where Ana's body is now so we can complete the ritual. We were hoping you could find out for us."

Oh, okay. This is an easy one. Although it would have been even easier for them if they'd put themselves down as Ana's emergency contact.

"I actually already know," I say. "She was picked up by Burton Funerals. She'll be there until the police clearance comes through and then she'll be cremated."

Alex is already on his phone searching for the funeral home's website. He stands up and, without looking up from his phone screen, walks into the bedroom. He reappears quickly with a small laptop computer which he places on the coffee table and taps away at the keyboard.

I lift up a glossy photo from my lap. I can see the woman Amber identified as my mother holding the hand of a young man. He's older than her, mid to late twenties with short dark hair and a medium build. I know who he is. This is the first photo I've ever seen of my father that isn't a grainy newspaper reprint. I've never searched for the newspaper articles myself, but since when have big sisters ever stayed out of their little sister's business.

My bio father is younger here; killing my mother must have aged him. He looks happy standing next to her, and normal. There's no hint of what's to come.

I look at the girl next to him. She is looking up at him, her large eyes combined with her small nose and chin, give her a look of melancholic longing. I wonder what she's thinking. Surely if she had generations of knowledge about how people behave, she would have seen he was dangerous.

"That's your mother, just after your dad asked her to marry him. She was twenty," Amber says quietly. "We're going to find her so you can control your ability, or it will start to control you."

I don't like the sound of that.

"And then we can finally lay her to rest."

I feel pity for the poor woman in the photo, but it doesn't feel real that I'm related to her. What is starting to feel real is that Amber and Alex are my family. They don't know me at all and they still want to help me.

Alex looks up from his computer.

"I've found us a way in. They use one of the security companies I've worked for. Their system is basic, so it won't be much of an issue. We'll go in tonight."

Alex turns to pin me down with the full force of his intelligent blue-grey eyes.

"We need your help for this part too, Lily. Amber and I have never had to do this before. Are you in?"

My commonsense is screaming at me to say no. They are talking about breaking into a business. I can count the laws I've broken on one hand and most of those were accidental.

"Please help us Lily." Amber's face is so hopeful I don't know how to let her down. "Once this is done, I'll be stronger and more able to help you in return."

I do need to get my time slippage under control. Even now, as I look at Amber, her face is starting to peel away at the edges again. I could end up seeing anything, anywhere, anytime.

A terrifying thought occurs to me. What if my nightmares are part of this and the killer who visits me in my dreams does exist. A shudder creeps its dirty fingernails up my back and under my hair. I shake my head to dislodge the feeling. I definitely don't want to be slipping into that shit.

Amber sees my head shake and her face falls. Alex opens his mouth to argue, but I beat him to it.

"I'm in."

Chapter 16

Afternoon - Alex's place

Amber and Alex agree to drop me home after some fairly intense persuasion on my part. They aren't keen on me staying in my room because Nathan knows where I live. But I'm not even nearly convinced he's the bad guy they think he is. And he knows where I work too. Do they expect me to give up my entire life?

Also, I have to go home because I'm still wearing a black evening dress. I'd stand out a bit at a funeral home after hours. I told them I'll change into a set of plain, nursing scrubs. Funeral home attendants always wear a suit when they're picking up bodies, but I can't imagine they wear them in the prep room. I'm hoping scrubs won't look out of place if we're sprung.

And I badly need a shower. I finally know what the deodorant ads mean by stress sweat. Not being able to smell all these years has had its benefits.

Alex steps out of his bedroom looking like a brooding model in a jeans commercial, except Alex's mood looks a lot darker. For the first time I realise under his openly hostile expression towards me, he might be okay-looking, handsome even.

He slides his wallet and phone into his front pockets as he walks between the lounges and out the front door. Amber hands me my shoes and purse and we follow Alex outside.

Amber's smirking because she happened to be looking at me when Alex walked through. I shake my head at her, frowning. She could not be more wrong. I'm not sure what my face was up to, but I'm not hot for her brother. I mean, lions and tigers look beautiful too, but no sane person wants to take one home as a pet.

We climb into Alex's dual-cab ute. The front seats are relatively clean, but the back seat and footwells are messy with cables, tools and folders with papers escaping from them. Amber sees me looking.

"Alex's had a lot of jobs. He's an electrician and a security guard amongst other things, under different names of course."

I nod knowingly, as if I've met loads of people with secret identities.

"But a lot of that's just for show," Amber continues. "You'd be surprised how many places you can walk straight into if you look like a tradie or security."

I remember assuming Alex was one of the demolition workers when I first saw him at the hospital. She's not wrong.

It's mid afternoon on a Saturday, so the roads are busy, but not big-city busy.

I don't recognise where we are immediately, but it's not long before I recognise the city centre ahead by its tall buildings and tram lines. We are through the CBD in minutes. I can already see the hospital I work at looming large in front of us. Alex turns right, away from where I live. Of course, he wouldn't want to drop me at my building in case anyone is watching. He would think of that; he's a stalker after all.

Alex sees me studying him in the rear-view mirror and his eyes narrow before looking away. I sink down in my seat so he can't see me as easily. My migraine is starting to spark back up due to being around so much unrelenting negativity.

I turn my attention to the scenery outside my window. We are passing the front of the old Royal Adelaide Hospital but it's the footpaths that attract my attention. They're filled with the shivering translucent lines I now know are trails left behind when a person, or possibly a ghost, has passed by.

The translucent web hangs over the footpaths near the road and every path leading into the hospital. The cobwebby mass is undisturbed by the cold breeze that is fluttering the leaves on the street trees.

Many of the lines lead away from the hospital, along the road and into the Botanic Gardens as well. I can't see far into the gardens due to the high stone wall surrounding it, but I search the skies above it for the ghost of the lunatic asylum. It's not there. If the shivery lines are a vision of the past, my power is being weirdly picky about what it chooses to reveal, and when.

We turn a corner and Alex pulls into a car park. Amber is quiet now I'm leaving them, so I give her a quick hug. I have to remind myself she's only young and she's always thought of me as family, even if I'm still getting used to the idea. After exchanging phone numbers and agreeing to be ready to go at eight, we part ways.

I consider walking around the front of the gardens and hospital, but the back will be quieter since it's off the main road. The fence here is more modern, with seven-foot-tall, galvanised-metal bars, so I've got a great view of the gardens from this side.

The shivering lines hanging in the air inside the grounds are so thick in places it reminds me of the haze from a bush fire.

I stop at an ornate cast-iron entrance. These gates are tall and similar to the Cinderella-like entrance at the front of the property, but a little less decorative. They certainly didn't spare any expense keeping people out of this place.

I look through the gates to the boulevard of towering trees beyond. An involuntary shudder creeps over the skin of my neck and back. I roll my shoulders and rub the sensation away with my hand. My imagination happily supplies a monstrous spider crouched down in the centre of the park, but I know that isn't right. There is a threat here, but it isn't a spider.

The right answer tickles in behind my right eye, in the same place migraines come from. I can't quite get to the information and thinking about it is causing my headache to ramp up. I have enough problems right now, this one will have to wait.

As I walk along the footpath thousands of fruit bats high up in the trees between the Botanic Gardens and the Zoo watch me curiously. I think they are cute at first, until I notice how many there are and how intently they watch me. I can hear their chittering and squeaking. Creepy. I'm definitely not coming this way at night.

After the craziness of the last couple of days, seeing the pollution-stained stonework of the old nurses' quarters provides welcome relief.

I'm home, where I can lock my door and pretend I know who I am and the world will seem stable and knowable, even if a thick mass of shivering webs leads straight in through the big wooden door.

It's weird that the lines are only in certain places. There must be a pattern. Is it places I've been?

Whatever the reason, they don't seem to be provoking one of those visions at the moment. I punch in the code for the door, wait for the click and shove my way inside.

Sam is home and either watching an action movie or having a shootout in his rooms.

I'm almost past his door when he bursts through it, fully dressed this time, in casual pants and a loose shirt.

"Hey, I thought it was you," he says with a big grin.

I know what he reminds me of, a border collie. It's the friendliness, and the fact he's got more energy than he'll ever be able to use.

"Hi," I respond.

This is good luck. Now I won't have to track him down.

"I was hoping to catch you," he says. "There are going to be a few workers in the building Monday morning."

"Oh?" I ask.

"I think they are just checking out what needs to be done before demolition starts. Seeing what's salvageable, stuff like that. I don't think they'll actually do anything yet."

"Oh, okay," I say.

I couldn't really care less about Monday. I might be in jail by then anyway.

"Hey Sam, what floor did you say Ellie lives on? I went upstairs last night to say hi, but I couldn't see which room was hers."

I don't mention I was running for my life at the time, mostly because I've no idea how I would answer those questions. Sam's dark eyes shift sideways for a second or two before he looks back at me with a perfectly reasonable answer.

"She moved down to this floor a couple of days ago actually. Said it was getting spooky up there, all alone on the top floor."

Sounds legit. Great. I ran away from safety last night.

"Of course," I say. "Which room? I'll go say hello."

"She left already. Said she's going to be out all night. She works a lot."

I nod and keep my face carefully blank. Sam is talking faster than normal and shifting on his feet a lot. Not to mention the extended eye contact is feeling a bit weird. I know he's lying, but I can't tell which part is dodgy.

More worryingly, some of the furniture behind Sam's fidgeting body is separating around the edges. I feel like I'm getting double vision, except Sam is still crystal clear.

Am I going to have a vision now? What happens then? Will I just stand in front of Sam, looking like I'm having a seizure, while my mind is off gallivanting around in another time?

Gotta go. I'm already halfway up the stairs when I call 'see ya' to Sam. As I get to the middle landing and turn the corner, I hear him walking along the ground floor in the direction of Ellie's new room.

I wonder what he's up to for a split second, but I'm so surrounded by intrigue at the moment that I just can't force myself to care.

I gather the things I need and head down the hallway towards the bathroom. It's ridiculous how non-threatening the hall seems in the daylight. I remember the shadow I saw in here yesterday morning and stop in what I think must be the correct doorway. The room is empty except for the fixed furniture and a whole mess of shivery lines. If the lines were being spun out by a spider, this would be its lair.

I head up to the ugly bathroom and climb into a steaming hot shower. When the water is perfectly set so I'll glow red for the next hour, I can think without distraction for a few minutes. I feel guilty wasting water though, the state only just got off water restrictions. Adelaide seems like a tiny pocket of green surrounded by dead and dying land. The lush green farm I grew up on seems so far away now.

How pathetic, barely four days and I'm homesick. What would my parents think?

And now I'm thinking about them, how much do they know about my background? They know about the trial and everything public of course. They've always said I can ask them anything I want when I am ready. Trouble is I never was.

I've got the thick, yellow envelope containing the transcript of my father's trial at the bottom of my suitcase. I've had it stored with my other important papers for so many years the outside has been worn soft and velvety. Maybe it's time to open that particular package of nope.

I've always felt like reading it somehow gives my biological father validation. Like me knowing his pathetic excuse for killing my mother might somehow excuse him. Or I might be contaminated by his reasoning.

My traitorous mind bitches at me, arguing I'm really afraid of agreeing with my father and what that might mean for my character, or my sanity.

But things have changed; knowing what happened isn't about him anymore. Too many people know who I am. How am I supposed to make the right decisions with only half the information?

Back in my room I drag the envelope out of my suitcase. The thick yellow paper was torn open a long time ago, not by me, and it's been resealed with a single strip of wide clear tape. I take a calming breath and pick at a corner of the tape and peel it off. The envelope is bulging with papers, most of them stapled into one big book, but there are some loose sheets as well.

I glance at the time. There's less than an hour until I have to meet up with Amber and Alex, not enough time to get through all of this. I look at my laptop sitting on the bench. Should I just google my parents? My overactive imagination helpfully supplies me with images of websites that glorify murder and murderers. Or even worse, websites that blame the victim for their fate.

Nah. It's about time I read this transcript anyway. I've been holding on to it for years.

My stomach feels like I've been storing heavy, drop-forged spanners in there all day.

I realise with relief I need food if I'm going to be getting up to trouble tonight. I don't have anything interesting in my little fridge, but I end up putting a frozen lasagne I'd forgotten I had in the microwave to heat up. Can I justify waiting until I've eaten to start reading? I check the clock. No.

All of the loose sheets are just admin' junk so I ignore those. The first few pages of the stapled bundle are all of the legal particulars and I quickly skim them.

I locate the charges, but there's not much in there I don't already know. It looks like Jak's lawyers didn't trust my father to speak in his own defence. Neither would I. He had a different story every time he spoke to the papers. One minute my mother is the love of his life and the next she's an actual monster.

The list of witnesses for the prosecution is long. I don't recognise any names for the defence, Ana's name isn't there. I should have known a family so private wouldn't want to get mixed up in a public trial. It's doubtful any of the defence witnesses actually know what happened to my mother, or my father wouldn't have been in prison for almost my entire life.

I flick through the papers to the prosecution witness's testimony. It's quite a thick section. I'll never get through all that in an hour. The first few are just police and experts making their cases. I skim a psychiatrist's testimony on my father's possible mental illness. There's nothing interesting. He never met my father until after the murder and it looks like my father wasn't, quote, rational at the time. I'll come back to the rest of the experts later.

I finally find what I am really looking for, the testimony of Bianca Bowler. I don't recognise the name, but apparently she actually knew my bio parents, Hope and Jak. I skim her testimony. A frisson of shock sweeps up from my toenails to my scalp.

My bio mother was a nurse. At the same hospital I work at.

Why didn't Mum and Dad tell me? Did they forget? I doubt it.

Yes, I always refused to discuss my bio family with them, but it feels like they could have made an exception for this.

Bianca was a nurse who lived in the nurses' quarters I'm currently sitting in and she worked with Hope. They were friends. Bianca testified that she heard my parents arguing in the days before she disappeared. She reported my mother missing and possibly dead when she didn't turn up for her morning shift. She tried contacting Hope on her mobile but there was no answer. When she tried the home phone Jak answered and refused to tell her where Hope was.

I'm nearly finished reading Bianca's testimony when my phone chimes. It's a text from Amber, they're around the corner waiting. I text back to let them know I'll be a sec.

I skim the rest of the page. Apparently, she saw Jak carrying something large enough to be Hope's body out of the building in the middle of the night. Other than that, Bianca doesn't have anything solid on what really happened to my mother.

I quickly rifle through the rest of the pages hoping something will stand out, but I don't find anything concrete. It seems like most of the evidence against my father was circumstantial.

Who knows what might've happened if Jak hadn't given up and pleaded guilty right before closing arguments? I need to read this thoroughly soon, but it doesn't seem like this is the best way to get to know about my family history. This is just a badly-filtered snapshot of one moment in time.

I put down the file, grab my things and head out the door.

Chapter 17

Evening - South of the city

Amber and I are sitting in a borrowed car, across the road and down a bit from Burton Funerals. We've been 'casing the joint' for about an hour now. I was pretty surprised to see Amber and Alex dressed as security guards when they picked me up in a small, white hatchback. I knew Alex sometimes works as one, but somehow I didn't really expect them to go all out with their cover story.

I've had plenty of time sitting here to notice some interesting details. For example, the badges on both of their uniforms aren't sewn on. I can tell because they are lifting slightly at the edges. Also, while Alex's uniform fits him perfectly, Amber's shirt is probably one of Alex's. It's several sizes too big, even though she's rolled up the sleeves and tucked the tails into her pants.

Even so, I was still shocked when Alex got out of the car twenty minutes ago, walked straight up to the front doors of the funeral home and knocked. I don't know what the plan was, but it worked because the door opened and Alex walked in.

These two are completely fearless.

Amber seems fine, but I sit in dread-laden silence for 564 breaths. Finally Alex walks back out of the front door and around the building, shining his torch into the shadows and eaves. When he finishes his careful inspection, he strides back down the street towards us. The car rocks as he yanks the door open and folds himself back into the driver's seat.

"How'd it go?" Amber asks.

Alex's habitually-grave face lightens for his sister; he almost looks happy.

"Better than I expected. Sean, the guy I called earlier, already told me they don't use C&T Security anymore." Alex points to the badges on his uniform shirt for my benefit. "But they haven't moved to another company, the alarms aren't monitored at all. The cameras just record to a hard drive in case they're broken into.

"All I had to do was tell him I'd just been at a break-in at another funeral home and was letting our old customers know about it in case they had the same weakness in their systems. He showed me their whole setup. They haven't upgraded in years."

"So are we gonna be able to break in?"

Alex is in a good mood, but he still rolls his eyes at my question and holds up a small set of keys.

"There won't be any breaking. These were just hanging on the wall of the office. Really, I can see why they don't bother having their alarm monitored when they have idiots like that working for them."

"And the cameras?" I ask.

I know it's pretty unlikely he's forgotten them, but I can't help myself. I've got trust issues.

"Off," Alex replies bluntly without even glancing in my direction.

Wow, he really doesn't like being questioned, or it's just me. Still, my anxiety can only be tamed by controlling all the details, so I just plough on.

"Won't they notice the cameras are off?"

Alex mutters something under his breath before turning to look at me.

"They aren't actually off. Okay? I set the program so the footage won't be saved to the hard drive. They don't have any remote-viewing programs set up so, unless we are caught in the act, no one will know we've been there."

I stay quiet after that. I'm comfortable knowing not everyone has to like me, but Alex seems to find me particularly repugnant.

About half an hour later the back gates open and a plain grey van rolls out. Amber and I look to Alex to tell us what happens next.

"Okay, he's going across town to a pickup. We have about an hour before he'll get back," he says, climbing up out of the little hatchback. "Oh, and bring that bag Lily."

A black sports backpack is well camouflaged in the darkness of the foot well.

"This one?"

Alex doesn't answer, but I can't see another bag. I haul the backpack out as I step out of the car. I automatically start to offer the bag to Amber, but I can see her a bit better now. Her security guard cover is barely passing as it is. She has her small black handbag slung over her shoulder. The bag is bulging as usual and it definitely doesn't look something a professional security guard would carry at work. If I give her the backpack as well, she'll look like some school kid dressing up for the Book Week costume parade.

I sling the backpack over my shoulder as we cross the road and approach Burton Funerals. The business has no front fences so we can walk right up to the building. There are several manicured garden beds bordering a spotless customer car park, not a single weed or stray leaf is in sight.

The reception area is a rendered stone building with big glass windows that have been tinted to keep out the heat of the Australian summer. I can't help looking up into the eaves of the building. Several security cameras stare down at us.

"It's fine," Alex insists in his rough voice.

I can tell he isn't used to being doubted. I roll my eyes at Amber.

We continue around the side of the building to the beige metal gates. Alex unlocks the small access gate with a key from his pilfered keyring. He holds the heavy gate open for us 'weaklings' and I make sure to give him a narrow-eyed look as I walk under his arm. He returns it with interest and I instantly regret provoking a man I know nothing about. Having his sister around is giving me a false sense of security. I doubt she could protect me if he got angry enough to get violent.

The other side of the fence is a stark contrast to the front of the block. The gates are designed to conceal two dull-grey, tin sheds that are big enough to hold a combine harvester or two. This area looks nothing like the front of the business, this is more like a tidy truck yard.

Except there isn't a vehicle to be seen. They must be in the bigger of the two sheds, because it has an enormous sliding door on the front and most of the tire tracks lead that way. The smaller of the two sheds is attached to the back of the reception area and has a large door about half-way down its length.

Alex strides past me, closely inspecting the keys in the harsh glare from several security spotlights. He unlocks the door and walks into the building. This shed is one big storage room, crammed with chairs, tables, all sorts of weird rolling contraptions and about a thousand coffins and caskets. The only empty floor space is directly in front of us which leads to a small walled off area with a large drain in the centre of the floor surrounded by cupboards, benches and sinks. It's a prep room where they get the bodies ready for burial. On the far side of this room insulated double doors lead into a room-sized, industrial fridge unit.

Alex opens the coolroom door. It's dark inside. My eyes are just beginning to adjust when a fluorescent overhead light blinks on. I close my eyes against the pain for a second and when I open them I'm confused. I was expecting a funeral home to have a wall of silver doors with bodies in drawers behind them, like you see on TV.

This setup is just a large coolroom with strong metal shelving on each wall. Bodies are stacked on the shelves. Most are bagged, but several are just laying there, either in the clothes they died in or dressed more formally in their Sunday best, with a layer of plastic over them to keep the condensation at bay.

It's unexpected. It feels wrong to have people lined up like stock in a supermarket, but not much more wrong than us being here. I'm still second guessing why I agreed to do this. It seemed so obvious that I had to help when Alex asked me too, but right now I can't remember why.

I still don't even know exactly what this ritual requires.

Alex and Amber start checking the racks on the right of the door. I take the left. I am about three bodies in when Amber calls me over. I look at the shelf that attracted her attention. A tiny form concealed inside a blue, hospital body bag is lying on a waist-high shelf. Ana's full name is printed on the bag's label. There isn't much other information. Just a couple of numbers. No personal belongings are listed, so I hope Amber and Alex weren't counting on stealing some family heirloom back.

"So what now?" I ask Amber. "Do you need to wave a candle over her and pray to your ancestors or something?"

She shakes her head, grabs the gurney from the centre of the room and wheels it alongside her grandmother's body. Following Alex's lead, I grab a corner of the bag covering Ana's body and haul it across onto the gurney. We move Ana into the centre of the room and carefully unzip the bag, exposing her head and neck.

She looks like a pale-blue, wax replica of herself. The funeral home hasn't started to prepare her for a viewing, and they probably won't if she's going straight to cremation.

Ana is not the first dead body I've seen, but this is Amber and Alex's Grandmother. I only met her twice, but I feel like I knew her. I need to force myself to stay detached.

This can't be easy for Amber either. Who knows about Alex? He seems cold enough to me, but even dickweeds must still love their Nan.

I look at Amber. Her eyes are shining as she leans in and gives her grandmother's waxen cheek a light kiss. She stays bowed over her grandmother, whispering quietly in her ear for nearly a full minute.

I hope this is the ritual she needs to complete. I'm desperate to get out of here. Time is getting away from us, and it's so cold I can't tell if my shivering is due to the frigid air or the excess adrenaline coursing through my veins.

All I need now is for the edges of everyone to start shedding.

Finally Amber stands up straight and looks silently at Alex. He stares back at her, his face darkening. They stand silently arguing for nearly a full minute until I hold my wrist between them and point to my watch.

"Please Alex." Amber whispers.

"Amber, you know we can't take her body," her brother replies in a firm voice.

"But he'll come for her."

"That's a chance we have to take. Besides, he probably already has what he needs."

Somehow that must make sense to Amber because her expression changes. She is all determination now.

"Fine," Amber says, holding a hand out towards me. "Can you pass me that bag please Lily."

I pass her the backpack and she digs through it and pulls out a needle bigger than anything I have ever seen. It looks antique, with a steel barrel and a thumb and finger rings making it look more like a dentist's needle than anything we use now. She holds it out to me.

"We need a piece of her brain."

Chapter 18

Evening - Burton Funerals

"Seriously?" I say, shaking my head in horror.

I thought they were going to wave some sage over her or put some crystals on her chest and chant or something. I'm in way over my head here.

"I knew this was a waste of time," Alex says, shooting me a dirty look. "Here Amber, I'll do it."

Alex reaches for the syringe, but Amber pulls her arm back, out of Alex's reach.

"No Alex. We only get one chance at this. You know it's too important. Please Lily." Amber has tears in her eyes again.

I feel terrible for refusing her, but this is crazy. I think there's an actual crime named for this scenario, interfering with a dead body or something. I shake my head again, or keep shaking it anyway, I'm not sure I ever stopped.

"Please Lily." Amber tries again. "Don't make Alex or me do it. This is what Ana wanted. This is part of our beliefs.

Your mother believed in this and she would want you to help us. Besides, if we get this wrong, we won't be able to help you either."

Great, an appeal to our new friendship, followed by guilt, followed by blackmail. Next I think she might try a threat, but when I glance at Alex's face I realise there is already enough menace in the room to get me rethinking my position. After all, I'm already here.

In fact, the longer I look at Alex the more reasonable the idea seems. I'm pretty sure the police will charge me with whatever these two get up to, even if I leave right now. And just maybe I can do this without leaving any trace of our actions and we can get out of here.

Tears are flowing down Amber's cheeks when I look back at her. I hold out my hand for the needle and she sobs loudly when she realises I mean to do this gross thing for her.

The truth is I'm not that repulsed by taking a sample from a dead body. One of the reasons I'm going into nursing is because biology fascinates me. I'm always begging Dad to let me help him with necropsies on the farm.

Amber gives me the needle and something heavy and cold starts clunking around in my stomach. I consider how to best go about this without leaving any evidence that a cursory exam would discover. We already know Ana won't be autopsied, so as long as nothing is visible on her skin when the funeral attendant prepares her for cremation we'll be good. So, eyes, ears, nose or mouth. I look carefully at each choice. I think the angle of the ears will be difficult. I check under the eyelids but I'm not sure I can face the idea, and I don't know how Amber would react. I decide to get more information.

"How is this usually done?"

"I don't know," she admits. "The stories say the community used to have an expert to help, but there really isn't that many of us left anymore. Even less of us have managed to keep our memory-chains intact. A few generations of nothing getting passed on and it's all gone."

"Do you at least know if it's a particular part of the brain you need?" I ask her.

I did learn where everything in the brain is in year twelve psychology, but it gets pretty complicated in the emotion and memory centres.

"Where the long-term memories are stored, we think. That's why we need your help. We only have this one chance. I'm so sorry to get you into this, but I promise we'll help you out next."

"Help me what?" I ask.

I'm pretty sure she means help me find a way to control my visions, but it never hurts to check. And I need a minute to prepare myself for what I'm about to attempt.

"Find your mum, of course."

That's right, she said that before. Trouble is my mother's remains have never been found. I envy people who have a grave to visit, because I imagine they feel closer to the person they lost. My bio mother has always just been a collection of my wishes and imagination.

I almost open my mouth to ask Amber what her plan is, but one problem at a time. First, I need to get this done and we can get gone.

"Can you bring up a picture of a brain on your phone for me? A cross-section, find one with all the areas highlighted in different colours if you can."

I am all business now. I compartmentalize my thoughts like this is a final exam and this procedure is all that exists right now.

I study the long needle again. I'm worried it's not strong enough to break through the bones at the back of the sinus cavity, or long enough to get the samples we need.

I look around for something else. There is nothing in this room, but I remember a large stainless-steel cabinet in the prep room outside the door. Amber protests as I turn from Ana's body, but I ignore her and search the cabinet until I find what I need.

When I walk back into the fridge Amber shows me an image of a brain she found.

"Do you need it labelled?" she asks me.

I expand the image and rotate it until I have a good idea of where I'm aiming. This isn't going to be precise surgery though. This is more just grab everything and run.

"If you can, it might help," I tell her.

I don't really need the labels, but I know the extra layer of complexity to the search should keep her occupied for a while longer. I don't want her to watch what I am doing.

"Sorry Ana." I apologise to the woman I barely knew.

I put the long thin metal tube up her nose until it touches bone and then I give the end a sharp hit with an unidentified piece of metal I'm using as a mallet. The bone breaks easily. Too easily and the metal tube pushes through a lot further than I expect.

Amber looks up from her phone, screws up her face and turns her back on us. Alex has folded his arms across his chest and is glowering. I don't know what he expects from me. I am being as respectful as I can.

I withdraw the tube and shake it clear onto a tissue and then return to probing Ana's brain. When I'm as close to the hippocampus as possible I turn the tube hoping it will provide a cutting action and collect a sample inside. I repeat the process nearby, just in case I missed the exact spot. The noise is disgusting and Amber puts her hands over her ears and runs from the room.

"How much do you need?" I ask, looking up at Alex.

His jaw muscles are working hard.

"A tiny amount, a pin head."

Good, I'm confident I have enough then. I remove the metal tube carefully and check the end. Alex hands me a small jar and I shake out the inch long sample of Ana's brain into it. He takes the jar and puts a lid on it before putting it in the backpack. I clean up after myself using a sink in the prep room. It feels wrong putting the equipment back in the cabinet without sterilising it, but we don't have time.

Amber's not in the prep room. I hear some noises from further away, near the shed door. It sounds a lot louder than any noise Amber should be making. I hope I'm not going to have to clean up out there too.

Alex has moved to stand next to Ana's head and is stroking his grandmother's hair back from her forehead. I hesitate. It's weird to see anything but hatred on his face.

"We have to put her back and get out of here," I remind Alex quietly.

I wipe Ana's face carefully and check her for any signs of what I've done. No, we're in the clear. I zip the bag back over her face and Alex and I push the gurney back over to the wall and respectfully shove her body back onto its shelf. With one look back over his shoulder Alex leaves the room. I don't know whether to be impressed or disturbed by his composure, but as someone who never had a grandmother, my understanding of appropriate behaviour is probably unrealistic. A little too children's bedtime stories.

I search the rooms for traces of our presence. Looks good. I pick up the backpack and sling it over my shoulder as I follow Alex out of the prep room. To my surprise Amber isn't waiting for us in the shed's storage area. I hope she hasn't gone outside into the yard to throw up or anything. There were no garden beds in the rear yard and vomit is hard to clean up on concrete. I've had experience. My sister isn't much of a drinker now, but she did more than her fair share in her teens.

A few of the folding chairs have fallen over but otherwise we've left no trace here. I'm still looking over my shoulder when I walk into a wall of Alex. He's stopped in the middle of the exit without any warning. I rub my sternum where his elbow connected.

"She's not here." Alex's voice rises towards the end.

He jogs to the fence line and puts one foot on a cross bar and lifts himself to peer over the top. I can't think of any reason Amber would leave without us. I spot something small and silver lying on the ground near the door, camouflaged against the tin shed's wall.

"Alex, look," I call.

"She's not at the car either."

Alex drops off the fence and turns to look at the brushed-metal drink bottle lying against the shed. A dark stain on the concrete that looks worryingly similar to blood leads to a silver lid a metre away. Our wide eyes meet.

"That's Amber's drink bottle." Alex looks wildly around before shoving me roughly aside and running back into the building we'd just left.

Chapter 19

Only a smidge later
- The funeral home

I don't follow Alex. I'm pretty sure Amber came outside, either feeling sick or just to put some distance between her and what I was doing to her poor nan.

I walk over to Amber's drink bottle and pick it up. It looks like the same bottle she drank from on the day I met her. It must've been in the tiny handbag that's permanently strapped to her body. I check the contents, hoping that dark, wet stain on the ground is just blackcurrant juice or even port.

There's a mouthful of some thick dark liquid left inside the bottle. I pour a few drops onto my hand. It's thick and sticky like undiluted cordial. It does look similar to the stain drying on the ground.

If this was a TV show, I would taste the stuff on the ground and in my hand to see if they matched. Hard pass. I pick the lid up off the concrete and screw it back onto the bottle.

I'm about out of ideas, so I stand in the yard staring blankly at the high fence line as I try to imagine what happened here. It would be super-convenient if I could have a vision of the last few minutes. I concentrate on the stain on the ground, trying to force the edges to start fraying, but my new 'ability' doesn't seem to work that way. I need to stop calling it an ability. Disability is closer but it's inconsistent. Maybe illness, weakness? Useless is what it is.

I look at my watch. The funeral home attendant will be back any time now. I'm considering bailing when Alex emerges from the shed door, his face dark red with rage.

My fight or flight response starts screaming loudly in my head in favour of flight. I take an involuntary step away from him. I want to ask what he knows, but the obvious danger in drawing the attention of a furious man, who is not my biggest fan by the way, clamps my jaw firmly shut.

With my heart pounding, I watch him pace the yard and wait for him to speak. Twenty-three normal heartbeats and five premature ventricular contractions later he finally breaks the silence.

"He took her."

I gasp automatically and feel stupid even as I do it. It's actually one of the more rational things that's happened around me lately.

"How do you know?" I ask.

I know immediately it's a mistake. Alex's eyes narrow at me and I see the muscles in his jaw working. I have his whole attention. I don't dare look away or I won't know where the danger is coming from. Alex's expressive face is so easy to read I see the exact second he decides I'm not worth his time and energy. He turns abruptly and stalks over to the front gate.

I consider my options, none of which are good. I quickly shut the door to the shed and follow Alex, staying carefully out of arm's reach.

He doesn't wait for me while I quietly shut the gate behind us and tug on it to check it's locked. I run a few steps to catch up to him before he can get in the car and tear off without me. I reach him just he stops near the driver's door. He makes no move to open it. I walk around him and stand in his peripheral vision so he knows I'm there.

"He's seen this car," Alex growls. "We can't use it."

The words 'who's seen the car' are bashing against my clenched teeth, but this time good sense and cowardice win the battle.

I glance at my watch. It's been seventy-one minutes since Alex said we have an hour before the morgue attendant returns and I'm not sure he's capable of making good choices right now.

"Maybe so, but we need to get out of here. And we can't leave this here for someone to trace either." I try to keep my voice firm and confident as I hold out my shaking hand, palm up. "Give me your keys."

He looks lost for a moment before he hands his keyring to me and walks obediently around to the passenger seat. I get into the driver's seat and have a look around the cabin for a minute. Alex is much taller than me and I need to adjust everything that moves but driving this car shouldn't be too difficult. It's about the same size as my faithful old Barina, just a lot newer.

Out of habit, I check Alex is strapped in before I start the car. I need to put some distance between us and the funeral home, but I have no idea where I'm going. As soon as I pull out into the street Alex bends forward and clutches his head in his hands. I keep an eye on him as I drive, not sure what to expect. He doesn't look the type to internalise his pain. He looks more like a ticking time bomb.

"I am so sorry Alex," I say quietly.

He stays silent, so I decide to leave him to his demons for now. Due to the lack of a better plan I drive in what I think might be the direction of his apartment. Hopefully I'll find a landmark when we get closer.

In less than ten minutes we pass a large church I recognise and I know we are close to Alex's place. I can't remember which side road to take, so I just turn into the suburb and find a quiet spot to park alongside a brush fence. We won't be disturbing anyone here while Alex gets himself under control.

We have been stationary for a few minutes and I'm already lost in my thoughts, when Alex straightens and coughs to clear his throat. He rubs his hands roughly over his face and sits back looking out the passenger window.

Now that I am not distracted by driving, my imagination is torturing me with everything Amber might be going through. My throat chokes up and it's not long before I am forced to speak. I have to know what's going on.

"Did you see who took her?" I ask Alex.

He shakes his head and looks around the car for the first time.

"Where are we?" he asks.

"Near your apartment I hope. I couldn't remember exactly how to get there."

He is silent again and my patience is only so good.

"Do you have any idea who it was, or why they took her?"

"Your boyfriend," Alex spits the words out. "Nathaniel bloody Cain. Who else would know we would come here?"

I shake my head. That can't be right. Yes, I find him intimidating with moments of outright scary, but I just can't imagine him kidnapping someone.

At the risk of setting Alex off again, I need to know more.

"You haven't explained how you know she was kidnapped."

Luckily for me, this time he doesn't take my question as an insult to his manhood.

"I checked the camera feed in the office. I couldn't tell who it was, but they carried her easily enough, so it was almost definitely a man."

"But the cameras weren't recording."

"The buffer was enough to go back five minutes, so I saw him carrying her through the parking lot. He put her in the boot of a black Audi sedan," Alex explains, his voice breaking on the last sentence.

I rack my brain for the make of Nathan's car. Nothing.

"If you're sure it was Nathan, maybe we can find him and get her back." I still don't think it's him, but doing anything would be better than nothing. "Do you know where he lives?"

Alex nods slowly.

"I don't think he'll take her straight back to his house though. It's too public. Anyway, it might not have actually been him who took her. He could have sent someone."

"So what can we do?" I ask.

I need to do something soon to control my rising panic. At least driving the getaway car I felt like I was achieving something.

"I don't know," Alex replies. "I need to think. All I know is we need to find her before he kills her, just like he killed Ana."

"No." I shake my head. "I don't know much about what is going on here, but I know whoever has her doesn't want to kill her. At least not yet."

Alex raises his eyebrows slightly.

"He would have just killed her at the funeral home, wouldn't he? There weren't any witnesses."

Alex thinks for a moment before replying.

"Maybe he thought the cameras were on?"

"You said you couldn't tell who it was anyway."

"Yeah, he was wearing dark, loose clothing and something covering his head."

We sit thinking for a minute. I have no idea what to do next. I don't even have to ask if we should call the police. Alex would have already done it if he thought it was a serious option. Yes, the police would ask awkward questions, but I think that would be a small price to pay to get Amber back safe and sound. But then I haven't spent my entire life hiding my true identity. At least, not in the same way.

Alex sits up straighter, closer to his normal self.

"Okay, I think I know where we are," he says looking around. "My place isn't safe anymore. We agreed that in a scenario like this Amber will give up where I live if she needs to, so she can protect our more important secrets."

I think for a moment.

"Do you think my apartment would be safe?" I ask.

"I think you need to go back there so everything looks normal," Alex replies. "Also, there's a good chance whoever took her has no idea you're with us and Amber would never give you up."

He sounds very confident, and his behaviour is unpredictable so I choose not to remind him that torture exists.

"Okay," I reply, letting my tone rise towards the end of the word to telegraph my scepticism to Alex.

"Don't worry, I'll keep watch."

I actually believe he intends to keep me safe, until he continues his sentence.

"That way, I'll see him when he comes for you."

I'm the bait.

Alex must have seen my horror because he corrects his last sentence.

"If he comes for you."

"It's fine," I say.

"Look, I have a plan to find Amber and I need your help," Alex tells me, looking straight into my eyes to reassure me. "So I'd have to keep you safe even if I wasn't programmed to do it."

"I said it's fine."

And somehow it is. Mostly because everything always seems okay while Alex is talking me into something, but also because there's a lot to unpack in what he just said. He has a plan? And he's programmed to take care of me? Is that because I'm renascent or whatever the word is, reborn?

Alex interrupts my unpacking before I've even framed my first question.

"First, I need to get some stuff from my place."

I drive, with Alex ordering me left and right, until we are a road away from his apartment. We abandon the car to walk the rest of the way. At the corner Alex touches my hand lightly and steps across next to the wall. I fall into line behind him as he checks down the road. There are a lot of cars parked on the street, but none look familiar to me.

"Do you think it's safe?" I whisper.

"Wait here." Alex jogs back to the abandoned hatchback, rummages around in the boot for a minute, before slamming the hatch and jogging back to me with a tire iron in his left hand.

"Okay, you go first," Alex says. "Just in case."

I frown. In this scenario doesn't the guy go first to keep the girl from harm? I guess he already admitted he isn't above using me as bait.

Barely two metres around the corner I notice a dark car parked on the road, two houses this side of Alex's place. It's not the car Nathan picked me up in, it's not sleek enough. And it's not an Audi either, so it can't be the car that the kidnapper used.

Still, as I continue walking, I can feel something wrong about it. It's too dark. It's like a hole has been punched out of the dark street.

As I get nearer, I can't tear my eyes away from the inky shape. I can't make out the interior, but I can't see much at all anymore. My eyes are burning and my vision is starting to blur as tears build on my lower lids.

My vision clears momentarily as the tears spill over and stream down my face, showing me that the edges of the car are starting to peel away. Everything around me is shivering.

My hands clench in a futile effort to keep myself present on this night with Alex, but it doesn't work. I slip backwards to a different night. I can tell because the moon is in a different place and the grass is longer now. But the inky black car remains parked in its place by the kerb.

My view changes again. It's warm now and I can smell flowers and freshly cut grass in the air around me. There's no moon this night, but I can see the car's silhouette in the darkness. A pale shape is illuminated by the car's dashboard instruments, sitting motionless behind the driver's wheel.

With the clarity of a nightmare, I know this is the man who pursues me from my dreams in the mornings. The man in my nightmares was never my father, it was always this man sitting there; and he has seen me.

The car door is opening and a dark silhouette stands up out of the car.

It's too dark to make out his features and I wonder if he can see mine. Maybe just like me, some primal instinct has awakened in him. Telling him his prey is near.

I tell myself I must be dreaming even if I don't remember falling asleep. I try to force myself awake, but just like in my nightmares, nothing happens.

The man who has been trying to kill me my entire life is still walking around the car towards me. He isn't rushing. He has all the time in the world because it looks like I am just going to stand here and wait for him.

He is halfway around the bonnet now. I feel a twitch in my legs, maybe I can move? I spin away from the car and start sprinting back down the footpath. I make it three steps when the timeline changes again. I can see the moon in front of me.

Am I back? In the movie of my life, would 'Present Day' be printed in large script across my fleeing ankles?

I see Alex coming around the corner about ten yards away from me.

"Alex," I croak as a dark figure steps out of the shadows of a tree in the yard beside me.

I am still drawing in a breath to scream, when something hard connects with my temple, and I drop to the concrete like a marionette with its strings cut.

Chapter 20

Quite a while later
- No idea again

I wake up with a scream and a screaming headache. Constant pain seems to be my new default setting. I'm sitting in the passenger seat of a moving vehicle, with a seat belt on. Hopefully that's a good sign.

I wrench my head to the right to see who's driving, but my rusted-over neck sets off an explosion of light and pain from my shoulder to my left eye. I can't even breathe for the next few seconds.

I slowly open my eyes again. I'm not surrounded by the black leather, or even pleather, I expect to see inside my nightmare killer's car. Instead I'm looking at a green glovebox coated in a thick layer of dust. Alex's four-wheel drive?

I shift in my seat, keeping my neck frozen, until I can see Alex's lovely, grim face. His jaw is clenched as usual. I wonder if he gets headaches from that.

"You're awake," Alex says, glancing over at me.

I think he might be an actual genius. I would laugh if I remembered how. Maybe I've got brain damage?

"What...?" My voice trails off.

I had a sentence formed before I started to speak, but the surge of pain that accompanied the echo of my voice in my head has completely erased it.

"I nearly had him," Alex says. "He ducked at the last minute, so I missed his head."

At least he's figured out what I wanted to know. That can't have been it though.

"I had to let him go. You sounded like you were swallowing your own tongue."

Oh, he took care of me instead of dealing with the attacker. I don't know Alex at all.

"Thank you," I say, shamefaced by my own nastiness.

Maybe I deserve all the dirty looks he gives me.

"Could you see his face?" Alex asks.

I shake my head slowly before remembering he's driving. "No, could you?"

"Too dark," Alex says. "So why'd he attack you if he couldn't tell who you were?"

He thinks on it for a moment before continuing.

"Night vision goggles? Just some random sicko looking for prey in the night?"

No. I have an idea, but how to explain it?

"He knew who I was. I think he's been watching you too, cos his car was there in the same spot months or even years ago." I bend forward and rub my knuckles over my forehead and eye sockets, seeking any relief as the pain flares even higher.

"What, really? How do you know?"

"Vision." I manage to mutter while scrubbing my palms over my temples and forehead. My head is so bad now I'm worried I've got a brain bleed.

"So my apartment's definitely not safe then. And now we know how he knew Amber exists." Alex looks grimmer than ever.

I can't respond.

"How's the head?" Alex asks.

I run a few answers through a filter for sarcasm and pettiness before deciding the less I say, the better.

"Bad."

"There's a flask in that bag at your feet that should fix you right up."

I can't think of anything short of a morphine drip that would make a dent in the pain I'm feeling, but I'll try anything. I gingerly bend at the waist, keeping my head and neck as still as possible and find a large duffel bag at my feet.

Hang on.

"When did you get this?" I ask Alex

"I went into my apartment after the guy got away."

"You left me on the road?"

"It was the footpath, and no, I locked you in my car first."

Oh, okay. Not sure how I feel about being dumped in a car straight after being knocked unconscious. I guess I should be thankful he rescued me at all. His priority should be finding his sister.

The bag crushing my feet is too big to lift onto my lap, so I unzip it and rummage until I find a stainless-steel drink bottle similar to the one Amber carries, but larger.

I unscrew the lid and sniff at the contents expecting nothing, but my new sense of smell doesn't let me down.

I'm reminded of the rich and tangy crust on a roast beef and a summer's barbecue. My mouth waters, but I hesitate. Since when does a drink smell like a barbecue?

"What is it?" I ask Alex.

"It's a natural medicine passed down for hundreds of years in our families. The drink version of that meal Amber cooked for you yesterday."

Amber's cooking was very good, and it did make me feel much better. Surely that can't be down to some traditional herbal remedy?

"What's in it?" I ask uncertainly. "There's nothing illegal is there?"

Alex shakes his head in frustration.

"There's no drugs if that's what you mean. Look, I don't know the entire recipe. I've never made it. That was Ana's job and now it's Amber's. Or yours. There's nothing in it you didn't already have yesterday."

He's right to think I'm an idiot of course. Someone just tried to knock my eye clear out of the other side of my head, Amber's been kidnapped, and I'm being picky about my food. If I can't trust Alex and Amber not to poison me, I have more problems than I can possibly survive. I bring the bottle to my lips.

The viscous liquid is savoury and sweet all at once, and it leaves a tangy aftertaste on my tongue. I take a large mouthful and wash it around in my mouth. There is definitely some kind of herb in it. Rosemary maybe? I swallow the mouthful and swig another. Alex looks at me with approval before turning his full attention back to driving.

Now that it's several swallows too late, a potential issue occurs to me. It was straight after eating Amber's home remedy yesterday when I had my first full vision of the past, rather than just seeing those shivery trails and peeling skin. And I started seeing the trails just after I ate at the restaurant with Nathan.

The food's definitely triggering the changes in my vision. Two incidences aren't a scientific sample size, but it's quite a coincidence. Is it some sort of weird reaction to the meat? It was the first time I've tried duck. Amber said her recipe used beef though and I grew up on a cattle farm, so I'm no stranger to that.

I test my sore neck by turning to look out the car's passenger window. My head swivels smoothly with no trace of the strained ligaments that hurt so badly when I woke up. And we are almost back at the old nurses' quarters. I can already see the corner of the hospital with its shivery trails hanging above the footpaths.

"Wait," I say.

Alex glances at me with his eyebrows raised.

"That man watching your apartment would know this car."

He nods unsurprised.

"That's why I'll drop you off round the corner and go dump this a few blocks away. I'll find us another car tomorrow."

I nod, wondering if I should tell him I have a car. I decide to wait and see how I feel about it in the morning.

"You are coming back, right?" I ask him.

I won't feel safe rattling around in that huge place alone all night. It's real late. The 'Hallway of Terror' will be in full swing by now.

In fact, I'm more worried about the building's general spookiness and ghostly encounters, than I am about Nathan knowing where I live. I still don't think he has anything to do with Amber's kidnapping, because now I know the attacker from my nightmares exists in the real world. Can there really be two bad guys, getting around in the same place, at the same time?

Oh, I actually forgot this is the serial-killer capital of Australia for a moment.

"Don't worry, I won't be too long," Alex says.

He pulls the four-by-four into a 'No Parking' spot between two trees and I climb down from the tall vehicle.

"I'll wait just inside so I can let you in," I tell him.

"Don't bother. I know a few ways into that building," he replies, before driving away.

My headache's almost gone as I walk around the corner. These people are really on to something with their home remedies. I look up the road to the front of the doomed old building I live in.

Oh yeah, the drink worked all right. The shivery lines that lead into the building's maw have increased in both number and size. The whole building is now shivering along with them.

I suck up all the courage I have, and some I've borrowed from Alex, and walk towards the building.

Now that I'm closer I can see movement deep inside the web.

At least I'm not alone now I think, as I follow the ghost of my mother into the darkness.

Chapter 21

Dawn - Nurses' quarters

I can't breathe. My corset is too tight, and my long petti-coats are sticking to my legs. It is so hot even the ever-present warbling magpies have fallen silent.

The unforgiving Australian sun is burning my fair skin, but that is nothing compared to the pain in my heart, and the anguish I can hear. The ringing in my eardrums and the scalding pain in my throat suggests I am the one who is screaming. But when I look down at the pressure I feel around my hips, I see my little girl's perfect wheaten ring-lets. She is clinging to my skirts.

I make the choice to let go of her delicate arms as she is torn away from me. Choosing to not hurt her in this fight might be the last gift I ever give her.

The girl's crumpled face is red and tear stained. She is crying and screaming in a hoarse voice. She has been upset for a while. I am not screaming, but I cannot hold back my own hot tears.

The two men holding my daughter are dressed in three-piece suits, complete with hat and tie, even in this weather. They drag her towards the door to the cottage and shove her inside so roughly she falls to her knees on the slate flagstones.

I have not entirely given up hope that my fate can be changed. I look to the man standing rigid near our cottage door. His face is hard and accusing. He sees me looking at him with tears streaming down my face and one corner of his mouth lifts in contempt.

I do not deserve that look from the man I took as my husband, the man I loved enough to have a child with. A beautiful, thoughtful daughter, who is locked behind the unpainted wooden door my husband now guards.

My body remains perfectly still while my mind races. I need to show these men that I am calm and rational, that this is all a terrible mistake. But still the unwelcome tears stream down my face.

I hear a crash of glass. My tiny daughter has thrown a heavy silver-plated candlestick through the window and is trying to squeeze her small body through the opening. The new hard-hearted version of my husband crosses the uneven timber veranda and slaps her hard across the face.

I breathe her name as she vanishes from my sight.

"Bridget."

She doesn't reappear. The two suited, mustachioed men advance toward me as if I am a skittish colt. They have taken in the chaos here and decided my husband is right. I am the one to blame. The men grab my arms and steer me roughly towards their black windowless carriage.

Only now, through the dark carriage's open door, do I spy the shadow of a man already sitting in the depths of the carriage. I cannot see much of his face in the darkness, but his narrow eyes glint at me in amusement and I can already feel his evil crawling across my skin.

I know now this is him. The man I have been running from. The man who scared me onto a ship and across the oceans, to find a place where he could not reach me.

I scream for my daughter. She needs to be warned. I rear back and try to wrench my arms from the rough hands dragging me towards my enemy. Instead I am lifted clean off my feet, carried the last few paces to the carriage and bundled inside.

In the seconds before the door blocks my last view of the home I have grown to love, I see the men tip their hats to my husband. He has puffed up his chest, proud at being back in control of his domain. He touches his cap to the men in return, keeping up the act they started. The pretence that my husband is a gentleman.

He and I know better. He is no gentleman by breeding or by character. He catches sight of me looking at him and scowls before turning his back on me.

I am afraid for Bridget. Will she be whipped for breaking that window? I hope she settles quickly, or he will be even angrier. I cannot believe I ever thought he would understand.

I almost told him my secret just after Bridget was born. I thought it might make life easier if he knew. But the beliefs of a devout man quickly turn into righteous anger, and my ribs ache with the bruises I was given when he finally stumbled upon my secret.

But physical pain is insignificant next to the molten grief I feel in my chest for my precious daughter. Who will protect her now?

I have seen the lunatic asylum they are taking me to. We have walked nearby when taking in the sights. It is a grand looking building from the front, but I have heard the noises coming from inside. And worse, I have heard stories.

I know our little farm cannot afford to pay for my care so my situation will be dire. But I have never expected anything more than hardship.

The temperature in the carriage is stifling as the driver cracks his whip and the horses begin the slow trudge back down through the mountain range towards the city. I cannot breathe.

The sound of a man clearing his throat a mere foot away in the darkness startles me. In my misery I had forgotten the man sitting on the seat in front of me. It's so dark when the silence returns, he could be a figment of my imagination. Then he speaks.

What he tells me of my fate is horrific, but not unexpected, so I sit and listen meekly. What choice do I have? It's when he begins to speak of my daughter I scream.

I'm still screaming when I wake up. The dream was so real it takes a moment before the fear begins to subside and then the door to my room explodes inwards. I cower under my quilts as Alex looks wildly around for the danger. I don't know exactly where he spent the night, but he was obviously close enough.

I'm sweating with the stress of the dream, and I kick back the covers as Alex asks the obvious question.

"What the hell, Lily?"

"Sorry, Alex. It was just a nightmare."

"Jesus, it musta been a bad one then."

"Yeah, and you're going to need to clear out, just in case the people who live downstairs heard it too."

"Nah. He left at daybreak."

"What about Ellie from room 14?"

"No one else lives here," Alex replies, giving me a strange look.

I don't fight him on it. If Ellie was going to investigate the noise she would've been here by now. I look closer at Alex's face. His eyes are bloodshot and his eyelids are swollen. It's obvious as hell he's been crying.

"Are you okay?" I ask, knowing he's not.

"Sure," he answers too quickly, trying to shut down my concern.

Fine. I drag myself from the bed and check the mirror. Just for drool and the like. I'm under no illusion I'll look like a supermodel after a few hours of restless sleep.

As usual I'm more tired now than when I went to sleep, but as I was feeling pretty good last night after drinking that home remedy, I am feeling unusually energetic now. Hungry though.

I drag a loaf of five-day-old bread out of the cupboard under the bench and pop two slices into the toaster.

"Do you get many nightmares?" Alex asks me.

"Yeah, heaps," I reply. "They're heaps realistic too, usually someone's trying to kill me."

I reach into the fridge to get out the butter when I see the container with Ana's brain in it is taking up the entire vegetable drawer. Suddenly I'm not as hungry. Alex must have put the jar there last night when he came to check on me before finding himself somewhere to sleep. I grab the butter and start hunting around for a plastic knife.

"How realistic? Who's trying to kill you?"

"It feels real," I say, picking the toast gingerly from the toaster and laying it on a paper plate.

I start spreading butter on one slice, distracted by the memory of the man waiting in front of Alex's apartment last night.

"Actually, I'm not sure who the killer is. But you know how sometimes people have different faces in your dream and you still know they're your dad or sister or something?"

Alex nods and I grab a small jar of Vegemite out of the cupboard and waggle it at him. He nods again. I scrape a tiny amount over his toast and pass him the plate as I continue.

"Last night, even though I couldn't see his face, I knew the guy who punched me near your apartment was the guy in my nightmares."

I'm so lost in the memory I burn my fingers on the metal trying to fish my toast out.

"So you always have the same dream?" Alex says around a mouthful of food.

"No, but it's variations on a theme. The bad guy has found me and is killing me. Sometimes I know it's a dream and I can force myself awake, but not very often."

"That'd suck. How often do you get them?"

"Usually once or twice a week, but since I moved back here it's every time I fall asleep. And it's the bad ones that don't stop."

Alex frowns a question at me.

"I'm awake, but I can still see the man from the dream. I can still feel him stabbing me or strangling me." I am starting to feel traumatised just talking about it to Alex.

I can hear how outrageous I sound. I expect Alex to laugh or something, but he just nods thoughtfully.

I skip the butter that's been in the fridge with human remains and scrape a smidge of Vegemite on my toast. I eat slowly so I don't have to talk. I've exposed myself enough to a guy who has little respect for me as it is. Also I'm feeling a little sensitive to being thought crazy, because it still feels like I was dragged off to an asylum ten minutes ago.

I'm not good at quiet though, so before I even finish my toast I break the silence again.

"This morning was different though. The man wasn't actively killing me this time, he was hauling me away to the old Lunatic Asylum that used to stand in the Botanic Gardens." I don't tell Alex I saw the asylum looking and sounding real enough on my very first night in town.

Alex's rough voice cuts into my thoughts.

"So do you know who he is?"

"No, his face used to change every time, usually the face of someone I'd seen recently. A psychologist said the killer represents my biological father, but I don't think he does."

"Me either," Alex says. "I think your ability is to see the past, but you're a bit defective because you haven't completed the ritual, so your past lives have been breaking through in your dreams."

Part of that makes sense. The dreams feel so real, I can believe they don't spring from my imagination. But I've still got some issues.

"I'm defective?" I ask him, raising an eyebrow.

He shrugs back at me.

"Also, I would've had to die a lot of times then, cos I've been killed in every way imaginable in my nightmares."

My confident tone falters when Alex's face shows no surprise.

"What, really?" I ask.

"Like Amber and I said, renascent women are quite vulnerable, so their powers help to balance that out a bit. Over the years rumours of those powers have got out and some people think they can steal them from you."

Oh. Amber and Alex's paranoia makes more sense now.

"So that's why you think Nathan killed Ana and kidnapped Amber, to steal their abilities?"

When Alex nods, I continue.

"The biggest problem with your theory about my dreaming my past deaths is I'm positive that man last night is the man in my nightmares. Every single time I'm killed, it's been him. So your theory would make him hundreds if not thousands of years old."

Alex's forehead wrinkles.

"We don't actually know he's the same man from your nightmares though," he says.

"You might not know it's him, but I do. I can't tell you how I know, I just know I'm right."

Alex's face is broadcasting doubt, so I excuse myself to go down to the bathroom and clean up for whatever the hell we are going to have to do today to find Amber.

Chapter 22

Morning - Bathroom at the end of the hall

Once I am clean and dressed in jeans and a t-shirt, I use the scratched mirror in the bathroom to slap a minimal layer of makeup on. I still have no idea what Alex's plan to save his sister is, so I need to be ready for all eventualities. Most of which I assume will require this extra-thick, line of dark black eyeliner. I roll my eyes at myself, zip up my makeup bag and head back to my room.

Today's non-threatening hallway has rays of golden sunlight shining innocently through every open door, making the tiny floating dust motes sparkle in the air. If I were an influencer, I'd be posting this view with the caption 'Blessed' or something about letting the light shine into your soul.

I wonder exactly where Alex spent the night. I had half-heartedly offered to let him stay in my room, but we could both see that sharing my tiny bed would be awkward, physically and mentally. There isn't enough room on the floor for Alex's tall frame and the chair is uncomfortable at any time.

Luckily, he keeps some basic camping equipment in his four-wheel drive in case he and Amber need to take off without warning.

I check the shadow-room or spider's lair halfway down the hall. There's no camping gear in sight. I'm relieved because that would be super creepy with all the cobwebby time trails in here. They are so thick I can tell where the missing furniture was by the absence of shivery lines.

There's a darker mass under the wooden desk which I assume is millions of chairs in millions of slightly different positions. As I concentrate on the dark blur it resolves into long brown hair trailing down the curve of a hunched back. I virtually teleport backwards out of the room.

Slamming the door shut makes me feel a tiny bit better. I hope I'm not a coward. Okay I am a coward, but this is getting a little too close to a Japanese horror movie.

I check the rest of the rooms as I scoot by and sure enough, a few doors up from my room, I spot a canvas swag rolled up behind the door. Makes sense. Close enough to hear if there's a problem, far enough away to avoid detection if Sam comes to say hello, or Ellie if she exists.

When I open the door to my room, Alex is sitting in my chair with his elbows on the bench, looking like someone taking an exam. He launches straight into his list of questions.

"When are the dreams set?"

"I can't always tell, but the two most recent dreams were definitely a while ago, like in the 1800s."

"Is there ever anyone else in your dreams?"

"Sometimes there's someone I'm trying to protect. This morning's had my husband and daughter in it. The bad guy of course, and two men who worked for the asylum."

Alex nods. "Tell me about them."

My dreams usually fade quickly, but this one rushes back in vivid detail. The thick heat weighing me down, the leaden weight on my chest caused by the betrayal of the man I had loved and trusted.

My voice becomes hoarse as I describe the beautiful face of my daughter as she is dragged away from me. I tell Alex about the cold and haughty appearance of my husband. I have no description of the man hiding in the shadows.

I start to think back in earnest. In all of my dreams he's in the shadows, or both of us are. Why would he keep his identity a secret when his prey is about to die?

"I think he knows renascent people can keep their memories over generations, or that I would have visions of my death. He hides his face so I won't recognise him when I'm reborn."

Alex's eyes widen, before his face gets that determined angry look he usually wears.

"I think you're right. And it appears he's found you again," Alex says as he stands up.

"And Amber too."

Alex looks sceptical.

"Come on, of course it's this guy who took Amber. His car's been out the front of your apartment for months."

"Maybe." Alex is non-committal. "But Nathaniel Cain isn't in the clear just yet. It's after lunch so we need to get some food into you and then I have something to show you."

"Oh? A way to find Amber?"

"Not exactly, but it does lead into my plan. At the very least it might jog your memory. At this point any new information is worth chasing down."

Alex strides from the room and I throw my keys and phone in my handbag and follow him out. I have to jog for a bit every ten steps or so to keep up with Alex's long stride.

"Where are we going?" I ask, around gasping for air.

Alex finally notices my discomfort and slows to half speed.

"We need to find a car," he finally replies. "I'm going to try a mate of mine who lives a few blocks over."

Is the guy a Neanderthal? Why does he just assume I wouldn't have one? I try to cut him some slack. His sister's young and Ana might have been a bit past driving. I pull my keys out of my handbag and jingle them in the air in front of us.

"I have a car," I say smugly.

Alex looks surprised and for one hot second I want to smack that misogynistic look right off his face.

"I thought you flew here from New South Wales."

His knowledge about me is patchier than I thought, considering he'd been tailing me for a while. I narrow my eyes at him, trying to decide if I'm still offended. He gets the hint because he hurries into an explanation.

"I assumed cos you started work the day after you got into town. Most people would allow a day or two off to recover after such a long drive, or for car trouble."

In that case I can't wait to see what he thinks when he sees the crappy car I drove the 1400 kilometres in. I reward him for his explanation with a small smile, relieved he's starting to notice when he's upset me. Working together to find Amber will be much easier if we aren't at each other's throats.

"Come on, it's this way." I turn and walk in the opposite direction, towards the lonely dirt block where I abandoned my car five days ago.

We haven't got far when I hear a phone chime. I have a new text.

It's from Nathan.

My heart skips a beat, and not in that pleasant romantic way. This was more my heart wobbling like a disturbed jelly for a few seconds before turning a toddler-standard somersault. You know, all arms and legs with a hard landing at the end.

When my heart is safely back on track, I glance up at Alex walking beside me. He shows no interest in the message, so I decide not to mention it until I know if it's a cause for concern.

I try to remember when I gave Nathan my number. Maybe before our date?

The message is kinda blunt.

Come 2 work early TMR. Surprise 4 U.

Okay? So it looks like Nathan doesn't regard the date as a disaster. I, on the other hand, thought it ended super awkwardly. What could he possibly be doing to surprise me? It must be something nice, if it was sinister he wouldn't warn me about it. And no matter what Alex and Amber think of him, and despite his slightly scary vibe, he's been textbook perfect around me.

Meeting at the hospital seems fairly public and safe, so I decide not to mention it to Alex for now. He would be dead against it of course, but I think this is a perfect opportunity for me to find out if Nathan knows anything.

Alex finally takes an interest in what I'm doing, so I turn my phone screen off and slide it into my pocket. Will it be weird if I don't say anything about it?

"Just Mum checking up on me."

I know it's believable, so I'm surprised when Alex raises an eyebrow at me. Oh, right.

"My adoptive mum, Margaret," I explain.

I know I guessed right when Alex relaxes back into disinterest. Everyone here thinks my adoptive parents need a qualifying clause with their titles. To me, who never knew my 'real' parents, it's them who need the qualifier bio.

I see my tiny, blue hatchback sitting alone and untouched as we enter the deserted car park. This area is obviously used by city workers and, as this might be the last sunny day before winter truly kicks in, everyone is literally anywhere else enjoying their weekend off.

I unlock my door and climb in, throwing my handbag over the seat into the back before unlocking the passenger door for Alex. His lip curls ever so slightly as he crams his tall frame into the space. I give him a look, daring him to complain. He avoids my eyes and fumbles for the lever before shoving his seat as far back as it will go. He's probably still a bit uncomfortable, but at least he doesn't look like a clown now.

"Where to?" I ask.

"Not far," Alex replies. "I'll tell you as we go."

Still not ready to trust me then.

"Hey, can I get something to eat?" I ask.

Alex flinches. Did I startle him?

"Uh, sorry I'm out," he replies after a moment's thought.

"Okay yeah... I mean I think there's a Maccas not far from here. I'm starving."

"Sure," Alex says to my great relief.
I put the car in gear and drive.

Chapter 23

Afternoon - Northern suburbs

We are high up in the metal stands of a shiny-bright, private school gym. Of everything I thought I might be doing today, watching a kid's ballet competition wasn't one of them. All the girls look so cute in their little leotards and tutus and there are a few boys looking proud of their suit pants and shirts. Pink is clearly the popular choice for the tiniest ballerinas, but the colours get a little more adventurous as the girls get older.

All of the kids are much more talented than I ever was. I only did ballet for a couple of years and I think everyone was secretly relieved when I quit in favour of swimming lessons.

Alex is sitting quietly next to me, even though he has signalled twice for us to leave. Part of me wants to leave now, because I have so many questions. I can't ask them here, it's too quiet, we'd be disturbing all the proud parents and grandparents. But I can't take my eyes off the little girl who is sitting in the front row with her friends.

I recognised her the second she walked onto the floor with her class. Even with her wheaten ringlets scraped back into a tight bun, she is unmistakable. It's my daughter Bridget. The emotions from my dream sweep back over me and I watch her routine through watery eyes and smouldering panic. She is a couple of years older here than in my dream, all of her puppy fat is gone and her cheekbones are more prominent. She has my eyes and nose.

The little girl's expressions and mannerisms are so familiar to me it's as if she's captioned. I see the moment she isn't happy with the timing of her leap or the angle of her kick. I see how proud she is of her turns. My panic rises when her dance finishes, but she doesn't leave the gym. Instead she follows her troupe over to the empty front row to sit smiling and fidgeting through the other dances.

I have to keep looking away from her to let my eyes refocus. The longer I stare at the girl, the more her edges begin to fray away and the longer her shivery trails become. Only the little girl is affected.

This is my biggest clue yet that my ability to see the past is restricted to people I have known. It explains why I don't get any visions around Alex now that Amber's missing. I've never met him before.

My need to know more about the restless little ballerina finally overcomes my reluctance to let the girl out of my sight. Between dances, Alex and I get up and leave the gym. I watch the heavy doors swing closed behind us so I can start talking at the earliest possible moment.

"Who is that? She was my daughter in my nightmare this morning."

"I thought so," Alex replies.

I can't tell if he thinks he's finished talking, or whether he's deciding what to say. He starts walking away from the gym towards the car, but I have no intention of leaving that little girl until I know what's going on. I move a few steps to the left of the doors and sit down on the concrete with my back leaning on the orange brick wall. I am still deciding between all of the questions racing through my mind when my mouth goes it alone.

"And?"

It gets the job done. Alex comes over and slides down the wall to sit beside me.

"Her name is Bridget. This time around she's the daughter of your mother's cousin."

I struggle with the relationship ties for a moment. Is she a second cousin then? I've never really paid much attention to those titles.

"I have family?" I ask incredulously.

"Well, Bridget yes," Alex answers.

I can hear the bad news in his voice, so I guess what's coming next, but his words still send a wave of disappointment crashing through me.

"Bridget's mother died during the birth. She had a reaction to the anaesthetic during the c-section."

"Shit. Does any Renascent make it into their thirties?"

I can't help the anger I feel at being dealt such a hard blow through my genetics. I wasn't a sickly child by any means, but I had slightly more than my fair share of health issues. And if I have to die young, I don't think visions of the past are much compensation.

"Not many," Alex admits. "Ana's the only one I know who got to old age and that's only because she was a healer."

I'm starting to see a path to depression forming right in front of my eyes.

"Tell me about Bridget," I ask.

"She was adopted by the anaesthetist who was at her birth, possibly because his wife is renascent. You know her actually."

"Who?" I ask a little too loudly.

"Sahra, Nathan's friend." Alex talks in a deliberately lowered voice like I'm a child. "She's safe."

"How does that work if you think Nathan is killing renascent women any chance he gets?"

"We think Nathaniel is killing the reborn for their powers and Sahra and Bridget don't have any. Ana said Bridget's mother had virtually no abilities left. Your family line has been broken too many times. She had no memories of her previous lives at all. The loss of the matriarch of your family back in the 1800s, not long after she arrived in Australia, was devastating for you all."

Alex is looking at me as if waiting for something. I think for a bit but only one possibility comes to mind.

"You mean me," I say slowly. "That's why you've been searching for me. In the hope I can fix us. Why though? What good is it for you?"

"Any knowledge about who we are and how we can control our powers will help us. Stop us from being picked off slowly by killers looking for some small chance at gaining the power of fortune telling, or healing, or persuasion."

Alex's voice rises towards the end of his speech. He is upset. A hot wave of shame washes over me. He's lost his sister and yet he's here teaching me about my heritage.

"Why did you show me Bridget? What does it have to do with finding Amber?"

He nods at me and looks straight into my eyes as he finally unveils his plan to save his sister.

"I'm trying to prove that everything Amber and I told you is true, because I need your help. If we can wake up your powers enough so you can control them, we can go back to the funeral home and you'll be able to see who took Amber, and even follow them to the place she's being held now."

Alex's plan seems so simple and right while his grey-blue eyes look straight into my soul.

Something's wrong.

I look away from him and think about what he said.

"And how do you intend to wake up my powers?" I ask him.

"Find the closest female relative you have who has died and get you to perform the ritual."

Ah yes, the cutting out part of their brain ritual.

"And what happens when I have a part of my mother's, grandmother's or great auntie's brain."

"You have to eat it."

My mouth pops open.

"What did you just say?" I mustn't have heard him right.

"That's how the powers are passed along. The memories too," he answers in a completely reasonable voice, as if he hasn't just gone bat-shit.

Okay, I can see this conversation is going to get complicated and this isn't the right place to discuss this. Someone is going to call the cops on us.

Also, there's nothing I can do to help Bridget right now. I can't just walk up and kidnap her, as much as my arms ache to hold the little girl I've never met. The best thing I can do for her right now is to sort my own life out, so I will be able to protect her if she needs me.

I stand up slowly. My everything is aching, sitting on the concrete wasn't such a great idea. Alex bounces up off the ground and leads the way back to the car. I creak and crack behind him jealously. We're halfway to my little car before I have warmed up enough to catch up.

And of course I'm starving again. The take-away burgers we got on our way here didn't even coat the sides.

"Food?" I suggest hopefully.

His brow furrows. He's thinking way harder about this than I expected, but when he speaks it's not even on topic.

"How's your vision? Can you see the past at all?"

I have to think for a moment. I haven't had a fully fledged realistic vision since last night, outside Alex's apartment before I got hurt. Except for that creepy hair in the nurses' quarters, today's just been shivery lines.

"Not really," I say. "Hints of it, but no proper episodes."

Alex was expecting my answer. He looks like he wants to tell me something, so I wait while his mouth opens once or twice reminding me a little of a fish. Normally I would've laughed.

"We need to get you some more of that home remedy," Alex finally says, as he stands by the driver's door of my car with his hand out for the keys.

I shake my head as I step around him, unlock the door and collapse into the front seat. I reach across and unlock the passenger door and Alex folds himself in still talking.

"...important ingredient should be okay, but it won't be the same."

I pull out of the car park and head in the general direction of the city. I assume we are heading back home because Alex hasn't said anything about a new destination. It worries me he's this determined to make more of his home remedy. Sure, I love its curative effects, but I don't like being thrown into the past without warning.

"Uh Alex, maybe I shouldn't be trying to get the visions back while I can't control them. What if I'm distracted by a vision when there is danger in the now."

Shit, I could have a vision while I'm driving. I should have given the keys to Alex like he wanted.

"I know, but we have to use what we've got to find a relative of yours for the ritual," Alex says firmly.

I have a brilliant idea.

"What about Bridget's mother, my cousin, Auntie? She should be easy to find, she died in hospital, we could look up her grave online."

"Cremated." Alex crushes my hopes in record time. "We've checked. There are no known burials for anyone related to you. We'll have to use your visions to find one."

"What if I can't see anything useful until I get more control?" I ask doubtfully.

"I think that's unlikely. Your past has been trying to find a way out your whole life. You had your dreams before you had any of our home remedy, or whatever Sahra and Nathan fed you on Friday night."

I think all of that through until I see a large shopping centre on the right. Without asking, I change lanes and pull the car into the nearest car park. Alex looks confused. I point to the clock. If we want to get supplies and food before everything shuts it'll have to be here.

Chapter 24

Late afternoon - Botanic Park

Alex and I are sitting in my hatchback in the long row of cars parked behind the Botanic Gardens. We're here because Alex agrees with me for once. All of my most recent dreams have centred around Lilijana. And I had a vision of the asylum before I was exposed to whatever Nathan and Sahra fed me. This place is my best chance of getting some useful information through a vision.

Alex could be a bit nicer about it though.

"The records say you were crazy and then you disappeared one night. The official theory is that you escaped, but Ana disagrees. You would've come to her for help if you were able to, and you never contacted her or your daughter."

"So what did Ana think happened?"

"That someone killed you. Personally, I think anything could've happened. You were mad." He shrugs.

Great. Just when I get used to having him around, I'm gonna have to kill him.

"Excuse me?" My voice is at least an octave higher than I usually talk. "It was extremely easy for a woman to get called crazy back then. All she had to do was have a different opinion to her husband, or even refuse to have sex with him and she could be locked up."

I know I'm overreacting, but I feel like I have to defend Lilijana's memory. She was perfectly sane when she was carted away from her home, and I felt her fear when the killer came into her cell in my nightmare. She wasn't insane at all, not until her very last moments alive.

Alex wisely stays silent so I decide to drop it. Educating cavemen isn't my job.

I'm hungry as usual, but this time I'm prepared. I bought a whole bunch of snacks while Alex was off sourcing ingredients for his home remedy. Packets of lollies, biscuits and chips are sitting on the back seat beckoning me. I give in and reach back for a packet of Fruchocs. I make a mess of opening the packet and offer it to Alex, secretly pleased when he shakes his head.

Instead, Alex shakes the large silver flask he's mixed the home remedy in vigorously for a minute and then hands it to me. I open my mouth to protest but he cuts me off.

"Just drink half of it. I don't know how quickly it'll wear off cos it's missing some stuff."

I'd feel better if I'd seen him make it, but it was all done by the time we met back up at the car.

Against my better judgment I lift the bottle to my lips and take a mouthful. This liquid is definitely different than the one I had before. It doesn't taste unpleasant, the sweet-savoury flavour is more prominent now. It's missing a few herbs and spices this time.

It's the texture that bothers me. It's cold and lumpy, reminding me of my mum's badly-made custard. I try to ignore the sensation of congealed fat sliding over my tongue and down my throat. When I force myself to swallow, a piece of slimy skin like you get on the top of warm milk is left, stuck to my soft palate.

Every muscle in my body convulses. I hand the flask back to Alex quickly and open my door and lean out over the bitumen. Alex is saying something, but I need to concentrate on swallowing for a few minutes.

When I have myself under control, I close the door and look at Alex. To my relief, he has put the lid back on the flask and put it at his feet.

"Yeah, that's lumpy," I complain.

"Sorry." He shrugs. "I told you I didn't know the recipe."

"What the hell's in that?"

"Nothing that can hurt you." Alex's voice is firm, but rough. For the eightieth time I have to resist offering him a cough drop.

"Fine," I say. "The Botanic Gardens closes in twenty minutes. Let's go see if it's worked."

I get out of the car and lock it when I notice Alex's expression has gone dark.

"All good?" I ask him.

He nods. "Just hoping this works."

Me too. If it doesn't, we don't really have a backup plan. At least I don't. Alex will probably go beat Nathan to death.

I get a pang of guilt that I still haven't told Alex I'm meeting Nathan tomorrow, but it might be our best chance to get some information without resorting to violence. There wouldn't be any winners of that fight, they're both big men.

We walk along the leaf-littered footpath under the shade of rows of enormous plane trees. They must be a hundred feet tall at least. The Botanic Gardens on our left is surrounded by a tall, galvanised-iron fence with spikes. We aren't getting over that even if we wanted to. I don't mean now of course, we're walking in the gates this time round. I mean later tonight when we come back.

On our right are lush green lawns and huge trees of every description. The map on my phone says that's Botanic Park where people gather to have weddings and family barbecues under hundred-year-old Morten Bay figs and mast-straight pine trees. Even this late on a brisk autumn day I can see a few gatherings rushing to pack up tables and chairs before the temperature drops with the sun.

The light wind moans through a nearby pine tree, somehow peaceful and ominous at the same time. We come to the decorative, cast-iron garden gates. The shivery lines I'm used to seeing in this area approach the entrance from both directions, showing me where I need to go.

I decide to see if my vision will work the same way now as it did on my first visit to the gardens. I touch a fingertip to the cold metal gate.

The avenue of rubber trees lining the road inside the gardens brightens. The sun is much higher now and the shade isn't as deep because the trees are much shorter.

A dark, horse-drawn carriage is stationary on the narrow dirt road in front of me. A man in a vintage, three-piece suit, with dark sweat stains under his arms, walks towards the vehicle. He climbs up into the driver's seat, shakes the reins once and the carriage rolls slowly forward. Dust disturbed by the wooden wheels rises lazily in the hot summer's air.

I'm not dreaming. This is very different to my dreams. This time I'm an onlooker rather than a participant. I recognise the carriage. It's the one that transported Lilijana away from her family in my dream. I can't see her inside the windowless box, but I feel like I'm watching her arrive at the asylum.

I drop my hand away from the gate and the vision disappears. I blink for a moment, trying to readjust to the real world when Alex's hard body slams right into me.

"Ugh, sorry," he says.

"Sorry, my fault." I walk further into the gardens looking around nervously, but the visions don't return.

"Why'd you stop?" Alex asks.

I explain what happened when I touched the iron gate. He looks at it sceptically.

"It's only when you touch the gate? Why?"

I shrug. I recently read a book where iron was fatal to fairies, maybe iron has special properties? I don't mention that theory to Alex. He already thinks I'm an idiot.

I turn and walk along the avenue of rubber trees with their wide trunks and anaconda-like roots running out from the base and into the ground. They were much smaller, younger, in my vision.

I have an idea. We are a bit exposed here in the entrance, so I gesture at Alex to follow and I walk until I find a narrow dirt path leading deep into a grove of trees and shrubs. About twenty paces in I decide we have enough cover for my test.

"Wait here," I tell Alex and step off the path towards the largest tree within reach. I touch its rough trunk tentatively. Nothing happens. I study the tree again. The trunk's only about a foot wide, maybe it's not old enough?

I walk around the tree and move further from the path. One of the tree trunks here is at least two foot wide. This should do. There are too many branches to get near the trunk, so I wrap my hand around the thickest low branch.

It works.

The scenery changes. I can feel the heat of summer again, but it's not as oppressive this time because it's dusk here. Thousands of crickets are welcoming the cooler air night will bring.

Keeping a tight grip on the now thinner and more supple branch, I look around. There are fewer trees here now and even less are mature. I can see further into the gardens and the small brick building near the entrance is visible too. Using that to orient myself, I look to where the asylum should stand. I can see a roof line in the distance, but rows of thick young pine trees block my view of the building. I need to get closer.

I let go of the branch and the vision disappears.

I'm making my way back to Alex when a couple with two young children in tow walk into view. The woman tuts her disapproval at me. I wonder if she thinks Alex and I have been up to something we shouldn't be. The man looks me up and down, before sneering and ushering his children away.

When I reach Alex he's still watching the family walking briskly away from us.

"It worked," I tell him bluntly, before changing my mind and giving him more details. "My vision is stronger if I'm touching something that was there then, in the time I want to see."

The worried look vanishes from his face and I immediately feel guilty for acting like a shit around him.

"Excellent. Let's go move the car to a place without cameras and wait until it's safe to come back," Alex says.

"About that, how are we going to get in?"

"Don't worry about that, we did it all the time when I was at uni."

Somehow that doesn't surprise me at all, except the part where he went to uni.

Chapter 25

Early evening - North Adelaide

We park my car a few roads away where there's no cameras or parking fees and grab some fish and chips from a takeaway. Back at my room there isn't much we can do to prepare for tonight's break-in. I change into a darker t-shirt. Alex's clothes are already dark blues and greys. I wonder if he does that to match his eyes?

Right now he's lying on my bed reading the transcript of my father's trial. I don't know if there's anything useful in there, but as Alex seems to know more about my birth parents than I do, maybe he will pick up on something I'd miss.

I'm sitting at the bench with my phone plugged into its charger while I research the asylum. My phone chimes an alert and startles me so bad I drop it onto my lap. Alex doesn't even glance my way. Really, his complete lack of interest in anything I'm doing is starting to get insulting.

I pick my phone up, curious to see who's texting me at this hour. Guilt washes over me as I realise I haven't contacted my adoptive family since the day after I got into town, and I just thought of them as somehow less than my real family. I haven't been here a week and now the family who raised me have a qualifier in front of their title. Also, if they are contacting me this late, they're either angry with me or there's an emergency.

I turn my phone on. It's Nathan.

My eyes flick guiltily to Alex but he's still ignoring me. I touch the message symbol.

Important! Come early. Don't forget

Do I tell Alex? Nothing's changed. Alex won't want me to go, but I'm not scared of Nathan.

I go back to studying the plan of the Adelaide Lunatic Asylum I found online. There are a few more buildings on the drawing than I saw in my vision, so either I wasn't paying enough attention or my vision is of an earlier time period than the plans.

I yawn and tears gather on my lower eyelids, so it must be late enough now. I close the map on my phone. It's 11:43 p.m.

"Time to go," I say standing.

Alex looks up from the transcript. He's got much further into it than I have.

"Nothing useful yet," he tells me.

I wasn't holding much hope out for it anyway. We gather the few items we need and head out of the building.

"Is there anything I should know about Lilijana before we do this?" I ask Alex.

He doesn't speak and I can't really blame him. I got a bit irate last time he said she was crazy.

"I know you weren't keen on Amber telling me this stuff. Is it a secret, or are you afraid you'll upset me?"

"I just knew how it would sound. I wanted to break it to you slowly so you had time to see we were telling the truth." Alex gives me a sad look. "When Amber told me you hadn't recognised her or Ana we knew you didn't have your memories, just like Amber. We figured it was because you had so many false starts over the years."

"False starts?" I interrupt.

"There's been a few miscarriages and deaths between Lilijana and you. And you haven't completed the ritual. Ana wasn't sure you would be reborn at all, after the last time. But then you turned up at the hospital, a nurse just like your mother. We hoped you'd kept your memories from this life at least, that the memory of your mother made you seek us out."

"I don't remember my mother at all, how could I? I was just weeks old." I shake my head in confusion.

"Renascent don't just remember their past lives. They remember everything from the day they're born. Their brains are different. You don't need to relearn everything from scratch every time you're born, so the learning areas of the brain can be pared back and replaced with larger memory centres. Lilijana could remember her life in the 16th century as easily as the day she was born."

"That's impossible," I gasp.

He's talking about brain plasticity, the flexibility built into the brain to build new pathways and culling of un-needed neurons. It's crucial for learning new things. He can't be right, I did fine at school. Then, I remember Maths. I hated it. It always took me longer than the other kids to understand what to do, but once I know something, it's there for life. I've never revised for exams and my marks are great.

"Now I've talked to you, I think the damage to your memories might not be permanent," Alex says. "Your dreams make me think your memories are still in there. The ritual is usually to bring out your special abilities, but it might bring your memories back too."

"Would it matter if they didn't come back?" I'm a bit ambivalent about getting my memories of past lives back. I am curious of course, but it's hard to miss something you've never had.

"We've lost so much of our culture already. Think how vulnerable we'll be when we know nothing about who we are and who our enemies are."

I can see his point, and the Botanic Garden's fairy-tale, front gates.

"So tell me what happened here then." I gesture towards the dark gardens.

"You were locked up for a few days and then you disappeared. We know that much for sure. Ana went to visit you at home one day and your husband said he'd had you carted off the day before."

I nod, thinking back to my nightmare a few mornings ago. I'm pretty sure I know what happened.

"We don't know why your husband turned against you so quickly. You went from happily married to being locked away in days." Alex continues, "Ana tried to get you out, but your farm in the hills was a long way from the city back in the horse and cart days. By the time she got to the asylum you were already missing."

Alex's words are hitting me hard. This doesn't feel like a story about someone I've never met, it's more like hearing something happened to me while I was asleep and vulnerable.

"Did you know Bridget was there when I was taken away?" I ask Alex.

I try to keep my voice casual, but I feel very invested in his answer.

He nods. "Ana spoke to her afterwards. Bridget said her dad stayed in from the fields that day and everyone was on edge because he was acting strangely. You were upset, but Bridget didn't know why. You were making lunch when her dad called you outside, she followed. You were dragged into a carriage by two strangers."

I'd been wondering how accurate my dreams are, now I know they're bang on.

"What about now, does she have her memories?" I ask him quietly.

"We've never been able to speak with her, not even Ana could get anywhere near her."

"Does Sahra know who Bridget is to me?" I ask.

Alex shrugs.

"Don't know, she might. Ana didn't know Sahra from any past lives here or overseas. We know nothing about her except that she's renascent of course. Ana could tell that much."

"How?"

"She could read a person's health, see what they needed and sometimes heal them. It was her gift. It'll be Amber's too if she ever completes the ritual."

"When she does," I say.

"We're here," Alex says, stopping with his back to the low stone wall surrounding the Gardens.

He studies the traffic. We're at a bend in the road, so we can only be seen by cars on the fifty-metre stretch of road right in front of us. It doesn't take long before there's a break in the traffic and Alex puts one hand on the stone fence and vaults over it and out of my sight.

Chapter 26

Evening - Botanic Gardens fence

The glow of headlights approaches from my left, so I have no choice but to follow Alex's lead and put one hand on the waist-high stone wall and scramble over. The ground here isn't as low as I thought and I land awkwardly, jarring my ankle.

"No flashbacks?" Alex asks as he stands up out of his crouch.

"Nope," I reply.

We pick our way across the mulched garden beds, keeping to the shadows and heading straight down into the centre of the gardens. We keep trees between us and any buildings we spot, in case of security cameras. Now that I'm trying to avoid them, the gardens have a lot more fountains, gazebos and greenhouses than I remember.

I get a fright when I come upon two tall, stone pillars I've never seen before. Luckily they aren't a warning of a building close by, or even some spooky vision of the past. They just frame a set of stairs leading down into the dark waters of a stream. We skirt the edges until we come to a large pond with a statue standing in its centre. Even in the dark it's beautiful. I stand still and focus my energy on trying to conjure up the past for a moment. Nothing happens.

I'm surprised. Edged with rushes whispering in the wind, that beautiful pond is screaming out for a ghostly woman in a long, white nightgown to walk slowly down its grassy banks and disappear into the water.

Disappointed, I catch up with Alex who hasn't even noticed I'd fallen behind. On the far side of the pond we cross a small, arched bridge and I finally see the parallel rows of old Norfolk Pines that once lined the lunatic asylum's driveway. No wait, they still do. At the end of the line of trees a gauzy, insubstantial building floats like smoke in the air.

I'm on a different angle this time, but I easily recognise the distinctive silhouette of the old asylum with its long roofline broken by four, pointed, Gothic-style gables. From here I can see the main building has a long wing attached to the back corner which continues back nearly fifty metres to a tall stone fence. When I look straight at it, the apparition fades away completely, but if I look down at the trees, the building becomes clearer in my peripheral vision.

Alex stops beside me.

"See anything?" he asks quietly.

I'm nodding and about to say yes when I remember the first time I saw this apparition and the woman's startled face when I touched her. Did she somehow see the asylum through me?

If I can get Alex to see what I can, I won't have to go through this alone. To be honest the thought of being all by myself in that asylum is scaring me stupid.

Alex is already looking in the right direction, so without warning him, I reach out and touch his cold right hand. He flinches away from me, letting out a guttural grunt and rubs his eyes and forehead roughly.

"What was that?" he demands.

"Sorry," I say. "I thought you might be able to see the asylum too if we were in contact."

Alex shakes his head, not as if he's answering my question, more like a dog shakes water off its coat.

"I did see something for a second there, but it felt like you hit me over the head with an axe."

Alone it is then.

The pine trees whisper their warnings as I trudge towards the place my great-great-grandmother was murdered. The closer I get, the clearer the building becomes in the corners of my eyes, but I still can't see it straight on. I feel spongy grass under my shoes, but when I'm looking straight ahead the grass is gone, replaced by a gravel driveway. With every step the pine trees beside me shrink in size, aging backwards until they are merely decades old.

Beautiful statues stand in the gardens in front of the building. It soothes my anxiety a little. Surely people who have gone to so much trouble to build such a solid structure, and decorate it so nicely, would be as concerned with the people committed to their care. Also, the sound of Alex's quiet footsteps brushing through the grass on my left, reminds me this place isn't real. It can't hurt me.

I see a couple of those shivery lines leading into the asylum's arched doorway. I hope the lines are remnants of Lilijana's movements here. If so, they will lead me straight to her.

Wondering if I can make my vision even stronger, I stretch my arm out to the right, reaching for the last pine tree in the row. As soon as my fingertips brush against cold needles I can hear the past. Misery like I've never heard before floods out of the structure in front of me.

My muscles creep and crawl under my skin. I need to help these people, anything to stop that noise pulling at my tendons and ligaments, urging me to run, to fight, to do anything except let that horrific sound continue on into the dark night.

I wrench my hand away from the tree and clench my arms around myself, securing my fear and my courage inside me so they can't escape.

The screams and cries settle down into a background murmur.

Cicadas and crickets alert me to the fact it's summer in the past. If I concentrate I can almost feel it's warmth on my skin.

I survey the asylum's delicate timber verandas and latticed windows, looking for a way in. I need to come up with a plan. I can't just walk in the front door, can I? Looking straight at the door makes it disappear, but it does bring the massive light above the door into the sharpest focus I can get outside my central vision. It looks like one of those old coach lamps you see on carriages. I see an actual flame burning inside.

Now I know why the building is so dark, it wouldn't be safe to leave flames burning in the rooms of mental health patients. Only the few rooms clustered around the front doors are lit with a flickering orange glow. Those must be staff rooms.

I switch to staring at the lamp so I can study the heavy wooden doors up close. Bad move, I should have looked down. My foot passes straight through the concrete step to the soft grass underneath. I whirl my arms for balance and look down at my feet, now ankle deep in the stone step.

I pause, contemplating a new plan. However, Alex is impatient and scares me with a whisper that tickles my neck.

"Do you think you should try the drink again?"

I shudder at the memory of the oystery chunks.

"No thanks. I want to try something first."

I put my hand out to test the solidity of the door. My hand wafts through like it's not there. Considering this place is designed to keep people in, this is perfect. I was wondering how I would get in and out undetected. If I can just walk through walls, this'll be easy. Assuming nobody can see me.

I look directly at the door so it disappears, hold my breath and step forward.

Chapter 27

1800's - Adelaide Lunatic Asylum

The foyer of the lunatic asylum isn't as grand as I expected from the outside. Also some idiot part of me thought it'd be black and white like you see in old photos.

My central vision is still showing me the real world, so I concentrate on the view around it. I'm standing in a small room with doors on both sides of me and a long hallway running across its far end. High ceilings and polished wooden floors remind me more of an old office building than anything medical. There's even a few pictures hung high up on the walls.

I follow the shivery lines into the left branch of the dimly lit hallway. There's lots of closed doors, but the lines continue on, so I do too. Towards the end I see a right-hand turn into what must be the long, multi-storey wing I saw from outside.

I flatten myself against the wall carefully, so I don't fall backwards through it, and sidestep up to the corner for a peek. The rustle of starched linen alerts me to approaching danger and I look around for an escape route. Stepping through any of the closed doors nearby isn't a great option. Who knows how many people are in those rooms?

I hold my breath as a woman steps into view. She doesn't react to my presence at all. She's about my height, but that's where the similarity ends. Wait, I forgot I'm halfway up my shins in the wooden floor. This woman is short. She's wearing a floor-length, dark-coloured dress covered by a long, white apron. A folded-cloth hat is pinned over her escaping hair.

When I start breathing again, I feel pity for her as she walks briskly past me. She must be boiling in that outfit if it's summer here.

The woman opens a door into a tiled room that must be a bathroom. At least I hope it is, or something is dead in there. Many somethings.

Some of the shivery lines I'm following lead into that room, but they also continue down into the building on my right. None of the trails here look particularly solid, so I think none of them are recent. Like recent then, where I am now. In the past. I give up trying to keep it all straight and decide to ignore the bathroom as a lead for now. I'll come back if I have to.

I follow the wing down into an area that looks a little more like the asylum I imagined. There are heavy wooden doors along its length that have small inspection holes in them at about head height. The faint trail of my great, great grandmother leads into and back out of one of these rooms, but one more distinct trail leads further down the hall as well.

I'll eliminate this room first before following the trail further. I rule out sticking my head through the door, because it would be a high traffic area and I don't want to touch anyone here if I can help it. I move to a piece of blank wall and look straight at it so it disappears. It takes me longer than it should to convince myself the wall doesn't exist, don't judge me, but finally I hold my breath and lean forward.

When I open my eyes I see a long room with lines of beds down each side. It's obviously late at night here, because nearly everyone is tucked up asleep.

With the dim light coming through the small windows set high into the outside wall, I can make out the shivery trail I'm following leads to an empty bed and back out of the room. She's not here. I close my eyes and straighten back up into the hallway.

The light from the gas lamps is weak this far down the hall and the wooden floor is higher up my legs here. I can't feel the wood, but habit makes me spread my feet and elbows for balance, like I'm wading through the ocean. I continue down the centre of the building until the shivery trail leads me to another door. This one goes outside to a high-walled yard.

Lilijana has been in this yard, going in and out of the building on the left and a door in the back wall. It also looks as though she has spent some time wandering in what almost looks like a clover pattern around the yard. Maybe getting some exercise or socialising? I hope they do something as normal as that here.

I check the building on my left first. It's more real than anything else I've seen here, less see through. And the closer I get to it, the warmer I feel. Even the sound of crickets and cicadas is louder here.

The windows are dark, so I risk poking my head through the wall. It's a dining room judging by the long table. There's a cloying, rotting smell in the air that I hope is the residue of the unwashed bodies of the women here and not the last meal they were forced to eat.

Outside again, I follow the trail through the door in the back wall to an industrial-sized laundry. The shivery, translucent lines are thickest around one of the large tubs. I can almost see a complete outline of a woman in the gauzy shape.

I walk over to the epicentre of the lines. Even looking directly at the copper tub in the centre doesn't make it disappear. Looks like my theory is right. The more connected I am to an event or object, the more clearly it will show up in my visions. I try touching the tub but it's less substantial than mist and my hand slips straight through.

A thin streak of lines leads off this thick cluster and I follow them out through a door on the far side of the room and into another large, walled area. Most of the shivery streaks lead to long washing lines which stand empty in the darkness. But a few silvery lines, so fresh they hum in the night air, lead to two small, wooden sheds huddled in the corner between the laundry and the deep ditch that extends along the inside of the exterior wall.

I check out the smaller shed first. It's a toilet and it's empty except for the smell.

That leaves the larger shed standing nearby. I can tell this rustic, wooden, afterthought of a building is important. Firstly, because it looks completely solid and real. And secondly, that's no ordinary door I can just make out in the darkness. It has a large lock and a peephole like the dormitories inside the main asylum.

It's some kind of outdoor cell. But why would a patient be held out here, away from the other patients?

None of the shivery lines lead to this door, so there must be another entrance on the far side. As I walk around the building I'm startled to hear my footsteps. It sounds like I'm walking on concrete with a thin layer of gravel on top, when seconds ago I was still on thick, spongy grass. My feet aren't sinking into the ground either.

I hear a soft grunt and the rustle of fabric from inside the small cell beside me and then a scraping noise as a door is opened. Instinct makes me dart back around the corner for cover. When I flatten myself back against the undressed wood I realise I can feel its rough surface through my light jacket.

If I can touch things here, can I be seen?

I quiet my breathing as slow footsteps cross the concrete barely two metres from my hiding place and I send an urgent plea to any god that might exist to let those steps belong to Lilijana. Unfortunately gods are not what's listening.

A dark figure holding a kerosene lantern steps into view with evil vibrating off him in waves I can see and feel. It's him, the man from my nightmares.

I hold my breath, but I feel like he must hear the pounding of my terrified heart. If he turns his head now he'll see me hiding here in the moon's shadow. As usual I can't make out his face, but I recognise his shape, the way he moves and even the way he seems to absorb the light from the lantern in his hand, as if nothing good can escape his corruption.

It feels like a lifetime passes before the man disappears into the laundry. I stay frozen until the door has been safely closed for a few minutes.

The terrible thought that I might've been following the killer's trail and not Lilijana's creeps out from under my long hair and into my right ear. I stick my finger in my ear and jiggle it roughly. Pain is far better than allowing that feeling to crawl deeper into my head. And no, I didn't see any of that man's skin sloughing off as he moved, and he left no lines in his wake.

Lilijana's here somewhere.

I creep around the small building to the far door. It's open. Is that good or bad?

I put out my hand and find the wood is warm and solid under my fingertips. I push the door further across, out of my way.

The small chamber is dark, but my eyes have adjusted well. I see what looks like a bundle of rags on a wooden platform in front of me.

"Lilijana?" My voice sounds hoarse, halfway between a whisper and nothing at all.

The misshapen bundle doesn't so much as twitch.

The scene before me disappears as a cold hand closes on my shoulder. I squeak and twist under the hand's cold grip until I see Alex beside me. He hasn't let go. I don't know if he means to give me reassurance or a warning, but he's interfering with my ability to see the past.

The grimace on his face tells me he's getting that axe-blow headache again. I shrug his hand off and whisper to him.

"Not now."

The heat and sour smell of the cell washes back over me and I step forward until my shins touch the edge of the wooden bed frame. I study the grey cloth bundle carefully. I can't hear any breathing and there's no rhythmic rise and fall of the fabric either.

There's no way to tell which end her head is at, so I grab the blanket corner closest to my knees and carefully lift it up and away.

It's her.

Me.

And I can tell by looking into her sightless eyes I'm dead. I stare at her sad face for a long moment until my vision blurs with tears.

I can feel all the doubt I had about being reborn falling away, but I'm not lighter. Instead, the certainty I am renascent, and all the danger that represents, drifts down onto me like heavy flakes of ash that get deeper and denser until I might suffocate.

Now I know why this specific moment appeared so clearly to me, but I spent so much time dicking about finding my way here that I'm already dead.

I know there's nothing I could have done to change the past, but maybe she wouldn't have had to die alone, again.

Chapter 28

1800's - Asylum laundry yard

I brush the hair out of Lilijana's staring eyes and hold her lids closed for a few seconds. Her eyes don't stay fully shut, but she looks more peaceful now. And even though my tears still fall, I feel a tiny bit better.

Too late I remember the world should've imploded into itself, all those time travel no-nos, but nothing happens. Looks like Sci-Fi stories aren't that accurate. Or as Alex said, this isn't time travel. I cover Lilijana's face gently with the scratchy blanket.

A heavy wooden door rasps across concrete a short distance away, and footsteps hurry towards the outdoor cells. I'm desperately hoping it's just Alex doing something random, until I hear a second set of footsteps. I check the walls, maybe I can just slip out the back and hide. The walls are completely solid. I'm trapped.

I know Alex thinks this is all in my head, but I'm not so sure. My mother noticed my presence in a supposed vision

Friday night. And last night, outside Alex and Amber's apartment, the killer saw me as well. I have to assume the people coming will know I'm here. And if the killer's with them and I can touch things, he can touch me too.

Not to mention getting caught in an asylum, where I look exactly like one of the inmates, will have its own unique issues.

Unless...

"Alex?" I plead in a harsh whisper.

"What?" His slightly louder reply comes from in front of me and to the right.

He's close. I grope blindly towards him until I feel the cool material of his sleeve. I wrap both hands around his bicep and he grunts in pain. Pain from his head obviously, I'm not that strong. I clamp on anyway.

I look around and the walls have become transparent. They're not gone like I'd hoped, because my connection here is still too strong. I can only hope it's weakened enough for me to escape this cell. The footsteps are so close now.

Asking Lilijana's forgiveness silently in my head, I wade through the bed in the area her legs must be and pass through the wall behind her. Luckily, the pain in Alex's head distracts him from asking any questions. He just backs up.

When I am safe in the adjoining cell my shaky legs give way. I let go of Alex, collapsing onto the rough bed behind me. To my horror my fall isn't silent, but the group outside are louder now and don't notice.

The rustling of a large volume of material and the clack of leather-soled shoes pass my hiding place. I hold my breath.

No one mentions the cell door I left wide open. Maybe they assume the wind blew it, it wasn't actually closed after all. Or maybe Lilijana's killer isn't with them.

The high notes of a woman's voice rises above the others.

"I'm so sorry about this doctor. You know I don't like keeping the women out here, but she gave me no choice."

I can hear the woman's scorn and disbelief. I don't know her, but I'm sure my instant hatred of her is justified.

"Do not fret about it Matron. Some people cannot be helped. Be glad I found her tonight. She would smell rather unpleasant by morning in this weather."

I recognise his voice immediately and the hairs on the back of my neck and arms prickle. It's the same voice that whispers so cruelly to me in my nightmares.

"There was no evidence of men interfering with them after hours anyway. I ask you, what man would have anything to do with a madwoman?" The matron says, digging her way under my skin like a tick.

If she keeps on like this, I'm going to have to find her grave, dig up her bones, and then salt and burn them.

"No, No. Don't concern yourself," my killer responds. "That one was never going to learn. I know her type. These degenerates are never very strong in the first place, her death will be from natural causes. If she had been inside when she died you would never have gotten the smell out of the woodwork."

I'm so angry I'm shaking. It's not enough he kills her, he has to destroy her memory too?

Their voices sound further away now, although I know they haven't moved. It feels more like my connection to this time is failing.

"If you're sure doctor." The matron seems satisfied she's not in any trouble now. "When will you do the autopsy? I will need to inform the Botanic Gardens' manager. You know how angry he gets when the creek smells."

"I'll do it straight away. It's too hot to leave the corpse laying around and this way the creek will flow clear by the time he gets up in the morning." The man stops speaking for a minute and I hear some rustling before he speaks again.

"Leave the paperwork on this one to me. I will make sure you don't get any trouble about the level of care here."

Okay, that might explain the lack of a death certificate and the story about an escape. But he is the doctor, who would question him? Was he over his death quota for the month and worried about attracting attention. Doctors were respected back then, they still are really. I'd bet he could kill a third of his patients before anyone would even raise an eyebrow. And serial killers weren't really on anyone's radar yet, so who was he hiding the death from?

I hear a distant door open and close again. More footsteps make their way over to the cells.

"Take this one to the morgue immediately." The killer orders the newcomers who, from what I can hear, set to work immediately.

The wooden platform beneath me is becoming spongy and insubstantial. I stand up as quietly as possible while the noise in the next cell gets louder and then quieter, as everyone moves away to their separate dark purposes.

When the door to the laundry closes, the cell I'm hiding in vanishes completely. I look around and the whole asylum is gone. My connection with that time is over.

If I leave and come back, would the vision repeat? If I could be inside the main asylum building at the right time and see the killer in the light, I could identify him and he wouldn't be able to hide in plain sight anymore. If he didn't kill me then.

Alex is standing a few feet away, quietly watching me, but also keeping an eye on our surroundings so we don't get caught. This vision was so overwhelming I'd completely forgotten we shouldn't be here. I don't know how I'm supposed to cope with my normal life if I can just get sucked into the past whenever. I could drive straight up the back of a truck and not even know why I died.

"Could you see me the whole time?" I ask.

"It's okay to be upset. Whatever you saw must've been really hard on you."

He thinks I'm embarrassed to cry in front of him.

"No." I shake my head and start walking back to the path. "I was just wondering if I become less real here, as my vision solidifies."

I need to find the morgue, the killer mentioned a creek. Alex follows me while he considers my question.

"You were always here, but towards the end it did get harder to see you, like it was getting darker."

"I know you think I'm just having visions, but I could touch things in that cell you know."

"I know," he agrees. "I saw you sitting on something, it was weird. Maybe your mind makes it real for you, like when people are hypnotized, they can do strange things."

I'm not so sure, but his explanation does sound reasonable, so I don't bother arguing. I step off the grass onto the bitumen path and look behind me, expecting the asylum to appear. Nothing happens, the lawns are as empty and dark as they should have been all along. I hope that wasn't my only chance to get information here, because I botched it by messing around like some sort of time tourist, not knowing what I was looking for.

"Are you gonna tell me what happened?" Alex asks, the impatience I'm familiar with finally breaking through his new tolerant facade.

I give him the dot points: I was too late; the killer is definitely the man in my nightmares; he was a doctor here at the asylum; and Lilijana's body was taken to the morgue for an autopsy.

"That one?" Alex asks.

I follow his gaze to a small square building sitting in the middle of a garden bed in front of a creek.

"Probably," I say.

The morgue is built of multi-coloured cut stone with red brick outlines and a corrugated iron roof. It worries me there aren't any shivery lines near it. And shouldn't it be creepier?

My limited experience with morgues is that they are fairly large due to the need for lots of refrigeration and sanitation. This building would barely hold a mortuary slab with room to walk around it.

"So what do I do now?" I say. "I can't just walk up to that building. If my vision takes me straight to the past and the killer's there, what's to stop him killing me."

Alex looks doubtful.

"I don't think he'd be able to hurt you. You aren't really there after all."

So I haven't convinced him I can interact with the past yet. I mean I'm not sure either. But I'm not keen on testing the theory with my death as a possible outcome.

I study the morgue. There's no sense of foreboding, no crawling skin. The total lack of any emotion connected with the building creates a new feeling of dread in me. What if I have no connection here at all?

I walk slowly towards the building, watching for signs of the past being overlaid on the now. Nothing happens. The trees stay old and majestic, and the paths are still bitumen, rather than gravel or dirt. I follow the little path right up to the double doors and put my hand against the cold grey paint. Still nothing.

I look around for Alex. He's a step behind me, looking at a plaque set into the garden bed.

"Is this definitely the morgue?" I ask.

"Yep, it's a dead house, built 1886, so it existed when Lilijana died."

He walks around me and checks whether the door is locked before doing a quick circuit of the building and coming back to stand beside me.

"What's up?" he asks. "Not getting anything?"

"Nothing." I shake my head for emphasis.

Alex digs something long and thin out of his pocket and points it at the long slide bolt and padlock attached to the doors.

"Want in?" he asks.

"Yes please." I nod and watch as he sets to work with what must be lock picks.

I'm not sure if that's a skill he picked up as a security guard or not, but it'd be a handy talent to have. I wonder if I can get him to teach me.

I hear a soft click and the padlock turns. Alex pockets it and slides the bolt back. The grinding metal on metal is horrifying in the cold night air. My first instinct is to freeze in place until I know it's safe, but Alex has one of the doors open and is heading into the pitch black room. We will be well hidden inside, so I scurry in after him and pull the door shut.

We stand in complete darkness for a few minutes until we're sure no one is coming to investigate all the noise. At least I assume that's what Alex is waiting for. I'm currently trying to stuff my rising panic over all the unseen creatures here in the dark with us, back down into my big-girl pants.

Finally I take out my phone and press the power button. As usual I'm looking straight at it when it turns on, blinding me. I turn my phone away and light up the room around us, there's not much to see. It's bigger inside than it looked. The walls have been painted white and there's no ceiling at all. I can see right to the rafters holding up the corrugated-iron roof. The only furniture in the room is a shelf built into a wall below two small louvered windows, and a trolley of some type standing in the centre of the room above a drain hole.

One glance at the trolley tells me that it's unlikely to be the original autopsy table because there's no lip around the edge to keep the blood from spilling onto your pants and shoes. I could be wrong of course, maybe back then they had to use what they could get.

I put my hand out and tentatively touch the cold metal. Again, nothing. Maybe I'm right and the trolley isn't original. I move to the bench along the wall to my left. It looks old enough, the wood has shrunken away from the wall and the strip of edging that runs along the front is loose. I touch it with a fingertip first and then lay my hand flat on the dusty surface and concentrate on how it felt to look into Lilijana's sightless eyes.

"Anything?" Alex asks.

"No," I sigh heavily.

Have I worn out my powers by using them in the asylum, or is it something to do with my connection to this building? We have no proof Lilijana's body was actually brought here. Maybe those guys were in on it with the doctor and they took her somewhere else.

I didn't know I'd put so much faith in the idea we'd find Lilijana's body and I'd be able to control my new psychic power. The disappointment has physical weight. I'm exhausted down to my bones, and hungry. I feel less than useless like this. And worse, I'm wasting Alex's time when he should be concentrating on finding his sister.

"I'm sorry, it's no good," I say to Alex as I walk dejectedly out of the morgue. "I think we should just forget about trying to strengthen my visions and find another way to get Amber back."

Even beating Nathan up is looking like a better option.

Alex shakes his head and squares his jaw as he sets about closing up the morgue and replacing the padlock. I'm worried. I know what stubborn looks like.

"You should be looking for Amber, not going on wild goose chases with me," I argue.

"You think I don't want to find my sister?" Alex's voice is too loud.

"Shhh."

Alex makes an effort to whisper in his rough voice, but it's not particularly successful. His voice cuts out entirely when he goes a smidge under normal talking level.

"Any possibility that you can improve your visions enough to go back to the funeral home and track the kidnapper's car, is the best chance we have. Unless I go and beat the shit out of Nathaniel to see what he knows."

Now I feel guilty for thinking the same thing less than a minute ago, difference is I wasn't serious. I still don't think Nathan is the kidnapper or the killer in my nightmares. It certainly wasn't Nathan who was watching Alex and Amber's apartment for months or years. I think we are dealing with one person and I already know he's a killer.

There's nothing left for us here, so I start walking in a southerly direction, heading to where we entered the gardens. Alex seems reluctant to give up on this lead. I stop and try to reason with him.

"I'm not getting anything here now." I sweep my arm around indicating the entire gardens. "The asylum is gone."

Alex's face falls as he finally gives in.

"This way though." He points in the opposite direction to where we came in.

He leads me back over the arched bridge and this time we head north, creeping through the bushes along the rushing waterway. I hear the familiar soft sounds and smells of ducks rustling their wings as we interrupt their sleep. What is less familiar, and far creepier, are the soft splashes and low gurgles emanating from the dark waters of the creek. I tell myself it's only turtles or fish, but I walk as close to Alex as I can. I step on the back of his foot twice and he turns around and gives me what I assume is a glare. I can't see his face. I back off about a quarter of a millimetre.

We move away from the water's edge and skirt around a small, round lawn complete with a statue that looks like a two-headed monster in this light. On the other side of the circular garden we find the long avenue of colossal Moreton Bay Fig Trees that line the road to the back gates. Several spotlights light the road, so we follow the outer edges of the trees, keeping to the deepest shadows.

About halfway down the line of trees I can see the tall, cast-iron gates in front of us. Even from here I know I don't want to climb those. They might be decorative, but they seem perfectly functional as well. And the fence on either side is just as bad. In fact, if the gates here are anything to go by, Adelaide is expecting a zombie apocalypse any day now.

Thankfully, Alex has a plan. Not far from the gates we turn left and follow a creek until we near the western side of the gardens. Here the creek passes under the fence and into the parklands beyond. Alex steps down into the water and gestures for me to join him. I hesitate looking at his legs. The black water is almost up to his knees. I'm going to get in, I just need to prepare myself for a second.

I'm looking down at the water when I should have been watching Alex. He sweeps me off the creek bank, holds me across his body as he wades across to the low dam wall and jumps down the five-foot drop. I'm so shocked I don't even fight him. I'm still lying in his arms looking up at his clenched jawline as he swings me away from his chest and places me feet first on the grass.

The whole process might have even been romantic if he hadn't immediately wiped his hands down his legs twice as if I'd contaminated him. He climbs up onto the bank and starts walking off in the direction of my room.

I wish I knew what his problem was, but it doesn't matter now, I'm not doing this for him anyway. I'm helping him because Amber, an innocent girl, needs help. And for me of course, it would be nice to be able to turn the visions on and off as needed.

I follow Alex through the parklands, just far enough be-hind him so he knows I'm doing it on purpose. About halfway home I get over myself and jog to catch up with him. It might be my imagination, but I think his slouched shoulders straighten slightly as I settle into a brisk walk beside his amble. Maybe he doesn't hate me that much then.

Chapter 29

Before dawn - My room

I'm in one of those deep, dreamless sleeps where I feel like I have to swim up through thick, black water towards life. It takes me nearly ten minutes to become completely conscious and even then it's only due to my extraordinarily full bladder.

Something's missing. Oh right, my nightmares. It's been a week since I was last nightmare free. What does it say about my life now that the lack of a nightmare actually worries me?

I check the window frame. It's still dark outside, so it's going to be the usual Hallway of Doom scenario out there. I drag my dressing gown on and stuff some fresh scrubs, makeup and a towel into my bathroom bag. Hauling the bag onto my shoulder I stand holding the door handle, psyching myself up for a few minutes of bravery.

After all that effort, when I open the door, the hallway doesn't even look that scary this morning. Knowing Alex is sleeping in his swag a few doors down has a lot to do with it. Apparently, all I need is a babysitter nearby. I should ask Sam if I can move downstairs closer to him and the possibly-mythical Ellie.

I strut down the hall like it hasn't seen enough of my childish behaviour in the past week. I'm over halfway to the bathroom before I even wonder why I am trying to impress wood and plaster with my bravery.

Feeling sheepish, I rush through my morning routine. It's freezing in here as usual and I'm through the shower in two minutes flat. Washing my hair can wait another day. Dressing would be quicker if I took the time to completely dry myself, but it's too cold. I struggle my damp limbs into my scrubs, leaving dark speckles all over the fabric.

Stepping out of the tiny cubicle to find a dry piece of floor, I bend over to pull my socks on. My feet are still dripping, so it takes me a bit longer than a sensible person would need.

My sock finally slides on and I stand up straight. Unfortunately, when my head stops moving, my eyes and brain don't. I stay dead still as the room rotates around me a few times. When the awful sensation eases, I tentatively open my eyes, but they're still not quite right. Everything is blurry. I close one eye to see what happens. Now the blurriness is just a few millimetres to the top-right of everything. I check with the other eye. Same thing. With both eyes open it almost looks like everything has grown a light coat of fuzzy mould.

Am I just dizzy? I haven't eaten anything in about twelve hours. Alex did offer me that disgusting chunky liquid in the flask when we got back here last night. Just the thought of the lumps made me gag right in front of him. Luckily, he just looked worried, not offended.

I think back to my dinner with Nathan. When things first went blurry it was only people, and then some of them started leaving those shivery time trails behind them.

This isn't that. This looks like the room has dropped down by almost half a centimetre and left a shadowy time trail of the building behind. Maybe that's why this place is condemned.

I fight the urge to get out of the drooping structure as fast as I can. It must be safe enough or we wouldn't be allowed to live here, hopefully.

I move my things over near the mirrors and work around the rust spots to apply the tiniest film of foundation to even out my skin tone, before adding a dash of eyeliner and mascara. My skin actually looks a lot smoother than normal, and I have a healthy pink glow on the apples of my cheeks. Misadventure seems to suit me.

I'm putting the mascara wand back into its tube when I catch movement out of the corner of my eyes. I miss the tube entirely and wipe dark mascara down the back of my thumb. It's a false alarm. There's nothing unusual in the mirrors. I get the wand back in the tube on the second try and wash my hands. I bend down to use my towel, moving slowly so I don't provoke my head again.

I don't even flinch when I stand back up to see a figure at the next basin. At this point it would be a bigger shock if nothing happened.

I recognise my mother immediately. She's a little see through, but not so bad I can't see that she looks a few years older here than in my earlier visions. Her cheeks are hollow and her eyes are red and puffy. She's dressed for work in a crisp, clean uniform, but she looks like she's already pulled a double shift. I don't think I've ever seen a person who looks this bad and wasn't headed for a hospital bed.

Every muscle in my body strains forward to comfort this desperately unhappy woman, but I keep my arms stiffly at my sides. I'm afraid she'll vanish like the last time we touched and I need to see what this vision has to show me.

I watch as the mother I never knew splashes water on her face and stands up to survey herself in the mirror. She turns her face left and right and when her frown deepens, I know she's not happy with what she sees. With a final small pout at her reflection she leaves the bathroom and walks down the still dark hallway.

The irony of being scared of the hallway when it was empty and not being afraid to follow my mother's ghost out into the dark makes me smile. The shade of my mother disappears through the closed door to the shivery, web-filled room on the right. The same room where I saw the woman crouched on the floor under the bench. Was that her?

I open the door. Sludgy disappointment settles over me. This room is as empty as the rooms next to it. I expected to see my mother in here, or at least her personal belongings. Some hint as to why this moment is important.

I jump when I feel breath on the back of my neck. I spin around to find Alex well within my personal space.

"What the hell are you doing?" I shout at him. "You scared me half to death."

"Seeing what you were so interested in." He shrugs back.

"My mother was here," I tell him. "She's definitely connected to this building somehow and the rate she keeps appearing makes me think we're missing something important. Would doing the ritual with her body work?"

"Definitely." Alex sounds more hopeful than I've heard him in a while.

"In that case you should probably finish reading the trial transcript. See if there are any clues."

I lead Alex to my room and dig out the soft yellow envelope for him again and throw it on my bed.

"Make yourself comfortable," I say. "I have to get to work, but hopefully there's something useful in there."

"Cool. After I check out a couple of other things I'm headed over to State Records to see if I can find out what doctor worked at the asylum when Lilijana was there. There was nothing online. Anything else I should look up?"

"Not really," I say. "I'll text you if I think of something."

I gather my things and I'm almost out the door before I remember we might have a problem.

"You'd better bring your swag in here or stow it in your car today. Sam told me a demolition crew is coming today."

I say goodbye to him and walk out of the building feeling strangely safe and secure. That's not right, I'm in more danger now than ever before. I'm feeling all warm and fuzzy because I'm not alone here anymore. Someone will notice if I don't come home tonight.

Hot and sticky guilt washes over me. Alex wouldn't need me at all if Amber hadn't been taken. That pleasant sense of belonging I feel is a direct result of her pain.

I'm a monster.

Chapter 30

Early morning - Hospital

The air in the hospital foyer is warm and thick after the brisk autumn air outside. There's something different in here today though, something besides all the shivery lines that seem almost normal to me now. Every blank wall has at least one A4-sized piece of paper with a Crime Stoppers Banner running across the top and a photo below. A small group of people are clustered in front of one muttering to each other.

I move closer to a poster near the information booth to check it out. Someone else is missing. The photo is a bit grainy like it's a copy of a copy, so at first I don't recognise the smiling face looking back at me. Then I notice her smile doesn't quite reach her eyes. The bottom half of her face is wrong, so I cover the smile with my hand. It's Jan, the woman from HR.

The poster says she missed her Sunday shift. It's weird that an admin would be working on the weekend, but what do I know? She was last seen at the hospital late Saturday night.

Jan, Janice on the poster, going missing on the same night as Amber seems like a pretty big coincidence to me. I get my phone out and text Alex the particulars to see what he thinks. Maybe he or Amber know the woman.

I drop my phone back into my bag before realising I should have texted Nathan back at some point. I've got no idea where I'm supposed to meet him now. I could try texting him, but I'm already at Information so this is an obvious place to start.

Luckily, the woman on duty this morning is quite trusting, probably because I'm in uniform, and she gives me directions to his office with a wistful look on her face. Obviously another of Nathan's many fans. Weirdly, Nathan's office is nowhere near the surgical ward or the theatres. Seems inconvenient.

I follow the woman's directions down so many hallways and through so many hospital buildings, I must almost be home again. A lot of this part of the hospital is now abandoned, with builder's tape and signage declaring the area off limits. When the hallway ends at a stairwell to the basement I know I've missed a turn. I guess I missed my chance to see what's down there now with Jan missing.

I know it seems particularly callous to worry about history tours right now with Amber and Jan both missing, but I have an almost supernatural ability to worry about more than one thing at a time. Like the fact a serial killer who wants my useless powers is after me. I'd give the damn powers to him if I knew how.

I backtrack a bit, find the turn I missed and finally I'm standing in front of a door plaque with Nathaniel's name on it. Knock or just go in? Knock for sure. Until Nathan's angry voice freezes my hand in space. I can't make out his words, but the hair on my arms stands on end at his tone. No wonder the guy unsettles me if this kind of rage is quietly simmering under the surface of his beautiful face.

There's a quiet reply. I can tell Nathan isn't happy with it because his voice gets even louder.

"I didn't call you in because I was on duty and it was a simple operation. He'll be out by tomorrow at the latest. There is no issue here."

Nathan goes quiet but I can't hear what he's listening to. I've just decided he must be talking to someone on the phone when I see the door handle move slightly, as if someone on the other side has put their hand on it.

I back up a couple of steps, making sure to place my feet softly as I hear Nathan's voice again.

I don't get what he says, but this time I hear the other man's reply. Not the words, just the timbre and it's enough. I get a physiological fear response similar to a moderate electrocution. I would know my killer's voice anywhere.

I'm outa here. I back up some more and then turn and sprint down the hallway, making sure to land on the balls of my feet to lessen the noise. Luckily this area of the hospital is almost deserted and I can run a good distance before I have to slow down and act normal.

Why does Nathan know the killer? Is he working with him, for him? Was this an ambush? Did Nathan get me here to hand me over to my enemy? It didn't sound like they were best mates though. Making that much noise as the prey walks up doesn't seem like a great plan either.

I hope Nathan won't get angry with me for not meeting him at his office, but then I never told him I would. I never even replied to his text. For all he knows I didn't get the message. If I have to, I can say I assumed we'd meet in Surgical.

I'm almost an hour too early for my shift, but I head straight to the ward anyway. At least I can put my jacket away and sit in a quiet corner for a while. Get my head on straight.

Jen's already in the staffroom when I go in to put my things away. She's bright and cheery as usual and I return her wide smile. I wonder if it's due to all the coffee I see her drinking, or if she's just naturally like that. Actually, I could really use a coffee from the kiosk now, but I'll settle for a Coke from the machine because I'd rather hide.

I'm digging around in the bottom of my bag when Kaye tracks me down.

"Ah good," she says. "Someone told me they'd seen you come in. Jen, can we have a moment?"

Jen gives me a quick worried glance and hurries out of the room.

"Sit down for a sec," Kaye says.

She gestures towards a chair on my right and pulls another one across from a different table, placing it about a metre in front.

I do as I'm told, my heart pounding. They must have found out about my descent into crime. Are the police on their way? What will my parents say?

When Kaye starts speaking, I learn that even if I can see the past now, I'm terrible at predicting the future.

"I need to talk to you about one of our patients."

I nod uncertainly.

"On Saturday night a prisoner at the maximum-security prison was injured and sent here for surgery."

I nod, keeping my face neutral. Is that all? This isn't a problem, I was taught about this in my cert' three. It makes things a little difficult as they are usually handcuffed, but there's always at least two guards to keep everyone safe.

Unfortunately Kaye just frowns at me. Somehow I'm not reacting the way she wants.

"The prisoner has asked to speak to you."

Oh. I can only think of one person I know in prison, but my biological father wouldn't know I work here, or what my last name was changed to after my adoption.

Could Amber have ended up in prison? I'm not sure what kind of cop would bundle you into a car boot, but if she has been arrested that might actually be good news.

"What's the prisoner's name?" In my eagerness for information my voice comes out a little louder than intended, making Kaye flinch.

My question almost sounds like a command. I clear my throat and try again.

"Sorry, do you know their name?"

"Jacob Anthony King. How do you know him?"

I don't know how to react. While my brain's still trying to think of the appropriate response, my mouth takes over unassisted.

"Jak," I hear myself saying. "He goes by Jak."

My head is spinning and not in a metaphorical way. I can't focus on Kaye's face, and I can feel myself tilting in the plastic chair. I stand up, walk over to my locker, grab a few coins and walk out of the door to the drink machine down the hall. Twice, I need to take an extra step to the right to correct my leftward lean. I hope I don't look drunk.

I can hear Kaye repeating my name to get my attention as she follows me out of the staffroom, but I just hold one finger up as I stick the coins into the machine and press the buttons to select a bottle. The Coke falls on cue but the machine is not defeated yet as the bottle wedges firmly at the bottom of the chute. I fight the machine for thirty seconds before Kaye huffs at me and extracts my prize with a practiced twist. She holds it hostage as she walks back into the staffroom.

When we are both sitting down again Kaye hands my drink over and I rip the lid off and scull the bottle, ignoring the pain in my throat.

Kaye sits and watches me for a moment and then, with the expertise of someone who has taken a ton of patient histories, she starts her interrogation with one word.

"Talk."

And I do. With short leading questions interjected every minute or so, Kaye has the whole story in no time. Well, everything up to the day I moved back here. Everything I've learned since, I keep to myself.

"This is quite the dilemma," Kaye says. "What do you want to do?"

Behind her the staffroom door opens and Nathan strides into the room looking around for something. When his eyes settle on me I'm filled with equal measures of excitement and suspicion. My heart does its best electrocuted jellyfish impression for a few beats.

"Sorry Doctor, can I help you?" Kaye asks.

"Kaye, Lily." Nathan greets us with polite nods.

There's no sign of his earlier anger, he is all politeness and civility now. He isn't wearing a coat or jacket and his dark tie leads my eye down his shirt to where it narrows around his waist, emphasising his wide shoulders. Both Kaye and I brush hair off our faces without thinking and my cheeks burn as I realise Nathan must see us preening. He would need to be blind to miss the effect he has on women. Even women who aren't on the market like Kaye who, I know by the silicone safety ring on her finger, is married. I resist the urge to check my scrubs are sitting nicely.

"Actually, I wondered if I could borrow Lily for a while," Nathan asks.

"What for?" Kaye asks, standing up from her chair and sounding territorial all of a sudden.

"Could you wait for us outside Lily?" Nathan gives me a quick reassuring smile.

I leave the room mildly annoyed I'm being ordered around before my shift has even started. I wait across the hall where I can see them talking through the small window set into the door. Nathan has moved closer to Kaye and has his hand on her arm now. Kaye's wariness has disappeared and she is smiling up at his face. It's less than a minute before they walk out of the staffroom together.

"Doctor Cain needs a hand Lily. Help him out and report back to me when you're done please," Kaye says, before walking away.

"How are you Lily? Feeling any better today?" Nathan asks, as he gestures for me to follow him, before walking up the hallway.

"Yes, thank you. I just needed to lie down for a bit. I think I ate something dodgy at lunch."

I know he or Sahra gave me something, most likely that renascent health potion, as a test and I'd love to know why. But I'm not sure work is the place for a confrontation. Also the hallway is so thick with lines here it's starting to look like a web again and it's creeping me out.

"Sorry I didn't reply to your text," I say, just to get a safe conversation going. "I was so busy over the weekend."

"I'm told you know your birth father is here in the hospital."

"Is that your surprise?" I ask him.

"I informed him you work here, yes."

There's no apology or shame in his voice at all. I stop walking, forcing Nathan to stop and look at me.

"Why would you do that?" I ask him, my voice rising in anger.

Nathan looks around us before stepping closer and putting his hand around my upper arm. I look down at his long fingers to avoid his face, which is much too close for normal brain function. His voice is soft, gooey caramel.

"Your father is a good man. He just wants to explain."

I don't look up. I don't want Nathan to see my simmering anger at being manipulated into something I said I would never do. We stand frozen like the plastic couple on top of a wedding cake, until Nathan loses patience and uses his free hand to force my chin up. His sincere brown eyes are so full of concern for me, my anger now seems like an over-reaction. Of course he wants the best for me. When I nod, Nathan lets go of my chin, but not my arm, as he leads me along the hallway.

Almost immediately a new argument against me meeting my biological father springs to mind.

"Jak's mentally ill." I need Nathan to understand I'm not just being stubborn.

"No," he says.

A bit blunt, but perfectly functional I guess.

"What's it to you anyway?" I ask him.

"I owe him," Nathan replies, looking down at me. "Tell me you'll give him a chance."

I give a tiny shrug, expecting Nathan to take that as a yes. Instead, he leans in close and whispers softly in my ear.

"Your father had someone stab him in the torso so he would be brought here. I spent my Saturday night removing his spleen and stitching up his large intestine just so he could see you."

My mouth pops open in an 'O' of horror.

"I'll distract the guards so you can talk to him. This isn't an approved visit, so you will need to flush his cannula and change his drip or whatever so no one gets suspicious."

"I can't do that, I'm a nurse's aide." I hiss at him.

"They don't know that," Nathan replies and opens a door I never thought I would choose to walk through.

Chapter 31

Morning - Dad's room

I hang back in the doorway as Nathan enters the room and greets the guards before making a show of checking the patient's dressings.

I shouldn't have worried about the guards; they don't even glance in my direction. As soon as they see Nathan doing doctory stuff they go back to talking about the weekend's upcoming footy showdown.

Nathan speaks quietly to the man in the bed, before stepping back and gesturing me forward. I walk around the guards and edge past Nathan as he seamlessly inserts himself into the guards' ongoing football analysis.

I turn my attention to the man waiting quietly on the bed for me to acknowledge him. He's nothing like I expected. He's small for starters, and lean but not skinny. Also he's got no tattoos or scars that I can see.

His lined face doesn't even look insane as he lies looking up at me. If anything, he looks sad.

His eyes seem a smidge unfocused, but that's probably just the morphine drip hooked up to his handcuffed right arm. I check the rate the medication is running through the machine. It's actually set quite low. He would have to be in a lot of pain after his operation. Either he's being brave for the nurses or someone has decided to be cruel.

I am acutely conscious of the other people in the room, so I try to keep my voice as normal as possible.

"Hello, my name is Lily. I'm one of your nurses today."

"Lily." The man on the bed breathes my name like a prayer. "I'm Jak."

I look into his eyes as tears collect on the lower lids and then flow silently down his cheeks. Yep, he knows who I am. I check myself carefully for love or even just sympathetic feelings towards this vulnerable man but find none.

"Are you in pain? Do you need your medication increased?" I busy myself checking his records, even though I know I can't legally adjust his drip. I wouldn't even know how anyway. I notice he's not on any medication for a mental illness, which now I look further, isn't mentioned anywhere on his admission forms. I guess that explains why he's in prison and not a mental health facility.

He shakes his head at me.

"No thank you. I am just fine." Jak smiles at me.

I'm not sure what I'm supposed to say next, so I set about keeping up appearances for the guards by taking my father's blood pressure and pulse. I don't record anything, I think the ethics board would be annoyed I'm even in here, without me actually caring for an estranged family member. If I get sprung doing any of this, I fully intend to throw Nathan under the bus and say he told me to do it.

I check how Nathan's doing. It appears he's morphed from superman surgeon into Port Adelaide's biggest fan. Somehow, around all of Nathan's other responsibilities, he must actually follow Aussie Rules. Enough to drop the right names anyway.

I look back down at my biological father and take the blood pressure cuff off his arm. For now at least, he seems content to watch me as I work. But my time here will be limited, I need to find out what really happened to my mother on the off chance it can help me find Amber.

"Is there a particular reason you asked to see me Jak?" I whisper.

He winces slightly. I don't think it was a pain wince, I think he didn't like me using his name. Surely he can't expect me to call him Dad?

I search his face and find no similarities between us. I guess that makes sense if I look exactly like my ancestor. I wonder if the renascent genes are so dominant that the father's genes don't ever get expressed, or if it's something even weirder.

Jak's quiet voice brings me back to the present.

"I'm so sorry Lily. I would've never hurt her."

This topic has been the undercurrent of my entire life and I can't think of a single appropriate thing to say, so I don't react at all.

"Please, you have to believe me. It doesn't matter that everyone else thinks I murdered her, but I need you to know the truth."

I feel the undertow sucking me in, this is the moment I've dreaded my whole life. I feel sympathy for my father now that he's begging for my understanding.

Still, it's not going quite how I expected. I thought he'd rationalise the murder, blame my mother or mental illness, not pretend he had no part in it. I feel my heart harden back up a little. How dare he lie to me now?

"Have you forgotten you admitted to killing her at your trial? I've read the transcript. You were seen with her body."

I actually haven't read those parts of the transcript. Someone at school told me in grade five, but he doesn't know that.

"No, I was seen with her suitcase at the nurses' dorms. She'd gone to stay in her old room there after we argued. I only took her suitcase so she'd have to come home."

Almost sounds reasonable until you see the huge hole in the story.

"Your own mother testified you'd been arguing with Hope."

"Hope dropped you off at my mother's the night before she went missing. Mum always took you when our shifts clashed. I don't know what Hope told her, but I would've never hurt my wife, no matter what Mum said.

I glance over at the Nathan. He's miming kicking a ball and the guards seem completely immersed in his actions.

My father's story sounds believable, but it still doesn't explain what happened to my mother. I consider his words for a moment before picking up a thread he's left dangling twice.

"If you didn't kill her, why do you keep saying wouldn't have, rather than didn't?"

Jak's expression changes to one I recognise. It's the face I pull when I'm caught doing something dodgy.

"My memory of that night isn't perfect, but why would I take her stuff to make her come home, if I'd just killed her?"

"Psychotic delusion, like the psychiatrist said?"

"I'm not psychotic." Jak's face is alternating between distress and stubbornness.

I watch his face with my eyebrows raised in silent disbelief.

"I might've said some strange stuff about your mother, but that was taken out of context."

I feel like I'm not getting anywhere here. It's pretty obvious he isn't planning on confessing his sins to me. I'd give up right now, but need drives me on.

"What did you and Hope argue about that made her leave us?"

"No. She was coming back for you once her weekend shift was over. It's me she left."

Jak sets his jaw and reveals some of the twenty-six-year-old he was when my mother was killed. Stubbornness is a long way from murderous though. He seems pretty harmless now, but I guess that's what a lot of murderers count on.

"And you argued about...?"

"I can't tell you. It sounds bad."

I was right, there's something there. My feelings must show on my face because Jak starts shaking his head at me.

"No, I wouldn't kill her over it. I loved her. I was shocked, yes. I've gone over and over it in my mind until I'm not even sure it was real anymore. But I would never have killed her."

And everything becomes clear, there's a parallel here. Jak learned my mother was a Renascent and just like Lilijana's husband he couldn't live with it. So he killed Hope in a rage, rather than a psychotic delusion.

Deep in my psyche I feel a tiny flicker of hope gutter and go out. I'm the daughter of a murderer.

I am just about ready to get out of here, but first I need one more thing.

"So what happened to the suitcase?"

"I took it home. It was still in the boot of my car when the police found it."

Okay, so I can assume my mother's body wasn't still in it at that point.

"Are you sure you don't remember going anywhere else, doing anything else with the suitcase before putting the clothes in it?"

I know I've made a mistake with my wording when his face crumples and he folds his free arm defensively across his chest. Despite his best efforts his handcuffed arm remains firmly secured to the bed.

"I'm sorry Jak, but I really, really, want to get her back. She was my mother," I say in a soothing half whisper. "There must be something you remember that can help me."

Even if Jak's got no memory of what he did, if I can get him to narrow down the location and time, I'll have a better chance of coaxing my visions into cooperating later.

"I waited until she finished her evening shift and I snuck into the dorms to talk to her. She was happy to see me."

My eyebrows rise involuntarily. I fight for control of my face while he continues.

"We talked for a while."

From the look on his face I translate his words to 'we argued.'

"Hope wanted to stay there another night. She said there was no point coming home now when she worked in six hours. I...disagreed." Jak looks down.

Here it comes.

"I packed her stuff and dragged the suitcase over to the door. She was trying to stop me. I opened the door and that's it."

"What's it? I don't understand. Did you push her? Did the door hit her?"

"Hey." One of the guards snaps at me.

He seems annoyed and I realise I've long given up any pretence at acting like an disinterested nurse. I give the guard a reassuring smile.

"Just trying to cheer up the patient," I say in my cheeriest voice while making a show of adjusting Jak's blanket.

It's pretty obvious I'm out of time, so I bend over and whisper in Jak's ear.

"Please, just tell me what you did."

"Nothing. I just took the case and left."

"No, you didn't. You weren't seen leaving for hours after the argument."

Jak shakes his head stubbornly as the guards move over to the bed and start taking a very keen interest in me. I give Jak a pat on his arm, hoping to come off as an affectionate mother-hen type. It should be believable, at least a quarter of the nurses I know are exactly that way.

"Okay," I say to him. "I think you're being discharged to-day." I send a questioning look in Nathan's direction. He's standing behind the two guards with a helpless look on his face. He gives me a quick nod, so I turn my attention back to my father.

"So you stay out of trouble now," I continue. "We don't want to see you back here again."

I meant the comment at face value, but I see a faint glimmer of hope on Jak's face. He wouldn't get himself hurt again would he? I frown at him and shake my head almost imperceptibly. Jak's face falls and he looks every day of his nearly forty-five years.

I turn away conflicted. It was easy to hate a monster I'd never met. It's much harder to hate the man who got himself stabbed just to have a chance of meeting me. Not that that says great things about his mental health.

Nathan says goodbye to the guards, keeping up the friendly banter, and follows me to the door. I'm distracted by the heat of Nathan's body on my back as I open the door, so I'm not paying any attention to the man in front of me, pulling gloves onto his bony hands. Nathan puts an arm around my shoulders and sweeps me backwards as he steps into the hallway, forcing the man there to step back. But it's too late, I've already felt the corruption coming off the old man's narrow face and long teeth. My body reacts instantly with a jolt of adrenaline, but my brain takes a few seconds to catch up. By that time Nathan has given me a shove along the hallway as he distracts the newcomer.

I hurry up the hallway and around a corner out of sight. So many things should be racing through my mind now, like my father and how to get Amber back. But instead my mind is almost completely blank. All except one thought that's lit up in blood-red neon.

My killer just saw me.

Chapter 32

Morning - Surgical ward

I consider faking an illness and leaving work early, but I'm probably safer here in a public place. Particularly as Nathan knows where I live and he could be working with the killer.

And what would I do in the long term? Quit my job? Go back to New South Wales like a kicked puppy and work on the farm?

Kaye's busy and sends me off to help Sophie, without even asking how meeting my father went. It's as if she doesn't even remember our earlier conversation.

Sophie is taking an elderly gentleman's blood pressure when I enter the room. She gives me a wide smile and gestures to the food tray beside the bed.

"Lily has come to give us a hand Mr Jones. She'll help you with your breakfast if that's okay?" She addresses the patient, but her words are meant for me.

I move a chair closer to the bed and pick up the bowl of cereal and a spoon. My hands are shaking badly from the excess adrenaline and I need to rest them on the table or my lap when I can.

"Weet-Bix okay?" I ask.

When the patient nods, I feed him his cereal while Sophie bustles around taking care of everything else.

Later, when we have taken care of a few patients, I take the opportunity to question Sophie about the killer.

"Oh, Dr Miles? I think his first name's Elijah, but I wouldn't use it if I were you." She doesn't seem to like him much either.

I knew I liked Sophie, she has good instincts. Also, she is very forgiving of all of the mistakes I'm making today. She thinks it's due to my father's visit because that's what I told her. I needed a cover story when I dropped a vase not long after tripping over my own feet in the hallway. I'm sure the news my father's a murderer is already spreading like wild-fire and this way I get to control the version people hear.

Sadly, while meeting my father is an important mile-stone in my life, it's just not my most immediate concern. Top billing in my thoughts goes to the certain knowledge my killer is walking around in the same building as me. I flinch every time a door opens and my heart keeps playing a strange syncopated beat.

It's almost lunchtime when Sophie knocks on the bath-room door. I flinch so obviously the patient I'm helping to shower thinks I'm hiding a PTSD diagnosis. Or I'm a com-plete wuss. She's probably right about me being a coward, but then I am still here, doing my job.

On my lunch break I hide in the staffroom with a Coke and a couple of chocolate bars from the machines, and text Alex. He hasn't replied to my earlier message about Jan's disappearance, so I assume he doesn't think there's any link to his sister's kidnapping.

I text him everything I now know about Doctor Miles, which isn't much. Alex still hasn't replied by the time I have to go back to work and I'm starting to get worried I've got the wrong number for him. I scroll back through my texts. None from him, only Amber's number appears.

At about two in the afternoon Kaye lets me know my father's been transferred back to prison. I feel a moment of disappointment, which I'll analyse later if I get the time, but questioning Kaye about the killer takes priority.

"I didn't recognise one of my father's doctors. Do you know him, a Dr Miles?" Hopefully she'll think I'm interested in the quality of care my father's getting.

"Oh him. He's worked here forever." Her tone is so carefully professional I wonder if they've had a run in at some point.

"Is he a good doctor?" I ask.

Kaye shrugs.

"Must be. He gets very few complaints."

A thought occurs to me.

"Was he the anaesthetist for Ana's surgery last week?"

"Probably, he usually works with Dr Cain."

"Really?"

"Yes, Dr Miles insists on it. He was Dr Cain's mentor when he was a resident you know. Dr Cain wouldn't be a surgeon today if Dr Miles hadn't pushed his application through."

Well this just gets worse and worse. If those two are so tight, there's no way Nathan is innocent in all this. And just when I thought I'd cleared him by finding a link between my killer and Ana's death. What I can't work out is, if they are working together, why hasn't the killer come for

me already? And why did Nathan seem to be running interference for me at my father's room? Add that to his role in
taking me on a date so I'd eat whatever woke up my psychic
powers and I'm thoroughly confused.

I work in a daze for the rest of the afternoon. The only
good thing that comes from my mind being overloaded is
the shivery lines begin to fade away. It's good to know exhaustion has at least one positive side effect.

The only time my racing mind gets a break is when I'm
asked to read to a patient who forgot to pack her glasses.
The plot of the crime novel is so poorly planned the patient
and I are soon picking it to pieces for entertainment. Unfortunately she is soon wheeled away for an x-ray, and I'm
back to worrying myself stupid.

I've nearly survived my entire workday when I see Nathan
and Kaye talking near the reception desk. Kaye points in my
direction. Instinct screams at me to hide, but he's already
seen me. All I can do is hope someone just shot his dog,
because if that expression has anything to do with me, I'm
in real trouble, witnesses or not. I step forward slightly so I
can be seen by the patient and his guest in the room next
to me and wait.

"We need to talk," Nathan says when he's close.

"Yep," I agree.

"When do you finish today?"

"Uh, in ten minutes," I answer.

"And what are you doing after?"

"Going home."

"No." Nathan's usually calm, reassuring voice is anything
but that right now. "I'll be in surgery for the next couple of
hours. Will you wait for me?"

"What, here?"

"I have an office you could wait in, if you like."

I have no idea what's going on right now. But I do know waiting alone in his office, deep in the deserted part of the hospital, sounds like a great way to have my photo appear next to Jan's on the foyer walls.

Of course Nathan would know if the killer recognised me today. He might be trying to keep me safe. Still, I'd be alone in the office while he's in surgery. I think I'll take my chances with Alex.

"Sorry, no." I make my voice firm so he won't bother arguing with me.

I also keep my eyes studiously on the floor. I don't have a good track record of sticking to my guns when I look this guy in the face.

Nathan steps closer to me and I counter with an overplayed step backwards to protect my personal space. Nathan takes the hint and backs off again.

"You don't trust me."

I risk a glance up at his impassive face.

"I'm just tired and I need to rest. Call me when you get out of surgery."

Nathan considers my offer for a moment.

"If you promise to answer."

"I will," I say.

Nathan hesitates with his mouth open to say more, but then he sees Kaye headed towards us. He mashes his lips together and gives me a frustrated look as he turns and strides away.

I wait for Kaye nervously, expecting her to ask how I've annoyed one of her favourite doctors. I'm wrong again. One day I'll learn to stop guessing. Kaye ignores the fact I've been the world's worst employee all day and tells me I can go home. I thank her and grab my things from the break room and get out of there quick, so I don't bump into my killer without Nathan around to protect me.

I'm walking so fast I'm puffing by the time I round the final street corner and spot the tired, old building I have come to think of as home. It's changed while I've been at work, and I feel like someone has ripped out the small roots I'm trying to put down in this place. The nurses' quarters is now surrounded by fencing: some temporary chain-link panels; and some eight foot tall wooden sheets. All of it covered in advertising for the state-of-the-art tower blocks that will be built over the old building's grave. My home, and the last place my mother lived, will soon be wiped from the face of the earth.

I wonder if the shivery time trails will disappear with the building. I step into the translucent web knowing this is as close as I will ever get to being wrapped in my mother's arms. For the moment, I do feel less alone.

I walk in through a small gap in the fence and push the old doors open to discover my second nasty surprise in as many minutes. The foyer's a demolition site.

Sam said the workers weren't supposed to touch any-thing yet, but someone didn't get the memo. There are holes here and there in the walls, exposing the brickwork and reinforcing behind the many layers of paint. I guess they're checking how solid the building is and what it will take to pull it all down.

I'm drawn to a pile of wooden cupboards stacked hap-hazardly opposite the stairwell. I run a hand over a piece of the smooth hardwood, the same as the fixed furniture in my room. Restored, or even just cannibalised for the wood, these things would probably be worth decent money. Someone's trying to get a head start on the salvage process.

I knock on Sam's door to see what he knows about the damage, but he's not home.

I head upstairs to check on my room. The door is still locked shut, but I can see many of the other rooms along the hallway have been disturbed. Some doors have even been removed and are leaning in a pile halfway to the bathroom. That'll make a nice obstacle in the middle of the night.

Alex isn't in my room, but his swag is neatly rolled up and standing in the small space at the foot of my bed. I'm not so sure I want to be here alone. What if Nathan was trying to tell me my killer knows where I live?

I press send on a text to Alex, asking for an update on his whereabouts and am immediately rewarded with a chime right outside my door. I open it to find Alex balancing an armload of takeaway food on one hand while he digs in his pocket with the other.

My cheeks tense into an anxious smile, but Alex isn't in the mood for pleasantries. I can understand why. Amber's been gone for two days now. He must be starting to lose hope.

He passes me a tray of drinks and a paper bag bulging with food and collapses face first onto my bed.

"You okay?" I ask.

"Sure," he grunts.

At least I think he said sure, could've been anything really. I would ask, but it doesn't seem right to nag a guy who's currently face down in my pillow, not caring if he suffocates. I seriously hope I didn't drool too badly last night. It's perfectly possible that pillow is still damp.

Before long he rolls sideways into a sitting position and shrugs out of his backpack.

"Eat." He gestures at the bag of food on the table.

"I'm not that hungry actually, but thanks," I say.

Alex rolls his eyes at me and sighs.

"Eat anyway," he orders. "Your ability is affected by the food you've eaten."

He leans forward and digs the silver flask of disgusting out of his bag.

"And drink this. I need you in as close to working order as possible."

Okay, that's a bit ominous. But first...

"Sorry, hard pass on whatever's in that bottle. Is it the same stuff as last time?"

Alex looks annoyed, which is an improvement on the black exhaustion he's been displaying since he got back.

As a compromise I hand him one of the drinks from the tray I'm still holding and then take a long drink from the other. The bubbles burn my throat, but the sugar and caffeine hit makes it worthwhile. I sit down in the chair and open the greasy bag. Two burgers; two large chips; chicken nuggets; and two desserts. Ah, you gotta love a guy who expects a girl to eat.

I hand Alex one of each item and then take a large mouthful of my burger before remembering all the news I have. Talking around my food and behind my hand I tell him everything that happened that day. I leave out a few specifics, like I knew in advance Nathan was up to something, and that he ever sent me a text.

When I finish, I expect Alex to start telling me what progress he's made, but he just shrugs. He's not finished eating though, so it's possible he's not a pig like me. We eat in silence for a bit until I can't stand it anymore.

"So, what do you think? Do we find out where the killer lives and go pay him a visit?"

Alex puts his empty wrappers back into the bag and shakes his head.

"I already know where he lives, and if he's the one who took Amber, he won't have taken her home."

"Why not?" I ask. "How do you know where he lives?"

"He's Bridget's dad."

Chapter 33

Late afternoon- My room

My heart is flip-flopping in my chest. I haven't felt a normal beat in the minute since I learned Lilijana's daughter, my daughter, is being raised by the same person who is hunting down Renascents and killing them.

He must know she's one of us. Is he raising her like a lamb for the slaughter?

And Sahra his wife is renascent too. Whose side is she on? I can't work it all out. A thousand motives jump to mind. Did the killer fall in love with one of his targets and spare her? Does she not know he's a killer? Is Sahra the real bad guy, getting rid of her competition and her husband is just following orders?

No wonder Alex is so quiet. He's trying to work through all this too. I give up trying to sort it out alone.

"What the hell is going on?" I ask him.

Alex finally relents and tells me about his fruitless search for records of Lilijana's death. He quickly abandoned that lead and searched for information on Jan from work. So he does think two people going missing on the same day can't be a coincidence. But other than the fact she's missing, Jan seems completely ordinary. One husband, two kids, house in the suburbs and no connection to any Renascents he can find.

I can't think of anything to add to his assessment of her. Surely the fact she's an insufferable cow isn't pertinent to her current situation.

After I sent Alex the text naming the killer, he spent the rest of his day researching Doctor Elijah Miles. Online was a waste of time, but Alex did visit the anaesthetist offices pretending to be a new customer so he could scout around. Unfortunately it was a dead end. The office is shared with other doctors, so it's too small and too busy for Amber to be hidden there.

The same applies to the house where the doctor, Sahra and Bridget live. It's a small heritage cottage with a new extension on the back in the posh area of town near the hospital. Even during the day the house isn't empty. There's a cleaner in the mornings and a cook is there all afternoon and into the early evening. Definitely not a great place for keeping secrets.

"So what now?" I ask Alex.

"I think we have two choices. We physically track Miles, see if he will lead us to Amber. Or we try tracking him with your psychic power. Do you think your connection to him is strong enough?"

I shake my head slowly.

"I really don't know," I answer. "I still have to be where the event took place. I don't know if going back to the funeral home and tracking Amber and the killer from there would work yet. But even if I could tune into the killer somewhere like the hospital and track him from there, how would I know it was the right day or time to lead us to Amber. We could end up following him to golf."

"So the funeral home's still the best option for the psychic thing then. Unless you think you could have a power nap and dream where Amber is?" Alex adds hopefully.

"I didn't dream at all last night. I might have been too tired, but that usually doesn't stop me dreaming. I think physically tracking the killer is our best lead."

"Maybe so, but there's no point doing that yet," Alex says. "I know where he is right now. Mondays are Bridget's ballet classes. He hangs around till she's finished and then they go to Sahra's restaurant for dinner. We're looking at nine at least before he'll head out to check on Amber. I'll trail him from his house then."

So if we have nothing better to do...

"I was thinking while I was at work."

Alex looks at me hopefully.

"You know how finding Lilijana's body was a dead end, what about if I could find my mother's?"

"You wouldn't get Lilijana's memories back obviously, but your psychic abilities would get much better. Why, do you know where her body might be?"

"Not exactly, but it's pretty obvious this is where my father killed her. Cos even when my visions are almost non-existent, I still see things in this building. I've seen my mother's ghost here multiple times."

"Where?" Alex asks.

"Down here," I say, moving out into the hall. It's still daylight outside and the hallway is a perfect picture of innocence. The cluster of shivery lines around my mother's room is barely visible now. The spider must've moved out.

I step inside the freshly-ransacked room. The wooden wardrobe and bench that used to be here has been ripped from the wall, leaving behind nothing but ragged holes in the plaster and brick.

But that isn't the only change.

My connection to the room is gone too. I don't feel anything. I stand still and focus my thoughts on my mother.

Nothing happens.

I pull focus so hard that wavy black and white lines appear right in the centre of my field of vision. I blink a few times to clear them.

I look around wondering what's missing until my gaze settles on the holes in the plaster. Something about that furniture was improving my connection to my mother. I need it back. I back out of the door into Alex's hard body.

"What's up," Alex asks me, stepping back out of my way.

"Something's wrong. I've been seeing things in here since the start, but there's nothing now."

"The cupboards are gone," Alex says as he catches on.

I'm already jogging down the hallway when he starts following me. I take the stairs three at a time and stop in front of the wooden pile I was drawn to earlier. I survey the pile from all sides. I can't see anything unusual, so I get down to floor level and look at the underside of everything. Nothing.

I start opening the little cupboard doors. I might have nothing more important than Vegemite and some stale bread in my cupboard, but maybe my mother left something more important in hers.

Sure enough, right at the back of the third cupboard I try, a small key is taped underneath the middle shelf. The tape holding it up is so old it falls off in my hand and the adhesive crumbles leaving a yellow powder on my fingers.

I hold the key up for Alex to see.

"Do you think that's your mother's?" Alex asks.

"Gotta be," I say confidently, and head back up the stairs with Alex trailing after me yet again. I feel sorry for him. He looks uncomfortable not being the doer in this situation.

My connection to my mother is stronger now. The funnel-web lines are back at their shivery best. The key is working. I stand still just inside my mother's room and try to get her to appear to me.

Nothing.

Is it too light? The sun is almost down. Maybe this will work better once the hallway has fully recharged its horror-movie powers.

"It's not working," I complain to Alex who is waiting just outside the room so he doesn't interfere with the vibe, his words.

"Maybe it's not her key," he suggests.

"Oh, it's hers all right. It's working, just not enough."

Alex looks like he wants to say something but doesn't know how to say it. I see him change his mind and he steps back to the hallway wall and slides down it into a sitting position. I take this to mean he's willing to wait while I try some more.

Soon the sun has set and the light takes on the apricot glow of sunset. I close my eyes for a minute and concentrate on my mother. I remember her smiling face in Ana's old photo album and the way her ghost looked when I saw her here. I slow my breathing and try to imagine this room as my mother saw it. Without opening my eyes I see how a bed might have looked under the window. Would my mother have stuck pictures on the wall?

I imagine the cupboards and long bench intact, a small fridge in its space, nursing textbooks in a neat pile. Would my mother have had a computer set up on the bench when she lived here? Did people have laptops in the early two thousands?

I open my eyes. Nothing.

"Yeah, this isn't working," I tell Alex.

"You might as well keep trying. At least until it's time to pick up Doctor Miles' trail at nine."

"No, it's just not working. This isn't helping either." I drop the key on the floor in disgust, making even the translucent lines disappear from sight.

"I'm getting weaker and weaker." I'm angry now.

I'd believed in Alex's confidence that my psychic powers were going to improve and become a useful tool for us. I'd trusted his belief I could find Amber. Now the realisation I have absolutely no control over this horror story settles on me like a cloud of cheap perfume. My eyes water and my skin crawls with the need to do something, anything, no matter how futile.

I give Alex a hopeless look. He's watching me closely. He's never been good at hiding his emotions and I can see several of them battling it out for control of his thoughts. Finally his features settle. His eyes are clear and direct, and his jaw squared as he looks at me. He draws himself up to a standing position and looks around.

"We're gonna need some privacy," he mutters to himself.

He looks briefly at the door, but it's hanging on a diagonal, with one of its hinges broken. I don't think it's much good anymore, and apparently neither does Alex, because he grabs my hand and leads me down the hallway, back to my room.

I'm shocked at the feel of his hand on mine. I've gotten used to Alex being around and I've even started to get comfortable in his presence. Not burping out loud comfortable of course. But Alex has never touched me before. He goes out of his way not to. I have touched him a couple of times when I was testing my power, or when I needed out of my vision at the asylum, but nothing as casual as this. As if this is normal for us.

My discomfort increases when he shuts my door behind us and turns the lever to lock it. We cross the tiny room and he sits down on the edge of my bed. My anxiety climbs as he uses my hand, still firmly in his grip, to pull me down towards him. I sit next to him, our shoulders and thighs touching in the small space.

Alex takes a deep breath and then allows his shoulders to slouch down so his head is a little closer to mine. I risk a glance sideways at him. Where the hell is this going? Alex moves away from me a little so he can turn his body to face me.

"I know why your powers aren't improving, and I know how to fix it. But you're not gonna like it."

His rough voice is even more gravelly than usual.

"Why?" I say slowly.

"When Amber and I were explaining what it means to be a Renascent, one of the reborn, we didn't tell you everything." He hesitates now, unsure of himself.

I nod encouragingly. I know you can't summarize the entire history of a race of people in a few minutes.

"We left out something important, something you need to know."

Alex goes quiet again. My skin starts to prickle with worry. If he's this anxious about telling me, it must be bad. Worse than telling me I'll probably die young of disease, if a murderer doesn't get me first. They also seemed fine asking me to desecrate the body of their own grandmother.

Yeah, this is gonna be bad.

"You remember we said renascent abilities are often misunderstood and that's where stories of witches came from?"

I don't nod, I don't even twitch. My mind is racing. What do I know about witches? I'm pretty sure he's not talking about Wiccans and love spells and putting witch hazel on your sunburn. He means the old-fashioned stories of curses, spells to drive you mad, and human sacrifice.

Oh, shit. Is that why we needed Ana's brain, as part of some kind of sacrificial offering?

I feel Alex's weight shift slightly on the bed. I pull myself out of my head and look at him unbuttoning his shirt cuff and I gasp as I put two and two together. We are sitting on my bed and killing something isn't the only occult ritual I've heard of. I spring off the bed like it burned my ass.

"I am not having sex with you."

Alex blinks up at me in surprise for a moment before the corners of his mouth turn up in the tiniest of smiles.

"Ouch," he says, his blue eyes twinkling at me. "But no, that's not it."

With my cheeks burning I sit back down next to him.

"Just spit it out then, you're only making it worse."

My tone is a bit snarky, but I can't help it. My emotions are all over the place and this has already been a very long day.

"Fine," Alex says, pulling a small knife out of his back pocket.

He uses the knife to point to a series of small scars on his left wrist.

"You need to drink my blood."

Chapter 34

Dusk - My room

"So I'm a vampire now?" I ask in disbelief.

"No." Alex shakes his head emphatically. "The vampires from the stories don't exist. Drinking blood is about the only thing they got right. But you can see how being reborn is kind of like being immortal."

"And you're telling me this now because...?" Dread is making me snappy.

Alex gives up his gentle approach and goes straight for coercion. "You need to do this for Amber. She's waited long enough for us to find another way."

The guilt trip partly works, but the rational part of my brain is still looking for a way out.

"I thought you said the ritual would make my powers work."

"That's what the lore says. But it's pretty clear the blood is working."

I gasp as I realise what he means.

"You think that's what Nathan and Sahra gave me Friday night. What, in the wine?"

I've got to stop asking questions two seconds before I work it out myself. It wasn't the wine. Even now the memory of the sour cherry sauce makes my mouth water.

"And there was blood in the stew Amber made? Human blood?"

Alex just looks calmly into my eyes while I think it through. I can feel the new knowledge changing me as it sinks deep into my psyche. I know he's right. This explains so much about me, my constant hunger, and even why Lilijana and my mother were so hated they needed to die.

"So vamp-"

"No." Alex rolls his eyes as he interrupts me. "Vampires are fictional. So are witches, probably. You won't grow fangs, you can definitely be killed, and so can Amber. Which is why you need to drink my blood now, so we can go find her."

He makes it sound so reasonable, but I can still see a few problems with his plan.

"Wouldn't this be a really bad time to make you weaker though?"

"You're still thinking of the movies. You won't drink much. Most of your nutrition comes from normal food or you wouldn't have survived this long. The blood's more like a vitamin supplement. I could feed five Renascents at once and be just fine." His voice is calm and even, like a YouTube tutorial.

I force the image of five women hanging off his arms like fat leeches out of my head and get back on task. I've saved my best argument for last.

"What about diseases?" I ask.

I don't want to insult him, but my nursing induction was pretty clear on how common blood-borne pathogens are.

"You can't catch diseases from drinking blood."

I open my mouth to argue with him, but he interrupts me again.

"Not anyone can't catch them. You can't." He clarifies. "I have no idea why, I'm not a doctor. Antiseptic saliva?"

He shrugs his shoulders at me, not interested in trying to make a better case. More than anything else, this reassures me he trusts his information.

I've run out of reasons not to give this a try, other than the general ickyness of it. We're in a pretty clear-cut life or death situation. Rescuing Amber versus not.

And Alex is still staring into my eyes, willing me to do it. Hang on.

"Are you trying to glamour me?"

I can tell I'm right, because he immediately breaks eye contact.

"Hey, that's not fair. I thought you guys didn't come with any powers."

Alex looks up at me, a defiant look on his face.

"I wouldn't have to if you weren't being so stubborn about helping me find my sister."

Shame overpowers my indignation. I was always going to help, wasn't I?

"You can't blame me for checking if this is really the best way, can you?" I say. "So what do I do now?"

The defiance falls from Alex's face, leaving him so vulnerable that I'm the one who breaks eye contact this time. The situation only gets worse when he takes his shirt off. I avoid looking at his bare chest, preferring to concentrate on the implication he thinks I'm a messy eater.

"Here, lean back against me," he says, opening his arms and flicking his fingers inwards towards his half naked body.

I start to lean sideways towards him, but he puts his hands on my shoulders and turns me, pulling me into him so my back is resting against his chest. I manage to smother a tiny mewl of surprise, but I can't control my racing heart. I wonder if he can feel my reaction to being this close to him, touching his body. Hopefully he thinks I'm worried about drinking his blood, which I am.

Both of Alex's arms wrap around me and the sharp steel of the knife glints in the light as he draws it lightly across the thickened scar on his left wrist. Deep red blood oozes from the thin wound. He drops the blade on the floor and puts his right hand on my shoulder holding me still. He holds his left arm in front of me at chest height. I stare at the heavy droplet that is threatening to fall down onto my clothes.

"Lily." Alex's voice is even deeper than usual and there's a pleading tone I can't ignore. I reach out to his arm and wrap my hands around his wrist, pulling it towards my mouth. I sniff experimentally, but there's no smell I can detect. Not even the coppery notes I read about in crime novels. Maybe it would help if I knew what copper smelled like.

My heart feels like it's going to break a rib as I lick up the heavy droplet. I feel Alex shift behind me. I sincerely hope he's right about the vampire stories being made up. If he finds this sexy, the rest of the evening is going to be hella awkward.

The blood tastes salty and sharp on my tongue. I swallow quickly, afraid to taste it properly. The aftertaste reminds me of sucking on keys as a child.

My saliva has caused the blood seeping from Alex's wrist to turn into a trickle now. A thin trail is running down his arm towards his elbow. I'm not sure what the etiquette here is, but the thought of licking all the way up his arm is a bit flirty for me. I'll let my scrubs catch it, that's kind of what they're for.

I bring Alex's wrist to my face and cover the tiny wound with my lips and suck lightly. My mouth floods with warm, savoury human juice. That enticing flavour I loved in the duck sauce is now almost overwhelming and my mouth waters so hard my cheeks hurt. My hands are no longer quite under my control and they clench tightly around the warm and tasty arm. Now I know why Alex faced me away from him.

I suck a little harder. Warmth floods my mouth again, more than there should be from such a tiny wound. I swallow and feel the path of the blood as it burns towards the centre of my being. A tingling starts there and spreads out through my body. I can feel it flowing under my skin like a shiver, but sparkly.

I suck on the wound again and Alex shivers. Am I hurting him? A pang of guilt pierces through my overwhelming desire to keep drinking. What is wrong with me? I tear my lips from his arm and try to push him away from me, but Alex's free hand leaves my shoulder and wraps around my chest, holding me close. It's all too easy to put his welfare out of my mind and press my mouth back onto the rivulet of dark-red blood.

The overwhelming sensations are fading a little now and my thoughts seem clearer and sharper than ever. I realise I've been missing so much. For starters, Alex isn't the only one who's been using his power of persuasion on me. Nathan's done it several times.

I'm not angry about it. Their power is very limited anyway, barely enough to influence someone. It can't change a person's mind or make them quack like a duck.

Also, I know their power won't affect me anymore, I can ignore it as easily as a verbal command. Right now though, I let Alex's power flow over me, reassuring me as I drink.

When the sparkler effect spreading through me reaches my fingertips and toes I know I've had enough. I push Alex's wrist away so I can see his wound, but he moves that arm out of my sight and lets go of me with his other arm. This is my cue to get off him. When I've moved a respectable distance away, he's already wrapped a small bandage around his wrist. He's done a pretty good job one handed. No blood is seeping through the white bandage, but I still feel an almost irresistible urge to redress it for him.

"You might want to put some pressure on that," I tell him.

"It's fine," Alex answers, not looking up at my face. "I heal quick."

I have no idea what to do now, but I know a little gratitude is never out of place.

"Thank you."

"It's all good," he says, while checking himself over for spills and stains.

He's fine, my scrubs however, not so good.

As Alex turns away from me to put his shirt back on, I notice he has a faint series of scars where his chest meets his neck. I get a little shiver of fright at how close a couple of them are to the main arteries leading to his brain. If those scars are from feeding someone, I hope he knows just how close he's been to a serious injury.

Involuntarily I get an image of just how personal it would be to feed from him that way. He's definitely not feeding his sister from those wounds.

I find myself a fresh pair of jeans and a t-shirt to change into and shove them into my shower bag.

"I'm going to head out to the bathroom for a quick shower," I tell Alex, who stays facing away from me.

He's been fiddling with his shirt for an unreasonably long time. Something is up, like maybe he can't look me in the face anymore. I wonder what the problem is. Alex has done this sort of thing before. Many times I would say from his ease with the procedure.

Maybe he has a girlfriend and he's feeling guilty about sharing his blood. I can't ask now though. He'll think I'm selfish and wanting to know if he'll be able to feed me on the regular.

I decide to pretend that whole thing never happened. I wait for a pang of shame at my cowardice, but it doesn't come. Instead I'm feeling a buzz of happiness or joy that I need to ignore, because it's so terribly inappropriate with Amber in the clutches of a killer.

Luckily, I can feel the strength of my psychic ability now. I can tell it's always been there, dormant and waiting for me to learn how to use it. Like when I learned to raise one eyebrow or wiggle my ears, I just had to learn where those muscles were.

I am filled with sudden confidence in our plan. As soon as I've had my shower and changed out of these stained clothes, we are going back to the funeral home and I am going to track the kidnapper's car all the way to his hidden lair.

I yank the door open and look out into the hallway.

It's like someone switched my eyeballs off. It's so dark out there now, even the light from my doorway is instantly absorbed by the blatant malevolence radiating towards me.

Well, shit.

Chapter 35

Early evening - My room

I stick my head out into the hallway and look down towards the bathroom. I know Alex and I left the door to my mother's room standing open, but it looks shut now. A dark rectangle there is framed by slivers of bright light escaping the room.

My new stronger ability knows what I'm looking at as easily as I can tell east from west, up from down. Here in my room it's nearly seven o'clock on a Monday, but down there it's 2:01 on a Saturday morning eighteen years ago.

"Alex," I whisper.

For a moment I'm afraid he won't hear me. I feel so connected to that earlier moment in time I might've left reality entirely.

Alerted by my tone, Alex moves beside me and looks out into the hallway.

"What?" he whispers back.

"There's a light on in my mother's room," I say quietly. "I wanna check it out."

I walk down the black hallway. Quiet voices reach me. Someone is definitely in that room.

Weirdly, the threat I feel here isn't coming from the bedroom. The darkness is absolute in the hall on the other side of my mother's door, the end that leads to the bathroom. There's something down there. Something evil.

With my feet positioned so I can sprint off at a second's notice, I examine my mother's door. Looks real. But when I reach out to test it, my fingers slide right through. I make a quick 'follow me' gesture before I remember the hallway would be pitch black for Alex. He'll either follow or he won't. I grit my teeth together, close my eyes and step through into my mother's room.

It's disorienting to open my eyes to a bright room, and I need to blink tears away before I can see.

The image here is strong, but more like a high-definition movie than real life. I'm disappointed. I'm still just an observer like Alex and Amber said.

My mother is sitting on her bed, dressed in lightweight summer pyjamas. Her red-rimmed eyes are filled with tears, and she looks down at her twisting hands while Jak towers over her. He is so young now. I wouldn't have recognised him as my father if I hadn't seen the photo in Ana's album.

Jak's face is red and tear streaked like my mother's. I can tell he's sad and frustrated, but not that angry yet. He looks harmless. But that doesn't stop him from yelling.

"I said that," he cries out.

My mother is startled and glances at the door. Does she see me?

No, now she's shushing Jak.

"Please Jak, I have to work with these people," she whispers.

My father is stepping from one foot to the other and his hands are shaking. Adrenaline overload. I'm surprised when, instead of erupting, Jak falls to his knees in front of my mother and puts his hands over hers.

"Then just come home with me, Hope," he pleads with her. "We'll get you some help. Mum has agreed to keep the baby for a few weeks. And our health insurance will cover a psychiatrist. We'll get you sorted out."

My mother sighs and her shoulders sag.

"I can't be fixed, I told you that. This is who I am, who we are."

Jak jumps back to his feet enraged.

"No," he barks out. "You will not bring our daughter into your craziness. You are not a vampire, and neither is she. Thank god I caught you yesterday before you fed her that blood. Where did you even get it? Please tell me you didn't hurt anyone."

"It was donated by a friend. It was perfectly safe."

"Do you hear yourself right now? Who was it?" Jak leans over my mother, his red face only inches from hers, but she doesn't answer. And she doesn't look frightened. How could she misjudge him so badly? She shouldn't be provoking him when he's this angry.

And why isn't anyone coming to check on her?

"Who gave you blood to feed to our daughter?" Jak's voice is low and tinged with menace now.

I can understand his need to protect me, but my heart is still hardened against him. There are other ways to deal with things. Just when I am steeling myself to watch Jak kill my mother, she finally answers him.

"Nate gave me the blood. He wanted to. He adores Lily."

Jak's mouth drops open and he takes a few moments to reply.

"Nathan? You dragged that kid into your stupid fantasy? What the hell were you thinking?"

I see my mother's face moving through several emotions before her jaw juts slightly. Oh great. She's going with defiance.

"I didn't drag Nathan into anything," she says. "He already knew. His cousin is like me."

"Sahra?" Jak shakes his head. "You really have an answer for everything don't you. You're sicker than I thought, but you need to know this isn't real. We'll get you some therapy. Maybe some drugs will sort you out."

My mother's looking scared now. She should be. The next words out of Jak's mouth send a shiver up my spine too.

"Maybe we can get you into a treatment centre for a little while, just until you feel better."

The blood drains from my mother's face. She must know she wouldn't be the first of her line to be locked away against their will.

Jak sees her face and drops back to one knee at her feet.

"It's going to be okay. I promise." He pats her hands paternally and then stands up and drags a suitcase out from under the wooden bench. He unzips it and throws everything he can see into it before zipping it up and crossing to the door.

"Come on," he says.

"Um." My mother gestures down at her pyjamas.

"Oh right." Jak's face cracks in a small grin.

I wonder if he actually thinks it's funny, or whether he is just relieved my mother isn't flatly refusing to go with him now.

As Jak bends over to unzip the suitcase we all hear a quiet knock on the door behind me.

That'd be right. Now that the danger is over someone decides to play the role of concerned neighbour.

Jak switches places with the suitcase and I step through the wooden bench deeper into the room to avoid him as he opens the door. The figure in the doorway is dressed in dark clothes and his face is covered, but I don't need to see his long-toothed sneer to recognise my enemy. Doctor Elijah Miles steps towards my father and I see the glint of metal in his right hand as he brings a weapon up and into Jak's chest. At first I think he's been stabbed, but when Jak's body collapses to the floor I see an empty syringe in the killer's hand.

My mind races to assimilate this new information. Jak never killed my mother at all and now I'm going to have to stand here and watch helplessly while the man who has killed me more times than I will ever remember, kills my mother as well.

The coward in me wants to leave now, but I'll never live with myself if I don't at least try to help. Hope stands and raises her arms to defend herself as the killer advances on her. I search for a lifeline. I have affected things in the past before and I'm much stronger now. I just need something to help me tune in better.

The key.

I squat down and skim my hands over the carpet in wide sweeping arcs.

I can't find it. I crab walk to my right, deeper into the bench, while keeping my eyes fixed on the scene unfolding before me. My mother tries to fight off the killer's bony hands, but he is much stronger than her. His hands easily close around her throat and he forces her down onto the bed. She kicks out at him, but he just twists his lower body out of reach and squeezes tighter.

My mother's face is turning purple as I watch the killer lean in and whisper to her. I can't hear what he's saying, but I've heard it a million times in my dreams: we're evil; no one cares for us; and the world is better off without us polluting it.

Hot tears of frustration roll down my face. What's the point of my ability anyway? It's cruel to make me a witness to the suffering of my ancestors if I can't do anything about it. My hands are still moving frantically across the floor when my arm is yanked sideways and a cool metal object is dropped into my palm.

Alex.

I'd been so absorbed by my vision I'd forgotten he existed. He figured out what I was looking for. I close my hand tightly around the key and stand up. At first holding the key makes no difference to the level of reality around me, but as soon as I step out of the bench into an unobstructed area, my vision solidifies. I feel the hardness of the wood behind me and the 2D effect drops away.

I am here. There.

With my mother in the room she dies in.

I launch myself at the killer.

If he'd been expecting me it would've never worked. But he's standing awkwardly to avoid my mother's kicks, so it's easy to overbalance him. As he falls, he lets go of my mother in favour of protecting his skull.

As soon as our bodies hit the bed, I switch targets. Wrapping my arms around my mother's warm body, I throw myself backwards, dragging her with me. My plan to save my mother hasn't developed beyond wrenching her from the killer's grasp, so I do the only thing I can think of.

I drop the key.

When my mother and I crash down onto the carpet, it's in a dark room eighteen years later, with Alex's dark silhouette looming over us.

Chapter 36

Evening - My mother's room

I'm still catching my breath when my mother struggles free of my arms and moves out of my reach. The rustle of my scrubs when I right myself is enough to scare a scream from the darkness. It doesn't help that Alex's silhouette is looming large in the window.

I force my shaking limbs across to the doorway and flick on the light.

My mother is backed into a corner with her arms up, protecting her head.

I have no idea if she saw me before I grabbed her and if she'll recognise me now. She'd have to look at me first.

I take in Alex's stance, standing frozen with his hands out towards Hope. To me he looks like he's trying to quiet a panicked horse. To my mother, that's the same position the killer used to choke her only seconds ago.

I need to get her attention so she doesn't look at him first. A dozen possibilities occur to me, but in the end I decide simple is best.

"Mum?" I keep my voice soft, but it's enough.

Our matching green eyes meet. After a heartbeat her eyes leave mine, sweep quickly over my body and then once around the room. Her eyes hesitate on Alex before moving back to my face. Her posture relaxes and her face goes blank as she thinks, but then she accepts the truth.

"Lily?" My mother's face lights up and she launches across the room, barely slowing as her body crashes into mine and her arms wrap around me.

I return her hug as well as I can, but I'm having trouble accepting this is real. I've had my whole life to wish this moment into reality and now I feel as if she might disappear again at any moment.

My mother releases me from her tight embrace so she can brush my hair back from my eyes and pepper my face with kisses. I look at her happy face. Her emotions right now seem less complicated than mine. She last saw me yesterday, but I've had decades to miss her.

Sometimes I even hated her for being stupid enough to get herself murdered.

A lone tear runs down my face and my breathing turns to gasps. Seconds later, I'm ugly crying. Not that pretty crying girls do in the movies, but the screwed-up-face crying you don't want anyone to see.

I sit down on the threadbare carpet to try and collect my-self. My mother sits beside me and holds my hand in one of hers while she strokes my wet cheek with the other.

"It's okay Lily, it's okay," she murmurs softly to me while keeping a wary eye on Alex.

Eventually, I feel my breathing starting to slow, my sobs becoming less desperate.

As soon as Hope sees I'm settling down she starts questioning Alex in the same gentle voice she's been using on me.

Alex shifts his weight as he stands awkwardly out of place against the far wall, but he answers all of her questions. He explains he is Ana's grandson and how Ana recognised me at the hospital. He tells my mother about Ana's death and that his sister was taken.

"Where are your parents?" Hope asks.

"Dead," Alex answers flatly.

I'm startled. I hadn't even thought to ask. I'm a terrible person.

"How?" I ask.

He shrugs.

"They went missing when I was eight; no one's seen them since."

"So you don't know for sure then?"

Alex sends us such a black look I know he's lost all hope for them. I guess that's fair, the alternative is they deserted their kids.

"I'm so sorry. They were great people," my mother tells Alex.

I can see Alex is upset, so I take over the explanation of our plan to get Amber back.

My mother nods along as I describe our intention to improve my psychic powers so I can track the car that took her.

When I get up to our attempt to find Lilijana's body at the asylum, my mother looks thoughtful.

"I think your powers were just too weak to follow Lili-jana's trail once she died. A blood drink would've fixed that right up."

I feel stupid when she says it all matter of fact like that. How was I to know?

Alex looks at me with an unreadable expression for once. He's probably angry with me for wasting his time when we could've found Amber sooner. If only he'd forced me to drink that disgusting coagulated blood in the bottle. Or he could've explained what was really going on a little earlier.

I can see why he was worried about frightening me off though. I would probably have hidden the truth as long as I could too. I can still hardly believe it now.

I'm glad we might be able to find Lilijana and complete the ritual one day. It seems important to my mother and Alex. I just think it would be nice to find her and make sure she is buried in a respectful manner. I'm not even sure I need to complete the ritual now; my psychic powers seem pretty powerful already. I decide to ask my mother.

"You have your powers because we had a tiny sample from a few hundred years ago that we'd been keeping aside for emergencies." My mother explains. "Keeping spare samples is a necessary precaution in case the lines are broken. Unfortunately we've needed to rely on these emergency backups for so long they've been used up."

"So why can't I control the visions?" I ask.

"The sample was too small and I couldn't complete the ritual; your father came home early. Without the blood-feed the sample wasn't properly absorbed."

Alex is nodding. This obviously fits with his knowledge of the ritual.

I however, still have questions.

"That doesn't explain why I'm so strong now. Alex and Amber said my powers are psychic only. If I'm not actually travelling in time, I shouldn't be able to touch anything back there. You shouldn't be here."

For the first time since I rescued her, my mother looks sad.

"They were almost right, but the difference is crucial. It's not that you can't interact with anything during a psychic vision, but that you shouldn't."

"What? Why?" I ask.

"Everything has consequences."

"Like changing the future?" Alex interjects.

"No thankfully," my mother answers.

"Then what?" I ask.

"I'm sorry, I can't tell you. I don't want to make it any worse."

"Imploding the world?" Alex tries again.

"No." My mother gives him a look that makes him rethink his next question.

"So," he says. "What do you think of our plan to get my sister back? Will you help us go back to the funeral home and track the car, or do you wanna wait for us here?"

I get a sudden wave of guilt. Here I am having a family re-union while Amber is probably being tortured somewhere. Which reminds me...

"Hope, I've been wondering. If Miles wants Renascents dead, why didn't he kill Amber right there at the funeral home. Why keep her alive at all?"

"Is she a hostage?" Alex asks.

"Maybe," Hope answers, before immediately killing my rising optimism with her next sentence. "But more likely he just wanted somewhere private to work on her."

She hesitates, before getting to her feet and crossing to Alex. She looks straight at him and bravely breaks his heart.

"He will want to torture her and drink from her for a few days. It's what he always does."

I nod. This fits with the dreams I've had.

Alex isn't buying it.

"But he killed you straight away."

My mother shakes her head.

"He had already loosened his grip on my throat when Lily crashed into him. I'm guessing they didn't find my body here?"

"No," I answer. "They never found your body at all."

I don't tell her that her husband, my father, is still sitting in jail for her murder. That's something we can deal with later.

My mother continues her explanation.

"The torture is just for fun, but the blood drinking strengthens him. It's why he only looks in his fifties or sixties when he is closer to three or four hundred years old."

Alex's face crumples in despair as we both silently count the days Amber's been gone. My mother reaches out and covers Alex's hand with her own.

"The good news is that she's almost certainly still alive right now, but we don't have long to find her."

Alex jumps to his feet and walks out of the room, talking over his shoulder as he goes.

"Come on then, it's half past eight. He'll be taking Bridget home soon. Are we gonna track him, or are we going to go to the funeral home and start there?"

"Maybe we should split up," I suggest.

I stand up and start to follow Alex, but my mother is standing still with a frown. Then her mouth pops open in an o.

"Wait Alex," I call.

As soon as Alex fills the dark doorway again my mother starts speaking.

"Why is this room empty?"

"They've built a new hospital. This one is coming down soon," I answer.

"But the hospital is still there now, the big main building in the centre?"

"Yeah," I answer. "I think they might have started ripping down the East Wing though."

"Why?" Alex asks.

"I know where he might have taken Amber."

"Where?" Alex and I are in perfect harmony.

"The last thing Miles said to me before Lily crashed into him was 'It's your turn on the slab.' And I think I know just which one he means."

Chapter 37

Still evening - Still my mother's room

"The dead house in the Botanic Gardens?" I ask Hope.

I'm doubtful. It's an appropriately morbid place to torture and kill someone, but it's a bit exposed, right in the middle of a popular, public space. If Amber was conscious, she'd only have to call out once and someone would come to the rescue. And we were in there last night.

"No," Hope replies. "There's an old surgical theatre down in the basement of the hospital. It's hopelessly out of date and the whole area has been locked for years."

"Really?" Alex says. "Seems like a great way to get caught. That hospital is huge. There must be hundreds of people who could just stumble over him."

"The theatre is pretty out of the way, past the morgue, so it's well protected."

"In what way? Cameras?" Alex asks, no doubt already devising a plan to get around them.

"Not in the unused rooms, but yes, morgues need good security so no one can tamper with a body before autopsy. Dr Miles used to work at the hospital, so he had access."

Alex is pacing the room now, his brow furrowed.

"I don't know. It still seems like a big risk to keep a captive at the place you work," he says.

"Not as big for Dr Miles though. Think about it. He's a senior doctor in my time. Even with an outrageous cover story, no one would think to question him. Anyway, he'd been trying to get me down to the basements for a while. I thought he'd heard my marriage was in trouble and he was trying his luck."

"He still works at the hospital," I tell her. "He's an anaesthetist."

"Not much has changed then," my mother says. "I just wish I'd discovered him earlier. Then this could have all ended with me. Ana would still be alive, Amber would be safe and your dad wouldn't have had to raise you alone."

I glance quickly at Alex, but he doesn't seem inclined to say anything, so I decide this is a conversation we can have later. Instead I move over to my mother and take her hand.

"I have you now though," I say.

Tears form in my mother's eyes. She must be thinking of all the years we've lost.

Alex interrupts us with his decision.

"I'm heading to the hospital," he says. "You don't have to come, but I could use some help finding that room you're talking about."

He's already out the door. I can't blame him, this is the best lead we've had in days.

I follow him out of the room, my mother close behind us. Alex is already at the end of the hall and vaulting down the stairs.

"Wait. Don't we need a plan? Or at least weapons?" I call out, but it looks like nothing's going to slow Alex down after two days of inaction.

I break into a run to catch up, but my mother is faster. She's at the top of the stairs when I pass my open door and my shower bag catches my eye. My mother looks to be the exact same size and weight as me.

"Hope, wait." I grab the jeans and top out of the bag and throw them to my mother. I strip off my stained top and replace it with a clean one from my wardrobe. Hope's feet look about the same as mine too.

"Size eight?" I ask as I hold out my runners.

"Close enough," my mother answers, shoving her feet into them and we are back out of my room in less than a minute.

Hope's better than me on the staircase too, taking the steps three at a time, but she lands heavily at the bottom, giving me time to catch up. Together we cross the foyer and crash through the heavy wooden front door to the sight of large men fighting dangerously close to us.

I push my mother aside and dodge left as an elbow skims my ribs. What the hell is going on?

"Alex," I yell. "Nathan."

It's like I'm not even there. I put out a hand and touch hard muscle. Cool. Even if this is another vision I can still affect the outcome.

I raise my knee and bring my foot down hard on the back of Nathan's thigh. He instantly crumples to one knee and I step around him and under Alex's arm and push up. The fist, which is aimed too high now anyway, clears Nathan's head by a good ten millimetres.

"Stop it," I scream.

Alex looks like he's happy to keep fighting, but Nathan stands up and backs off, holding his palms out in front of him.

"He hit me first," Nathan says, proving even an expensive suit and haircut aren't enough to stop you looking like a toddler.

"Why are you here?" I ask him, while trying to keep Alex in sight at all times.

"You didn't answer your phone," he replies.

Oh yeah.

Alex gives up on us and starts jogging up the road. I assume he intends to go around to the emergency entrance, that's the only way into the hospital at this time of night. My mother and I can catch up in a minute.

"Sorry. I left my phone in my room. We're a bit busy."

"That's what I need to talk to you about. Do you know of anyone that's missing?"

I'm still not sure if I fully trust Nathan yet so I act dumb.

"You mean Jan from work? I only met her a couple of times. Why?"

"No. A young reborn girl. I don't know her name."

"Amber," I say. "What do you know?"

"I know who's got her and I know she doesn't have much time left. He'll kill her tonight."

"Help us find her," I beg him.

"That's why I'm here," Nathan answers.

I look up the road. Alex is almost at the corner.

"Alex," I yell.

Nothing.

I put my fingers in my mouth and whistle like I'm calling the cows in. Alex looks over his shoulder.

I use both arms to wave him back towards us. As soon as he starts jogging our way I turn back to Nathan.

"Nathan, this is Hope, a friend of mine." I'm still not sure how much to give away, so I've settled for a version of the truth.

My mother steps into the bright circle of light near the door, politely offering him her hand to shake, but Nathan's face is a mask of shock mixed with horror. His jaw drops and his voice is lower than ever as he repeats my mother's name.

"Hope?"

My mother studies his face.

"Nate?"

Nathan nods, his eyes shining under the light. I still can't tell what the expression on his face is. Maybe guilt? Fear? Wait. He's crying.

Alex reaches us just as my mother steps forward and gives Nathan a tight hug. Nathan seems awkward about returning it. That might be because Alex is now standing less than a metre away looking as confused as I feel. I see Nathan's shoulders hitching slightly, but I have no idea if he's laughing, crying or something in between as he finally returns my mother's embrace. He lifts her off the ground as she laughs happily. What the hell is going on?

"Apparently Nathan knows my mother, and that Dr Miles has Amber," I tell Alex, while looking to Nathan for confirmation.

Nathan looks surprised when I say the kidnapper's name, but he nods and puts my mother down, keeping a hand on her shoulder as if to convince himself she is real.

"Do you know where he holds his victims?" I ask Nathan.

"No, but I should be able to find out."

"Please do, but in the meantime we think it's the old demonstration autopsy room in the hospital basement."

Nathan nods slowly as he considers our theory.

"It makes sense. It's secure and he has reason to be in the vicinity if he's caught there. I can get us in."

"Let's go then," Alex says turning back to the road.

"No, this way." My mother reaches out and grabs my hand and drags me in a run down into the darkness beside the condemned nurses' quarters and through a gap in the temporary fencing.

We're closer to the hospital than I realised, only metres from a multi storey building at least a hundred metres long. This too is fenced off, but we find a gap and squeeze through. My mother leads us to a small door.

"Back entrance for us nurses," she tells us. "Let's see if this still works."

My mother punches in a four-digit code into the mechanical lock on the door handle and the door clicks open.

Luckily the power to this building has already been cut. Even if the security cameras are working, we'll be harder to identify in infra-red. Alex and Nathan get their phones out and turn on their flashlight apps. My mother and I follow them through the maze of corridors and junctions.

About two buildings in I realise I'm not seeing any shivery timelines, which is a shame. It'd be nice to know we're headed in the right direction. As soon as the thought forms in my mind the translucent web appears around us. It's thicker than ever, but not as useful as I had hoped because every time we reach a junction the lines are thick in every direction. I'm guessing most of them have been left by my mother, but it's possible I'm seeing the paths of other Re-nascents as well.

I wish the time trails away and they immediately vanish. Even if drinking Alex's blood hadn't allowed me to save my mother, this control is worth the awkwardness.

We soon reach an area of the hospital that's still in use. Nathan suggests my mother and I wait in a recently vacated office while he checks the morgue is quiet and Alex deals with the security system. I'm annoyed at being stored away like a useless lump of meat, but he makes a good point.

At best, a group as large as ours will attract unnecessary attention. At worst, someone will call the cops on us.

As soon as we're left alone, I worry this is all a trap and Nathan has led us here like lambs to the slaughter. He could be having Alex arrested right now.

"How do you know Nathan?" I ask my mother who's standing so close beside me, we're touching.

She was holding my hand earlier, but she let me go when she saw I was uncomfortable. I'm not used to the touchy-feely stuff, particularly when I'm stressed.

"I knew his parents. Nate was a great kid; he was only ten when I last saw him."

When she died she means.

Finally the office door opens and Nathan ushers us back out into the hall.

"Where's Alex?" I ask.

"Still in the security room, sorting out the cameras. He said not to wait for him."

We make our way down a few more long hallways before we reach a set of stairs with a door labelled 'Staff Only.' I expect Nathan to get keys out, but the door isn't locked.

Two flights down and we are deep in the bowels of the hospital. We reach the locked doors of the morgue. Luckily, while it's obviously still in use, there's no one else here right now. Nathan punches in a code and we're in. We don't bother searching through the bodies here, too many people use this area. Even if Amber is dead, an extra body wouldn't go unnoticed. We cross the room quietly and open yet another door. Prep rooms. I get guilty memories of desecrating Ana's body.

Down another hallway things start looking more promising. This area is old as hell. The clean lino floors have given way to vintage, green tiles and there's more wood than stainless steel around now. The rooms are small and the doorways narrow and impractical. Efficiency was either unheard of back then, or things just worked way differently in those days. Maybe people were smaller?

Soon we are standing in front of a double-width door that looks promising. I use my vision to check we are in the right place. A handful of shivery translucent lines appear around me, all leading in through the heavy door in front of us.

Wait.

I examine my previous thought and find it to be true. I can tell that these lines lead into the room, not one of them comes back out. While I hope there's another door out that these trails could have left through, the lead weight in my gut is telling me the lines end not far from here.

And it's not just one person who's entered this door and never come out. Now that I examine them closely, I can make out subtle differences in the qualities of the shivery lines. These belong to at least six or seven different people.

I push on the door. It's locked. It's a big old-fashioned lock I could see through if it wasn't pitch black in there.

I wish Alex was here with his lockpicks. Should we wait for him?

Nathan takes a step away from the door, so I think he has the same idea as me.

I'm wrong as usual.

Nathan steps forward into a perfect turning kick and smashes the door open.

Chapter 38

Later that evening - Hospital basements

Nathan's phone light moves around the room. First I scan for immediate danger. On the second sweep I'm looking for Amber. When she's not immediately visible, I take in the rest. Tiered viewing stands dominate the large room. They're wooden, which means they're old. Steel has been the standard in hospitals since before even my mother worked here.

The stands besiege an antique autopsy table in the centre of the room. I only know it's old because I can see its legs. The top of the table is shrouded in fabric. It's not flat, there's a shape there that's consistent with a small body.

Amber.

I race over to the table and wrench the sheet off, revealing Amber's battered body. She's tied down with several straps. Some that came with the autopsy table, as well as a few extra just to make sure.

"Light Nathan," I demand. I know checking the rest of the room for danger is important, but that'll have to wait.

Nathan moves towards us with his phone. Amber's skin and lips are pale and bruised. There are several fresh wounds that need stitching and my throat aches as I realise none of them are actively bleeding. This is a very bad sign.

Nathan checks for a pulse while I work on the chest strap. The old buckle isn't budging. I look around for something sharp. At the foot of the autopsy table is a small trolley laden with surgical equipment and vials.

Perfect.

I grab the first blade I see, it's a small surgical scalpel coated in blood. I scan quickly for a better option, but this will have to do. I'll just have to be extra careful not to nick Amber or myself.

I move back to Nathan's side just in time to see him raise Amber's eyelids with his fingers.

She has pin-point pupils.

"She's been drugged," Nathan says, before catching my eyes and nodding towards the trolley at the foot of the table. "What've we got over there, Lily?"

I'm back at the trolley in a heartbeat, checking the little vials I'd ignored earlier. It's too dark.

"Light please."

Nathan turns his phone my way. I find Propofol, Fentanyl and Morphine vials among a few old, brown bottles with faded labels. A half-filled syringe catches my eye. I pick it up and examine it. It's disposable with a safety cap still on it, but there's no writing or labelling of any kind.

I have to assume Miles filled it from one of the vials on the trolley and may have even used it before putting the cap back on. There's no way of knowing what's in it. It might be something to reverse Amber's sedation so she's alert for her torture, but it could just as easily be a sedative. I lay the syringe back on the trolley. I can ignore the old medicine vials; Narcan and such are too new to be in that type of container.

"Sorry Nathan, I can't find anything but sedatives."

I'm crossing back to where Nathan is trying to wake Amber, when my mother's voice calls to me.

"Lily, can you bring the light here for a minute."

I search the dark for her and see she's standing on the top tier of the viewing stands, right at the back. I consider taking the phone with me like she asked, but I can't leave Nathan to work on Amber in the dark. Nathan didn't want the lights on earlier, but surely it's fine now we know no one else is in here. I cross to the door and flick the large toggle switch down and the room is flooded with light.

My mother is partially hidden by the wooden handrails that run along each level of the wooden stands, but she appears to be crouched beside a crumpled pile of hospital linen. I climb the closer of the two staircases, make my way around the stands and crouch down beside my mother. She lifts away a handful of the crumpled fabric to reveal the milky stare of a corpse. I don't bother checking for a pulse. It's clear Jan has been dead for a while.

I'm flooded with remorse for thinking she was a pain, but I was right, it wasn't a coincidence she went missing on the same night Amber did.

"She worked at the hospital," I say. "She was giving history tours down here. She must have seen something she shouldn't have."

"Or invited the wrong person to join her," my mother replies.

An explosion of sound reverberates around the room's hard surfaces.

I look over my shoulder to see Nathan falling to one knee, before dropping out of sight behind the autopsy table. Movement draws my eye to the doorway. My killer is standing there, with a triumphant grin on his face and a gun in his right hand.

"Ah, Lily," he croons to me like a lover. "Come here."

I hesitate. Walking willingly towards my death seems like a bad plot twist in the horror movie of my life, but I do need to move away from this spot. My mother is lying flat on the floor beside Jan's corpse. If I stay here Miles will see her.

My mother grasps my ankle. Her intention is clear. Don't sacrifice myself for her or Nathan. But I'm out of options. I step away from my mother's hand and walk slowly, trying to keep the killer's eyes on me, while I think of a better plan.

I delay too long because Miles crosses to the autopsy table and his body jerks like he kicks something. I hear a thud followed by a deep groan.

"He's still alive, but I can make that change."

I speed up point zero, zero, zero one miles an hour. I'm conflicted, I don't want Nathan hurt, but there's still a chance he's not actually on our side. Or he's bait in the killer's trap. I'm also trying to make as much noise as I can, to cover the escape attempt I'm hoping my mother will make. Maybe she can sneak around the opposite side of the horseshoe shaped stand and slip out behind him. I hear a small noise coming from behind me. More cover is needed.

"You might have to explain to me why I'd care if Nathan is dead. I already know he's your minion," I say as confidently as I can.

"He admitted he gave your mother up to me, did he? I'm surprised. Was he trying to gain your trust?"

I try to cover my shock. I was right to be suspicious of Nathan. My mother was betrayed by a boy she thought was her friend. My eyes automatically flick in her direction before I drag them back to the killer's face.

Dr Elijah Miles looks no different from when I saw him in my mother's room earlier, but that was twenty years ago. He has no extra lines. No less hair on his balding head. Still, whatever he's doing to prolong his life isn't working perfectly. His teeth look exactly four hundred years old.

Revulsion crawls up my back, but I shake it off. I don't know what difference I can make to my fate now, but I refuse to go out weak.

"Nathan was right to keep you hidden from me," Miles croons. "You look just like you did the last time I tasted you and I've been waiting for you to come back for so long. I assume it was you that stopped me from killing your mother?"

When I don't answer, he continues on undeterred.

"Your powers are truly spectacular. What a shame it was a total waste of time."

This time I speak.

"Is that what this is about? You think you can take our powers?"

"I still haven't found a way to transfer your powers onto myself yet. But drinking your blood does have marvellous benefits. I'm 376 years old."

Hmm, younger than his teeth.

He pauses like he expects a compliment. Personally I wouldn't want to live to that age if I had to look like that. Or kill innocent people.

I am stepping off the stands onto the tiled floor when I hear a rustling noise to my left. I walk swiftly around the autopsy table to Nathan's side in the hope of distracting Miles, but it's too late.

"Come on out Hope. I know you're up there."

My heart sinks as my mother rises to her feet on the far side of the room. Actually, maybe this is a good thing. Miles will have to turn towards her at some point and I might be able to get the gun.

Except he doesn't. Miles keeps the gun pointed straight at me, trusting my mother won't risk my life.

I figure I can check on Nathan. The knowledge the killer will want to torture me gives me a little confidence he won't shoot me immediately, unless I force him to.

"Where are you hurt?"

Nathan lifts his hands from his thigh for a second, so we can both see the wound is bleeding profusely. It doesn't look arterial though, so he'll live. I assess what we're both wearing. Nothing will make a great bandage, but I remember seeing one on the trolley. I'm already pushing myself to my feet when someone grabs a handful of my hair and drags me upwards.

"Just leave him." Miles' face is so close, I can smell his rotten teeth. "He would've turned you in eventually, believe me."

"No, I wouldn't." Nathan's voice has lost its smooth, chocolatey tones. "Sahra doesn't want anyone else hurt for her sake."

That explains a lot. Sahra is some sort of hostage, used to force a ten-year-old boy into betraying my mother and who knows how many others? Ana and Amber surely.

"We'll see if she changes her mind when I bring her down here, shall we?" The killer taunts Nathan.

Miles lets go of my hair and steps back, so he can point the gun at me.

"Get down here Hope, be with your daughter while you can," Miles sneers at my mother.

The killer crosses to the trolley and selects a crepe bandage and throws it down to Nathan.

"And you. Bandage your leg. You're no use to me dead."

Nathan starts winding the bandage around his thigh over his pants. I don't know how I feel about him anymore. I can understand him wanting to protect Sahra, she's his family. But how can he live with himself after betraying my mother for her. And having done it once, the odds are he'll do it again.

Miles certainly seems confident Nathan's no threat to him, as he steps over Nathan to stand near Amber's head. I back up a few steps towards Amber's feet and the medical trolley. My mother has reached the bottom of the stands and is making her way across to me while I survey the trolley for anything that might make a good weapon.

I'm now the furthest from the door and the only person facing that way, so only I see the wooden door crack open.

Alex.

I keep my eyes firmly on the killer, so I don't give anything away, but it's a wasted effort.

This place is ancient, and so are that door's hinges. The metal-on-metal squeal is like a siren in the quiet room. As the killer's head turns, Alex throws the door wide and lunges for the light switch.

In the last second before we are plunged into darkness, I see Nathan wrap his arms around the killer's legs and heave himself backwards. At the same time, my mother launches herself between me and the killer.

A second later I'm deafened by the sound of the gun and my mother's silhouette is seared into my retinas.

Chapter 39

Later still -
Autopsy theatre

I think Miles just shot my mother.

I hear scuffling and grunts in the dark. I remember the equipment on the trolley. I step to my right with my hands out until I find it. I hear the little vials clinking together as I run my hands lightly over them. I can't find anything sharp, and I left the scalpel next to Amber on the autopsy table. I consider abandoning the trolley when my right hand touches a thin cylinder of cold plastic.

It's the syringe from earlier, the one filled with some anonymous drug. I think there's a better than fifty-fifty chance this is a sedative of some kind. Why would the killer need to prepare a syringe in advance if the person was sleeping peacefully? No, this must have been prepared to quiet a noisy victim quickly.

I pull the safety cap off the syringe and hold it carefully in front of me while I use one hand to guide myself along the autopsy table to where I last saw the killer standing.

When my feet touch something soft and large I stop and crouch down. This person isn't moving at all. I brush my free hand quickly over the slim, denim-covered legs. This can only be my mother. I feel a hand touch mine and hold it firmly, before a flat, palm-sized object is pressed into my grip and then my hand is pushed away. It couldn't be clearer that she means I should leave her and deal with more urgent matters.

After a quick feel of the thing in my hand, I recognise it as a phone. Nathan's I guess. I don't know the code for it so I won't be able to use the flashlight setting, but just pressing the on button will give me some light.

I scoot around my mother towards the noise of grown men fighting for their lives. When I'm close enough to the action that I've been kicked twice, I press the phone's power button.

Nathan, Alex and the killer are a tangled, writhing mass in the dim light. For a moment I can't make out who belongs to what. Nathan's arms are still wrapped around the killer's legs and it looks like Alex is fighting for the gun.

The killer is stupidly strong, much stronger than a balding, old man should be. And by the look of Alex's grimace, he won't be able to hold the gun for much longer.

I crouch beside them and time my strike perfectly. When the needle is deep in Miles' thigh, I push the medication in. The killer's body goes limp almost instantly. It was a sedative. I shake the leg roughly, but there's no response.

"It's okay," I say. "He's out."

Nathan shoves the unconscious killer out of the way and drags himself across the floor to lean, panting, against the autopsy table.

Alex rips the gun from the killer's unresponsive hand and tucks it into his pants pocket, before running to the light switch. Once the overhead lights are on, he calls his sister's name as he runs in her direction.

My eyes are having trouble adjusting to the quick change in light levels and I squint and blink as I survey the damage.

The killer is sprawled out in front of me breathing deeply, so he's still alive. The tiles are covered in blood, Nathan's I assume.

He doesn't look too bad though. The blood hasn't even seeped all the way through the bandage yet. He doesn't seem too worried about it either; his wide eyes are fixed on the floor behind me.

I whip around. My mother is lying flat on her back with her head propped awkwardly against the bottom step of the viewing stands. Her eyes are closed. I hope she hasn't hit her head too badly.

I scan her body for other injuries. There's a tiny tear in the middle of the long-sleeved t-shirt I loaned her. The small hole has a thin red outline. That's not enough blood to be a gunshot wound, surely.

I drop to my knees beside her as Nathan crawls over to us.

"Mum?" I try to rouse her by gently tapping her arm.

"Mum?" I speak louder the second time and I'm rewarded with a tiny flicker of my mother's eyelids.

Nathan carefully stretches the neckline of my mother's top out from her body and looks down at the wound. I hear his sharp intake of breath, but I refuse to look. It can't be bad, there's almost no blood.

Unless it's leaking into her lungs and chest cavity. Okay, my imagination might be making it worse than it actually is.

I'll look.

I lift her shirt from the waistband. It's bad. It does look like a bullet wound and it's right over her heart. Nathan puts his hands over the wound and leans his weight into it. My mother's dark green eyes pop open.

"It's okay Mum. We're in a hospital. We'll get you help."

I look back down. Dark blood oozes out from under Nathan's large palms. I look around for something to stop the bleeding, but all I see is the filthy sheet covering Amber. Nope. I strip off my scrubs top, ball it up into a tight knot and ask Nathan to move his hands.

For a moment it looks as if he will resist, but then he raises his hands and lets me cover the hole in my mother's chest. I push the balled-up shirt onto the wound with all my strength, trying to press my mother's back onto the tiles hard enough to stop the flow of blood from what I know might be a much larger wound there. There's nothing I can do if it's just leaking into her chest cavity or lungs though.

Nathan checks my mother's breathing and pulse, while I look helplessly into her pale face. Her lips part and I can see blood in her mouth. She gives a tiny cough trying to clear her airways, but her breathing is shallow. Too shallow. I am torn between turning her to let her catch her breath and keeping pressure on the wound.

"It's okay Lily," my mother's now blue lips manage to whisper. "It's too late. You have to let me go."

I shake my head stubbornly.

"No, there is no too late anymore. Even if you die before we can get help, I can go back and save you again."

My mother shakes her head, but then stops, grimacing at the pain.

"I'm sorry Lily. He was always going to kill me. This is the natural consequence of trying to cheat fate."

"No, it wasn't inevitable. You jumped in the way. He wasn't even aiming at you."

"Because I know how it works. Trying to change the past is like trying to cut a path through a tsunami. The flow of time just closes back around your efforts, leaving the result unchanged. At least this way my death saves you."

"No," I argue. "That's not fair. And if nothing can be changed why bother saving me. Surely I'm destined to die now too."

"No, it's not the same. You acted in the past, I acted in the present. The future isn't set."

I look up at Nathan who is kneeling quietly beside me.

"Do something," I beg him. "Feed her your blood."

"The bullet hit her heart," he tells me in a soothing voice. "Even if we were already in theatre I wouldn't be able to save her."

I want to slap him. He must be a crap surgeon if he's this practiced at giving out bad news.

"So go get someone who can."

"No," my mother breathes to Nathan. "Stay and help my daughter."

Nathan nods solemnly, as if he has just taken a vow. For all I know he did.

"You can't save me," my mother says. "The timeline needs to reset itself."

I have to lean in now to hear my mother's soft voice.

"Please don't leave me again," I beg her with hot tears running down my cheeks.

This can't be right. I only just found her. Wait.

"You knew," I say, looking at mother. "Why didn't you tell me?"

My mother's sorrow-filled face is so pale she looks like a marble angel.

"Forgive me," my mother whispers. "You're all grown up and such a beautiful, strong woman. I couldn't bear to break your heart. I was selfish."

Her words only make me feel worse. How could I judge her when she knew this whole time she was doomed to die, and yet stayed so strong for me and Alex and Amber. My hands have come away from my mother's wound, and while we both know there's nothing that will make a difference now, Nathan replaces my hands with his.

I swipe my mother's blood off on my pants, before gathering her icy hands in mine.

"Of course I forgive you Mum," I say through my sobs.

Hope's breathing is almost undetectable now. I kiss my mother's cheek as she draws her final breath, sighing with her as she leaves me, finally and forever.

I collapse down beside my mother's dead body, still holding her hands while I sob uncontrollably. After a moment or two Nathan puts his hand on my shoulder to show his support, strips off his shirt and lays it over me, before leaving me to grieve.

My mind is consumed by my loss, but some small survival instinct is still aware of my surroundings. I drag Nathan's shirt on as he joins Alex at the autopsy table and the two of them work on getting Amber unstrapped. It's not long before I hear a groan. Amber's waking up.

I know Alex and Nathan have got this. Who better to take care of Amber than her brother and a surgeon. I'm not hurting anyone by snatching this selfish moment to stay with my mother for a few final minutes.

Then I see a foot twitch out of the corner of my eye.

My mother's murderer is waking up.

I pull Nathan's shirt on, get to my feet and locate the syringe I used to put him out earlier. Walking over to the trolley, I scan the vials there until I find the one I need. I draw up a full syringe of the strongest sedative and make my way back over to the killer lying helplessly on the floor. Without ceremony I inject the medication into the killer's vein and then put my fingers over his pulse and wait.

When I'm sure he's gone, I put the syringe down and return to pay my respects to the mother I barely knew.

Chapter 40

Sunday - My room

"Jeez Lily, you eat a lot of crap."

Amber holds out my little rubbish bin as proof.

I look down at all the chocolate wrappers and chip packets and shrug.

"It's not like I could do much in here." I gesture around my tiny room in the old nurse's quarters. "I promise I'll cook proper meals for us in our new place. When I'm not on the evening shift that is. Then, you'll just have to fend for yourself."

Amber's face falls. She's happy we've all agreed she should live with me for a while, but I can't be around twenty-four seven. I haven't even been able to go to the bathroom alone since we rescued her a week ago. Not that I blame her. It'd take anyone a while to get over being kidnapped and tortured, even a sassy teenager. I'm constantly watching her carefully for any aftereffects of her trauma, but this time at least, she recovers her usual happy mood quickly.

She puts the whole bin in a moving box and starts cleaning out the fridge while I strip the bed. I hope part of her happy mood is because Alex has found a fake ID good enough for her to go back to school and finish year 12. It's my only condition on Amber moving in with me.

I think we all know I would have caved eventually. Living with Alex while he works three jobs using two different names is just too disruptive. But they both seem happy enough to go along with my demand for now.

I did suggest Alex could settle down a bit and have a more normal life now the danger is gone, but he's lived his whole life running interference for the reborn. Making sure we're safe. And so far I haven't been able to convince him to stop.

Amber carefully extracts a jar from the top shelf of the tiny refrigerator and puts it in Alex's car fridge to stay cold. I'd completely forgotten the brain sample until this morning when Alex told us Amber and I will complete the ritual tonight.

You'd think something like that would be pretty memorable, but you can't blame me for being distracted. It turns out hiding three bodies is a pretty complicated process. Luckily for me, somebody needed to stay with Amber and she was most comfortable with me.

After Nathan gave her a blood feed to help with her healing, Alex and I brought her back here and I've been her primary carer ever since. Nathan gave me a sick certificate so I could take a few days off, but I finally got back to work on Friday when Alex took over Amber's care for the day.

Alex and Nathan buried Miles and Jan separately in bushland a couple of hours north-east of the city. When I heard that area had already been used as a serial killer's dumping ground back in the seventies, I argued against burying them there. But the guys said the north of the city was too close to a more recent site where eight murder victims were found. After that I just let them deal with it. I still can't decide if it was smart or stupid to use an area that's already infamous. I guess we'll find out.

My mother isn't there of course. I couldn't just dump her like garbage. She was buried properly. We even had a funeral for her, under a false name of course. Nathan arranged for Burton Funerals to pick her up from the hospital with another patient's paperwork. Alex just had to break back into the funeral home and steal that paperwork back, duplicate some records and arrange my mother's transfer to a smaller company for burial. Easy, so Alex says.

I hear heavy footsteps in the hall before Alex's tall frame blocks the door.

"What's next?" he asks.

I point to the car fridge.

"That's about the last of it. We've got the rest."

Alex takes the fridge and heads out to his car which is parked illegally on the footpath out the front. He's pretty confident he won't get a ticket. He's wearing hi-vis work gear, so he might be right. Apparently he's placed some witches hats around too. I assume he's talking about those orange traffic cones, but I didn't get time to ask.

Sam's really the only person who would be affected by Alex blocking the door anyway and he hasn't complained. Mostly because Sam and Alex are getting along like long-lost brothers. They met when Sam heard us bring Amber back here that night. It took some time to convince Sam we didn't need an ambulance, but after that he was a great help with Amber. He had some excellent painkillers and wound dressings, and he even ran out and got us food while Alex was out.

Alex was super grateful of course and that's morphed into a proper friendship. I should have known someone who knows how to blend in would make friends easily, but I've only had the pleasure of meeting suspicious Alex. This new relaxed and happy Alex feels like a stranger.

Their friendship has been useful though. Sam admitted to Alex our elusive house-mate Ellie never existed. Sam wasn't keen on living in this spooky building by himself and he can't move into his new flat for another three weeks. He invented Ellie because he thought I wouldn't agree to live here if it was just me, alone with a strange guy. I don't have the energy to be angry at him, also he's not wrong. I probably wouldn't have moved in here if it was just Sam and me. It's impossible to be scared of him now I know him a bit, but I didn't know that when I agreed to move in.

Amber and I pick up the last of my things and follow Alex out of my room. I don't bother closing the door.

I'm sad about leaving the old nurses' quarters, but at least some of my off mood is because I'm nervous about what comes next. Not the moving bit, or the new responsibility I have of taking care of Amber. No, the butterflies drunkenly careening about inside my gut are due to the ritual Amber and I have to perform tonight. Amber has her sample from Ana and Nathan is going to meet us at my new apartment with the sample he took from my mother.

I'm so grateful he was there to collect the sample properly for me. My mother deserved to be treated with respect by someone who knew what they were doing, not a hack like me. I still feel guilty for the mess I made of Ana's collection.

I haven't seen Nathan much in the last week, mostly because he and Alex still can't be left alone for a minute without an argument breaking out. Nathan seems to be making an effort to get along, but his newfound sense of humour seems designed to annoy Alex. And Alex isn't trying at all. He's still openly hostile to Nathan. Hopefully they can rein it in tonight at the ritual.

Thinking about yet another potential argument sends my stomach butterflies into a flailing panic. Then again, at least a few of those terrified insects appear every time I think of seeing Nathan again.

I still have no idea where I stand there. I do think he's on our side, but was his interest in me just because I'm reborn and he's wired to protect me, or is there something more?

He's offered to take me to the prison to see my father. I told him I'd think about it. I know my father is innocent now, but the prejudices of a lifetime are hard to drop. I will go and see him. I just need to sort myself out a bit first. Particularly the part where I am now more of a killer than he is.

Amber and I reach the bottom of the stairs when we hear a light knock on the door in front of us.

I cross the worn, tiled floor and pull the heavy door open for the last time. A green-eyed child with wheaten coloured ringlets is standing there, looking up at me.

Bridget.

Our connection is real and instant. I may not have my memories yet, but my DNA knows this is my daughter.

I bend down and sweep her up off the ground. Her little arms wrap around my neck and we cling tight to each other. I feel an all-encompassing, unconditional love that every parent must recognise. Suddenly I want my memories back.

It hasn't mattered until now that I can't remember my past lives, but now I have an idea of what I am missing.

I put my daughter back down so I can see her face. I hope I haven't scared her.

"Hello Bridget," I say, offering her my hand to shake. "I'm Lily."

Too late I realise a formal introduction is probably a bit weird after the bear hug. Bridget must think so too, because she laughs and makes no move to shake my hand.

"I know who you are." She rolls her eyes at me and points to Amber. "I know who she is too."

"Hello Bridget," Amber responds politely.

"I've got all my memories and all of my powers." Bridget's appearance changes into a tiny replica of Amber for a split second, before morphing into a perfect, but tiny, version of me.

My mouth drops open and Amber breaks out in surprised laughter.

Bridget puffs up with pride. "It will look better when I'm grown up of course. That whole conservation of mass law is a bitch."

I'm still speechless, but some forgotten motherly instinct rises in me at the sound of the swear word coming out of that tiny mouth.

Bridget sees something in my face and hurries ahead.

"I couldn't come see you before cos it was too dangerous, but you need to see this."

Bridget slips a pink backpack decorated with unicorns off her back and pulls out this morning's newspaper. She unfolds it and pins it against her body with one arm and points to the headline with the other.

NEW SERIAL KILLER FEARS AS HUMAN REMAINS FOUND IN ADELAIDE HILLS.

I take the paper from my daughter and read the few paragraphs that accompany the headline. It doesn't give much away, so it's hard to tell exactly how much trouble we are in until I look at the picture below the fold. It's a recent photo of the detective in charge of the case, and he's smiling.

All the warmth drains from my face as I'm transfixed by his long, stained teeth.

They look at least four hundred years old.